CW00419081

A
QUAINT
&
CURIOUS
VOLUME

A QUAINT & CURIOUS VOLUME

TALES AND POEMS
OF THE GOTHIC

Introduction
by Sarah Perry

**WILLIAM
COLLINS**

William Collins
An imprint of HarperCollins*Publishers*
1 London Bridge Street
London
SE1 9GF

www.WilliamCollinsBooks.com

First published in Great Britain by William Collins in 2019

1

Introduction copyright © Aldwinter Ltd 2019

Sarah Perry asserts the moral right to be identified as the author of the introduction
to this work in accordance with the Copyright, Designs and Patents Act 1988

A catalogue record for this book is available from the British Library

ISBN 978-0-00-835182-3

Typeset in Portrait by Palimpsest Book Production Ltd, Falkirk, Stirlingshire
Printed and bound in Great Britain by CPI Group (UK) Ltd, Croydon CR0 4YY

MIX
Paper from
responsible sources
FSC™ C007454

This book is produced from independently certified FSC™ paper
to ensure responsible forest management.

For more information visit: www.harpercollins.co.uk/green

There is something at work in my soul,
which I do not understand.

Mary Shelley, *Frankenstein*

CONTENTS

PART V: THE DEVIL

INTRODUCTION

I n 1764, an astonishing and disturbing manuscript by a certain Canon Onuphrio Muralto was brought to light. Discovered in the library of an ancient Catholic family and first printed in Naples in 1529, it had been translated into English and published under the enticing title *The Castle of Otranto*.

It was quite unlike any other narrative to hit the shelves of the British reading public. Revelling indecently in fear and transgression, it opened with a young prince crushed to death by an immense helmet on the morning of his wedding, after which his wicked father Manfred, fearing that the bloodline was cursed, pursued the bereaved bride. An instant sensation across Europe, it caused the poet Thomas Gray to write that it made 'some of us cry a little, and all in general afraid to go to bed o'nights'.

It was not, however, an ancient document – but rather a novel by Horace Walpole, Member of Parliament for King's Lynn, who had concealed his authorship out of concern that its reckless disregard for good taste and good morals would cause a scandal. Having observed its popularity, he hastily claimed ownership, stating that he had intended to 'blend the two kinds of romance, the ancient and the modern'.

Walpole subtitled his novel *A Gothic Story*, and in doing so instituted a genre whose subtle and irresistible grip on the public imagination has never quite been loosened. This was the first application of the word 'Gothic' to literature, and indicates Walpole's understanding that he was dealing in an aesthetic and a mode of thought which has a very particular – and a very dangerous – power. The 'Gothic' until then had been a pejorative term, used by the Renaissance taste-maker Vasari to describe the effect that the immense Romanesque cathedrals of Europe had on his sensibilities. With their gargoyles, buttresses, pinnacles, crypts and hidden places, these edifices were – he felt – as barbarous as the Goths and Visigoths who had literally dismantled 'civilisation' at the Sack of Rome in 410 AD.

Story, Walpole suggested, could have the same effects: visiting on the reader the destabilising sensation that everything which seems set in stone – morally, sexually, socially, politically – can be broken down and rebuilt, and that narrative can offer crypts and hiding-places where the reader's desires may be concealed, and their fears delightfully and horribly encountered.

In the years that followed, the Gothic has developed and altered, like a stone gargoyle acquiring moss and weathered by rain. Often it deals in the sublime, that aesthetic quality identified by Edmund Burke as something beyond the merely beautiful, but which operates in a manner analogous to terror . . . productive of the strongest emotion which the mind is capable of.' It is a sensation which operates at a deep psychological level, often trading on that uncanny feeling identified by Freud, in which everything which is known and familiar becomes strange, and 'everything . . . that ought to have remained secret and hidden . . . has come to light.' It is dangerous, because it refuses the ordinary binary of good versus evil, but rather presents the possibility of transgression deliciously, seductively: often, our sympathies are with the devil. It is political, allowing the exploration of notions of feminism, colonialism and the frail nature of the status quo, often finding its largest and most avid readership at times of national upheaval.

As with sensations like hunger or desire: the reader knows when they encounter the Gothic, but it is difficult to account for it, since its power does not lie in the deployment of certain motifs, but in the irresistible evocation of a certain kind of feeling. *The Hound of the Baskervilles*, for example, may give to the reader any number of moors, candles, beasts and curses, but it is not Gothic: one never fully encounters that feeling of delicious unease, because it is compromised by the presence of Sherlock Holmes, the embodiment of reason. Hilary Mantel's novel *Beyond Black*, on the other hand, may begin prosaically enough with a rush-hour traffic jam in North London, but before long its subtle operation of unease begins to give off the Gothic sensation like a faint mist rising from the pages. The Gothic is at its truest when the reader begins to feel as if a cold hand is reaching out, grasping theirs and tugging them in – as if they, too, are entering Castle Dracula with a packet of legal documents, or waking to find the Woman in Black standing in a gust of sea-fret at the foot of the bed.

The reader who opens *A Quaint and Curious Volume* holds the key to a cabinet of Gothic curiosities. Here they will encounter that irresistible sensation which invites them to meet transgression with fear and delight in equal measure, and to bring to light all the strange concealed turns of their own psychology. There is a very particular pleasure in store – though it may be that, like Thomas Gray, they find themselves 'afraid to go to bed o'nights'.

Sarah Perry, 2019

A
QUAINT
&
CURIOUS
VOLUME

THE LOVERS.

PART I

THE LOVERS

THE RAVEN

BY
EDGAR ALLEN POE

Once upon a midnight dreary, while I pondered, weak and weary,
Over many a quaint and curious volume of forgotten lore,
While I nodded, nearly napping, suddenly there came a tapping,
As of some one gently rapping, rapping at my chamber door.
"'T is some visiter," I muttered, "tapping at my chamber door—
                      Only this, and nothing more."

Ah, distinctly I remember it was in the bleak December,
And each separate dying ember wrought its ghost upon the floor.
Eagerly I wished the morrow:—vainly I had sought to borrow
From my books surcease of sorrow—sorrow for the lost Lenore—
For the rare and radiant maiden whom the angels name
   Lenore—
                      Nameless here for evermore.

And the silken sad uncertain rustling of each purple curtain
Thrilled me—filled me with fantastic terrors never felt before;
So that now, to still the beating of my heart, I stood repeating
"'T is some visiter entreating entrance at my chamber door
Some late visiter entreating entrance at my chamber door;—
                      This it is, and nothing more."

Presently my soul grew stronger; hesitating then no longer,
"Sir," said I, "or Madam, truly your forgiveness I implore;
But the fact is I was napping, and so gently you came rapping,
And so faintly you came tapping, tapping at my chamber door,
That I scarce was sure I heard you"—here I opened wide the
    door;—

                    Darkness there, and nothing more.

Deep into that darkness peering, long I stood there wondering,
    fearing,
Doubting, dreaming dreams no mortal ever dared to dream
    before;
But the silence was unbroken, and the darkness gave no token,
And the only word there spoken was the whispered word,
    "Lenore!"
This I whispered, and an echo murmured back the word,
    "Lenore!"

                    Merely this and nothing more.

Back into the chamber turning, all my soul within me burning,
Soon again I heard a tapping, somewhat louder than before.
"Surely," said I, "surely that is something at my window lattice;
Let me see, then, what thereat is, and this mystery explore—
Let my heart be still a moment and this mystery explore;—

                    'T is the wind and nothing more!"

Open here I flung the shutter, when, with many a flirt and
    flutter,
In there stepped a stately Raven of the saintly days of yore.
Not the least obeisance made he; not a minute stopped or stayed
    he;
But, with mien of lord or lady, perched above my chamber door—

4

Perched upon a bust of Pallas just above my chamber door—
                    Perched, and sat, and nothing more.

Then this ebony bird beguiling my sad fancy into smiling,
By the grave and stern decorum of the countenance it wore,
"Though thy crest be shorn and shaven, thou," I said, "art sure
    no craven,
Ghastly grim and ancient Raven wandering from the Nightly
    shore,—
Tell me what thy lordly name is on the Night's Plutonian shore!"
                    Quoth the Raven, "Nevermore."

Much I marvelled this ungainly fowl to hear discourse so
    plainly,
Though its answer little meaning—little relevancy bore;
For we cannot help agreeing that no living human being
Ever yet was blessed with seeing bird above his chamber door—
Bird or beast upon the sculptured bust above his chamber door,
                    With such name as "Nevermore."

But the Raven, sitting lonely on the placid bust, spoke only
That one word, as if his soul in that one word he did outpour.
Nothing further then he uttered—not a feather then he
    fluttered—
Till I scarcely more than muttered, "Other friends have flown
    before—
On the morrow he will leave me, as my hopes have flown before."
                    Then the bird said, "Nevermore."

Startled at the stillness broken by reply so aptly spoken,
"Doubtless," said I, "what it utters is its only stock and store,
Caught from some unhappy master whom unmerciful Disaster

Followed fast and followed faster till his songs one burden bore—
Till the dirges of his Hope that melancholy burden bore
                Of 'Never—nevermore.'"

But the Raven still beguiling all my sad soul into smiling,
Straight I wheeled a cushioned seat in front of bird and bust and
    door;
Then, upon the velvet sinking, I betook myself to linking
Fancy unto fancy, thinking what this ominous bird of yore—
What this grim, ungainly, ghastly, gaunt and ominous bird of yore
                Meant in croaking "Nevermore."

This I sat engaged in guessing, but no syllable expressing
To the fowl whose fiery eyes now burned into my bosom's core;
This and more I sat divining, with my head at ease reclining
On the cushion's velvet lining that the lamplight gloated o'er,
But whose velvet violet lining with the lamplight gloating o'er
                She shall press, ah, nevermore!

Then, methought, the air grew denser, perfumed from an unseen
    censer
Swung by seraphim whose foot-falls tinkled on the tufted floor.
"Wretch," I cried, "thy God hath lent thee—by these angels he
    hath sent thee
Respite—respite and nepenthe from thy memories of Lenore!
Quaff, oh quaff this kind nepenthe, and forget this lost Lenore!"
                Quoth the Raven, "Nevermore."

"Prophet!" said I, "thing of evil!—prophet still, if bird or devil!—
Whether Tempter sent, or whether tempest tossed thee here
    ashore,
Desolate yet all undaunted, on this desert land enchanted—

On this home by Horror haunted—tell me truly, I implore—
Is there—is there balm in Gilead?—tell me—tell me, I implore!"
Quoth the Raven, "Nevermore."

"Prophet!" said I, "thing of evil—prophet still, if bird or devil!
By that Heaven that bends above, us—by that God we both
    adore—
Tell this soul with sorrow laden if, within the distant Aidenn,
It shall clasp a sainted maiden whom the angels name Lenore—
Clasp a rare and radiant maiden whom the angels name Lenore."
Quoth the Raven, "Nevermore."

"Be that word our sign of parting, bird or fiend!" I shrieked,
    upstarting—
"Get thee back into the tempest and the Night's Plutonian
    shore!
Leave no black plume as a token of that lie thy soul hath
    spoken!
Leave my loneliness unbroken!—quit the bust above my door!
Take thy beak from out my heart, and take thy form from off
    my door!"
Quoth the Raven, "Nevermore."

And the Raven, never flitting, still is sitting, still is sitting
On the pallid bust of Pallas just above my chamber door;
And his eyes have all the seeming of a demon's that is dreaming,
And the lamplight o'er him streaming throws his shadow on the
    floor;
And my soul from out that shadow that lies floating on the floor
Shall be lifted—nevermore!

PORPHYRIA'S LOVER

BY
ROBERT BROWNING

The rain set early in to-night,
    The sullen wind was soon awake,
It tore the elm-tops down for spite,
    And did its worst to vex the lake:
    I listened with heart fit to break.
When glided in Porphyria; straight
    She shut the cold out and the storm,
And kneeled and made the cheerless grate
    Blaze up, and all the cottage warm;
Which done, she rose, and from her form
Withdrew the dripping cloak and shawl,
    And laid her soiled gloves by, untied
Her hat and let the damp hair fall,
    And, last, she sat down by my side
    And called me. When no voice replied,
She put my arm about her waist,
    And made her smooth white shoulder bare,
And all her yellow hair displaced,
    And, stooping, made my cheek lie there,
    And spread, o'er all, her yellow hair,
Murmuring how she loved me — she

Too weak, for all her heart's endeavour,
To set its struggling passion free
    From pride, and vainer ties dissever,
    And give herself to me for ever.
But passion sometimes would prevail,
    Nor could to-night's gay feast restrain
A sudden thought of one so pale
    For love of her, and all in vain:
    So, she was come through wind and rain.
Be sure I looked up at her eyes
    Happy and proud; at last I knew
Porphyria worshipped me; surprise
    Made my heart swell, and still it grew
    While I debated what to do.
That moment she was mine, mine, fair,
    Perfectly pure and good: I found
A thing to do, and all her hair
    In one long yellow string I wound
    Three times her little throat around,
And strangled her. No pain felt she;
    I am quite sure she felt no pain.
As a shut bud that holds a bee,
    I warily oped her lids: again
    Laughed the blue eyes without a stain.
And I untightened next the tress
    About her neck; her cheek once more
Blushed bright beneath my burning kiss:
    I propped her head up as before,
    Only, this time my shoulder bore
Her head, which droops upon it still:
    The smiling rosy little head,
So glad it has its utmost will,

That all it scorned at once is fled,
  And I, its love, am gained instead!
Porphyria's love: she guessed not how
  Her darling one wish would be heard.
And thus we sit together now,
  And all night long we have not stirred,
  And yet God has not said a word!

THE SONG OF
WANDERING AENGUS

BY

WILLIAM BUTLER YEATS

I went out to the hazel wood,
Because a fire was in my head,
And cut and peeled a hazel wand,
And hooked a berry to a thread;
And when white moths were on the wing,
And moth-like stars were flickering out,
I dropped the berry in a stream
And caught a little silver trout.

When I had laid it on the floor
I went to blow the fire a-flame,
But something rustled on the floor,
And someone called me by my name:
It had become a glimmering girl
With apple blossom in her hair
Who called me by my name and ran
And faded through the brightening air.

Though I am old with wandering
Through hollow lands and hilly lands,
I will find out where she has gone,

And kiss her lips and take her hands;
And walk among long dappled grass,
And pluck till time and times are done,
The silver apples of the moon,
The golden apples of the sun.

BERENICE

BY
EDGAR ALLEN POE

Dicebant mihi sodales,
si sepulchrum amicae visitarem, curas
meas aliquantulum forelevatas.

—*Ebn Zaiat*

Misery is manifold. The wretchedness of earth is multiform. Overreaching the wide horizon as the rainbow, its hues are as various as the hues of that arch—as distinct too, yet as intimately blended. Overreaching the wide horizon as the rainbow! How is it that from beauty I have derived a type of unloveliness?—from the covenant of peace, a simile of sorrow? But as, in ethics, evil is a consequence of good, so, in fact, out of joy is sorrow born. Either the memory of past bliss is the anguish of to-day, or the agonies which *are*, have their origin in the ecstasies which *might have been*.

My baptismal name is Egaeus; that of my family I will not mention. Yet there are no towers in the land more time-honored than my gloomy, gray, hereditary halls. Our line has been called a race of visionaries; and in many striking particulars—in the character of the family mansion—in the frescos of the chief saloon—in the tapestries of the dormitories—in the chiselling of some buttresses in the armory—but more especially in the gallery of antique paintings—in the fashion of the library chamber—and, lastly, in the very peculiar nature of the library's contents—there is more than sufficient evidence to warrant the belief.

The recollections of my earliest years are connected with that chamber, and with its volumes—of which latter I will say no more. Here died my mother. Herein was I born. But it is mere idleness to say that I had not lived before—that the soul has no previous existence. You deny it?—let us not argue the matter. Convinced myself, I seek not to convince. There is, however, a remembrance of aerial forms—of spiritual and meaning eyes—of sounds, musical yet sad—a remembrance which will not be excluded; a memory like a shadow—vague, variable, indefinite, unsteady; and like a shadow, too, in the impossibility of my getting rid of it while the sunlight of my reason shall exist.

In that chamber was I born. Thus awaking from the long night of what seemed, but was not, nonentity, at once into the very regions of fairy land—into a palace of imagination—into the wild dominions of monastic thought and erudition—it is not singular that I gazed around me with a startled and ardent eye—that I loitered away my boyhood in books, and dissipated my youth in reverie; but it *is* singular that as years rolled away, and the noon of manhood found me still in the mansion of my fathers—it *is* wonderful what stagnation there fell upon the springs of my life— wonderful how total an inversion took place in the character of my commonest thought. The realities of the world affected me as visions, and as visions only, while the wild ideas of the land of dreams became, in turn, not the material of my every-day existence, but in very deed that existence utterly and solely in itself.

Berenice and I were cousins, and we grew up together in my paternal halls. Yet differently we grew—I, ill of health, and buried in gloom—she, agile, graceful, and overflowing with energy; hers, the ramble on the hill-side—mine the studies of the cloister; I, living within my own heart, and addicted, body and soul, to the most intense and painful meditation—she, roaming carelessly through life, with no thought of the shadows in her path, or the silent flight of the raven-winged hours. Berenice!—I call upon her name—Berenice!—and from the gray ruins of memory a thousand tumultuous recollections are startled at the sound! Ah, vividly is her image before me now, as in the early days of her light-heartedness and joy! Oh, gorgeous yet fantastic beauty! Oh, sylph amid the shrubberies of Arnheim! Oh, Naiad among its fountains! And then—then all is mystery and terror, and a tale which should not be told. Disease—a fatal disease, fell like the simoon upon her frame; and, even while I gazed upon her, the spirit of change swept over her, pervading her mind, her habits, and her character, and, in a manner the most subtle and terrible, disturbing even the identity of her person! Alas! the destroyer came and went!—and the victim—where is she? I knew her not—or knew her no longer as Berenice.

Among the numerous train of maladies superinduced by that fatal and primary one which effected a revolution of so horrible a kind in the moral and physical being of my cousin, may be mentioned as the most distressing and obstinate in its nature, a species of epilepsy not unfrequently terminating in *trance* itself—trance very nearly resembling positive dissolution, and from which her manner of recovery was in most instances, startlingly abrupt. In the mean time my own disease—for I have been told that I should call it by no other appellation—my own disease, then, grew rapidly upon me, and assumed finally a monomaniac character of a novel and extraordinary form—hourly and momently gaining vigor—and at length obtaining over me the most incomprehensible ascendancy. This monomania, if I must so term it, consisted in a morbid irritability of those properties of the mind in metaphysical science termed the *attentive*. It is more than probable that I am not understood; but I fear, indeed, that it is in no manner possible to convey to the mind of the merely general reader, an adequate idea of that nervous *intensity of interest* with which, in my case, the powers of meditation (not to speak technically) busied and buried themselves, in the contemplation of even the most ordinary objects of the universe.

To muse for long unwearied hours, with my attention riveted to some frivolous device on the margin, or in the typography of a book; to become absorbed, for the better part of a summer's day, in a quaint shadow falling aslant upon the tapestry or upon the floor; to lose myself, for an entire night, in watching the steady flame of a lamp, or the embers of a fire; to dream away whole days over the perfume of a flower; to repeat, monotonously, some common word, until the sound, by dint of frequent repetition, ceased to convey any idea whatever to the mind; to lose all sense of motion or physical existence, by means of absolute bodily quiescence long and obstinately persevered in: such were a few of the most common and least pernicious vagaries induced by a condition of the mental faculties, not, indeed, altogether unparalleled, but certainly bidding defiance to anything like analysis or explanation.

Yet let me not be misapprehended. The undue, earnest, and morbid attention thus excited by objects in their own nature frivolous, must not be confounded in character with that ruminating propensity common to all mankind, and more especially indulged in by persons of ardent imagination. It was not even, as might be at first supposed, an extreme condition, or exaggeration of such propensity, but primarily and essentially distinct and different. In the one instance, the dreamer, or enthusiast, being interested by an object usually *not* frivolous, imperceptibly loses sight of this object in a wilderness of deductions and suggestions issuing there-from, until, at the conclusion of a day dream *often replete with luxury*, he finds the *incitamentum*, or first cause of his musings, entirely vanished and forgotten. In my case, the primary object was *invari-ably frivolous*, although assuming, through the medium of my distempered vision, a refracted and unreal importance. Few deduc-tions, if any, were made; and those few pertinaciously returning in upon the original object as a centre. The meditations were *never* pleasurable; and, at the termination of the reverie, the first cause, so far from being out of sight, had attained that supernaturally exaggerated interest which was the prevailing feature of the disease. In a word, the powers of mind more particularly exercised were, with me, as I have said before, the *attentive*, and are, with the day-dreamer, the *speculative*.

My books, at this epoch, if they did not actually serve to irritate the disorder, partook, it will be perceived, largely, in their imagina-tive and inconsequential nature, of the characteristic qualities of the disorder itself. I well remember, among others, the treatise of the noble Italian, Coelius Secundus Curio, *"De Amplitudine Beati Regni Dei;"* St. Austin's great work, the "City of God;" and Tertullian's *"De Carne Christi,"* in which the paradoxical sentence *"Mortuus est Dei filius; credible est quia ineptum est: et sepultus resurrexit; certum est quia impossibile est,"* occupied my undivided time, for many weeks of laborious and fruitless investigation.

Thus it will appear that, shaken from its balance only by trivial things, my reason bore resemblance to that ocean-crag spoken of by Ptolemy Hephestion, which steadily resisting the attacks of human violence, and the fiercer fury of the waters and the winds, trembled only to the touch of the flower called Asphodel. And although, to a careless thinker, it might appear a matter beyond doubt, that the alteration produced by her unhappy malady, in the *moral* condition of Berenice, would afford me many objects for the exercise of that intense and abnormal meditation whose nature I have been at some trouble in explaining, yet such was not in any degree the case. In the lucid intervals of my infirmity, her calamity, indeed, gave me pain, and, taking deeply to heart that total wreck of her fair and gentle life, I did not fail to ponder, frequently and bitterly, upon the wonder-working means by which so strange a revolution had been so suddenly brought to pass. But these reflections partook not of the idiosyncrasy of my disease, and were such as would have occurred, under similar circumstances, to the ordinary mass of mankind. True to its own character, my disorder revelled in the less important but more startling changes wrought in the *physical* frame of Berenice—in the singular and most appalling distortion of her personal identity.

During the brightest days of her unparalleled beauty, most surely I had never loved her. In the strange anomaly of my existence, feelings with me, *had never been* of the heart, and my passions *always were* of the mind. Through the gray of the early morning— among the trellised shadows of the forest at noonday—and in the silence of my library at night—she had flitted by my eyes, and I had seen her—not as the living and breathing Berenice, but as the Berenice of a dream; not as a being of the earth, earthy, but as the abstraction of such a being; not as a thing to admire, but to analyze; not as an object of love, but as the theme of the most abstruse although desultory speculation. And *now*—now I shuddered in her presence, and grew pale at her approach; yet, bitterly lamenting her fallen and desolate condition, I called to mind that she had loved me long, and, in an evil moment, I spoke to her of marriage.

And at length the period of our nuptials was approaching, when, upon an afternoon in the winter of the year—one of those unseasonably warm, calm, and misty days which are the nurse of the beautiful Halcyon (*1),—I sat, (and sat, as I thought, alone,) in the inner apartment of the library. But, uplifting my eyes, I saw that Berenice stood before me.

Was it my own excited imagination—or the misty influence of the atmosphere—or the uncertain twilight of the chamber—or the gray draperies which fell around her figure—that caused in it so vacillating and indistinct an outline? I could not tell. She spoke no word; and I—not for worlds could I have uttered a syllable. An icy chill ran through my frame; a sense of insufferable anxiety oppressed me; a consuming curiosity pervaded my soul; and sinking back upon the chair, I remained for some time breathless and motionless, with my eyes riveted upon her person. Alas! its emaciation was excessive, and not one vestige of the former being lurked in any single line of the contour. My burning glances at length fell upon the face.

The forehead was high, and very pale, and singularly placid; and the once jetty hair fell partially over it, and overshadowed the hollow temples with innumerable ringlets, now of a vivid yellow, and jarring discordantly, in their fantastic character, with the reigning melancholy of the countenance. The eyes were lifeless, and lustreless, and seemingly pupilless, and I shrank involuntarily from their glassy stare to the contemplation of the thin and shrunken lips. They parted; and in a smile of peculiar meaning, *the teeth* of the changed Berenice disclosed themselves slowly to my view. Would to God that I had never beheld them, or that, having done so, I had died!

The shutting of a door disturbed me, and, looking up, I found that my cousin had departed from the chamber. But from the disordered chamber of my brain, had not, alas! departed, and would not be driven away, the white and ghastly *spectrum* of the teeth. Not a speck on their surface—not a shade on their enamel—not an indenture in their edges—but what that period of her smile had sufficed to brand in upon my memory. I saw them *now* even more unequivocally than I beheld them *then*. The teeth!—the teeth!—they

19

were here, and there, and everywhere, and visibly and palpably before me; long, narrow, and excessively white, with the pale lips writhing about them, as in the very moment of their first terrible development. Then came the full fury of my *monomania*, and I struggled in vain against its strange and irresistible influence. In the multiplied objects of the external world I had no thoughts but for the teeth. For these I longed with a phrenzied desire. All other matters and all different interests became absorbed in their single contemplation. They—they alone were present to the mental eye, and they, in their sole individuality, became the essence of my mental life. I held them in every light. I turned them in every attitude. I surveyed their characteristics. I dwelt upon their peculiarities. I pondered upon their conformation. I mused upon the alteration in their nature. I shuddered as I assigned to them in imagination a sensitive and sentient power, and even when unassisted by the lips, a capability of moral expression. Of Mademoiselle Salle it has been well said, "*Que tous ses pas etaient des sentiments,*" and of Berenice I more seriously believed *que toutes ses dents etaient des idees. Des idees!*—ah here was the idiotic thought that destroyed me! *Des idees!*—ah *therefore* it was that I coveted them so madly! I felt that their possession could alone ever restore me to peace, in giving me back to reason.

And the evening closed in upon me thus—and then the darkness came, and tarried, and went—and the day again dawned—and the mists of a second night were now gathering around—and still I sat motionless in that solitary room—and still I sat buried in meditation—and still the *phantasma* of the teeth maintained its terrible ascendancy, as, with the most vivid hideous distinctness, it floated about amid the changing lights and shadows of the chamber. At length there broke in upon my dreams a cry as of horror and dismay; and thereunto, after a pause, succeeded the sound of troubled voices, intermingled with many low moanings of sorrow or of pain. I arose from my seat, and throwing open one of the doors of the library, saw standing out in the ante-chamber a servant maiden, all in tears, who told me that Berenice was—no more! She had been seized with epilepsy in the early morning, and now, at the closing in of the night, the grave was ready for its tenant, and all the preparations for the burial were completed.

I found myself sitting in the library, and again sitting there alone. It seemed that I had newly awakened from a confused and exciting dream. I knew that it was now midnight, and I was well aware, that since the setting of the sun, Berenice had been interred. But of that dreary period which intervened I had no positive, at least no definite comprehension. Yet its memory was replete with horror—horror more horrible from being vague, and terror more terrible from ambiguity. It was a fearful page in the record of my existence, written all over with dim, and hideous, and unintelligible recollections. I strived to decypher them, but in vain; while ever and anon, like the spirit of a departed sound, the shrill and piercing shriek of a female voice seemed to be ringing in my ears. I had done a deed—what was it? I asked myself the question aloud, and the whispering echoes of the chamber answered me,—"*what was it?*"

On the table beside me burned a lamp, and near it lay a little box. It was of no remarkable character, and I had seen it frequently before, for it was the property of the family physician; but how came it *there*, upon my table, and why did I shudder in regarding it? These things were in no manner to be accounted for, and my eyes at length dropped to the open pages of a book, and to a sentence underscored therein. The words were the singular but simple ones of the poet Ebn Zaiat:—"*Dicebant mihi sodales si sepulchrum amicae visitarem, curas meas aliquantulum fore levatas.*" Why then, as I perused them, did the hairs of my head erect themselves on end, and the blood of my body become congealed within my veins?

There came a light tap at the library door—and, pale as the

tenant of a tomb, a menial entered upon tiptoe. His looks were wild with terror, and he spoke to me in a voice tremulous, husky, and very low. What said he?—some broken sentences I heard. He told of a wild cry disturbing the silence of the night—of the gathering together of the household—of a search in the direction of the sound; and then his tones grew thrillingly distinct as he whispered me of a violated grave—of a disfigured body enshrouded, yet still breathing—still palpitating—*still alive!*

He pointed to garments;—they were muddy and clotted with gore. I spoke not, and he took me gently by the hand: it was indented with the impress of human nails. He directed my attention to some object against the wall. I looked at it for some minutes: it was a spade. With a shriek I bounded to the table, and grasped the box that lay upon it. But I could not force it open; and in my tremor, it slipped from my hands, and fell heavily, and burst into pieces; and from it, with a rattling sound, there rolled out some instruments of dental surgery, intermingled with thirty-two small, white and ivory-looking substances that were scattered to and fro about the floor.

THE WEDDING-KNELL

BY

NATHANIEL HAWTHORNE

There is a certain church, in the city of New York which I have always regarded with peculiar interest on account of a marriage there solemnized under very singular circumstances in my grandmother's girlhood. That venerable lady chanced to be a spectator of the scene, and ever after made it her favorite narrative. Whether the edifice now standing on the same site be the identical one to which she referred I am not antiquarian enough to know, nor would it be worth while to correct myself, perhaps, of an agreeable error by reading the date of its erection on the tablet over the door. It is a stately church surrounded by an enclosure of the loveliest green, within which appear urns, pillars, obelisks, and other forms of monumental marble, the tributes of private affection or more splendid memorials of historic dust. With such a place, though the tumult of the city rolls beneath its tower, one would be willing to connect some legendary interest.

The marriage might be considered as the result of an early engagement, though there had been two intermediate weddings on the lady's part and forty years of celibacy on that of the gentleman. At sixty-five Mr. Ellenwood was a shy but not quite a secluded man; selfish, like all men who brood over their own hearts, yet manifesting on rare occasions a vein of generous sentiment; a scholar throughout life, though always an indolent one, because his studies had no definite object either of public advantage or personal ambition; a gentleman, high-bred and fastidiously delicate, yet sometimes requiring a considerable relaxation in his behalf of the common rules of society. In truth, there were so many anomalies in his character, and, though shrinking with diseased sensibility from public notice, it had been his fatality so often to become the topic of the day by some wild eccentricity of conduct, that people searched his lineage for a hereditary taint of insanity. But there was no need of this. His caprices had their origin in a mind that lacked the support of an engrossing purpose, and in feelings that preyed upon themselves for want of other food. If he were mad, it was the consequence, and not the cause, of an aimless and abortive life.

The widow was as complete a contrast to her third bridegroom in everything but age as can well be conceived. Compelled to relinquish her first engagement, she had been united to a man of twice her own years, to whom she became an exemplary wife, and by whose death she was left in possession of a splendid fortune. A Southern gentleman considerably younger than herself succeeded to her hand and carried her to Charleston, where after many uncomfortable years she found herself again a widow. It would have been singular if any uncommon delicacy of feeling had survived through such a life as Mrs. Dabney's; it could not but be crushed and killed by her early disappointment, the cold duty of her first marriage, the dislocation of the heart's principles consequent on a second union, and the unkindness of her Southern husband, which had inevitably driven her to connect the idea of his death with that of her comfort. To be brief, she was that wisest but unloveliest variety of woman, a philosopher, bearing troubles of the heart with equanimity, dispensing with all that should have been her happiness and making the best of what remained. Sage

24

in most matters, the widow was perhaps the more amiable for the one frailty that made her ridiculous. Being childless, she could not remain beautiful by proxy in the person of a daughter; she therefore refused to grow old and ugly on any consideration; she struggled with Time, and held fast her roses in spite of him, till the venerable thief appeared to have relinquished the spoil as not worth the trouble of acquiring it.

The approaching marriage of this woman of the world with such an unworldly man as Mr. Ellenwood was announced soon after Mrs. Dabney's return to her native city. Superficial observers, and deeper ones, seemed to concur in supposing that the lady must have borne no inactive part in arranging the affair; there were considerations of expediency which she would be far more likely to appreciate than Mr. Ellenwood, and there was just the specious phantom of sentiment and romance in this late union of two early lovers which sometimes makes a fool of a woman who has lost her true feelings among the accidents of life. All the wonder was how the gentleman, with his lack of worldly wisdom and agonizing consciousness of ridicule, could have been induced to take a measure at once so prudent and so laughable. But while people talked the wedding-day arrived. The ceremony was to be solemnized according to the Episcopalian forms and in open church, with a degree of publicity that attracted many spectators, who occupied the front seats of the galleries and the pews near the altar and along the broad aisle. It had been arranged, or possibly it was the custom of the day, that the parties should proceed separately to church. By some accident the bridegroom was a little less punctual than the widow and her bridal attendants, with whose arrival, after this tedious but necessary preface, the action of our tale may be said to commence.

The clumsy wheels of several old-fashioned coaches were heard, and the gentlemen and ladies composing the bridal-party came through the church door with the sudden and gladsome effect of a burst of sunshine. The whole group, except the principal figure, was made up of youth and gayety. As they streamed up the broad aisle, while the pews and pillars seemed to brighten on either side, their steps were as buoyant as if they mistook the church for a ball-room and were ready to dance hand in hand to the altar. So brilliant was the spectacle that few took notice of a singular phenomenon that had marked its entrance. At the moment when the bride's foot touched the threshold the bell swung heavily in the tower above her and sent forth its deepest knell. The vibrations died away, and returned with prolonged solemnity as she entered the body of the church.

"Good heavens! What an omen!" whispered a young lady to her lover.

"On my honor," replied the gentleman, "I believe the bell has the good taste to toll of its own accord. What has she to do with weddings? If you, dearest Julia, were approaching the altar, the bell would ring out its merriest peal. It has only a funeral-knell for her."

The bride and most of her company had been too much occupied with the bustle of entrance to hear the first boding stroke of the bell—or, at least, to reflect on the singularity of such a welcome to the altar. They therefore continued to advance with undiminished gayety. The gorgeous dresses of the time—the crimson velvet coats, the gold-laced hats, the hoop-petticoats, the silk, satin, brocade and embroidery, the buckles, canes and swords, all displayed to the best advantage on persons suited to such finery—made the group appear more like a bright-colored picture than anything real. But by what perversity of taste had the artist represented his principal figure as so wrinkled and decayed, while yet he had decked her out in the brightest splendor of attire, as if the loveliest maiden had suddenly withered into age and become a moral to the beautiful around her? On they went, however, and had glittered along about a third of the aisle, when another stroke of the bell seemed to fill the church with a visible gloom, dimming and obscuring the bright-pageant till it shone forth again as from a mist.

This time the party wavered, stopped and huddled closer together, while a slight scream was heard from some of the ladies and a confused whispering among the gentlemen. Thus tossing to and fro, they might have been fancifully compared to a splendid bunch of flowers suddenly shaken by a puff of wind which threatened to scatter the leaves of an old brown, withered rose on the same stalk with two dewy buds, such being the emblem of the widow between her fair young bridemaids. But her heroism was admirable. She had started with an irrepressible shudder, as if the stroke of the bell had fallen directly on her heart; then, recovering herself, while her attendants were yet in dismay, she took the lead and paced calmly up the aisle. The bell continued to swing, strike and vibrate with the same doleful regularity as when a corpse is on its way to the tomb.

"My young friends here have their nerves a little shaken," said the widow, with a smile, to the clergyman at the altar. "But so many weddings have been ushered in with the merriest peal of the bells, and yet turned out unhappily, that I shall hope for better fortune under such different auspices."

"Madam," answered the rector, in great perplexity, "this strange occurrence brings to my mind a marriage-sermon of the famous Bishop Taylor wherein he mingles so many thoughts of mortality and future woe that, to speak somewhat after his own rich style, he seems to hang the bridal-chamber in black and cut the wedding-garment out of a coffin-pall. And it has been the custom of divers nations to infuse something of sadness into their marriage ceremonies, so to keep death in mind while contracting that engagement which is life's chiefest business. Thus we may draw a sad but profitable moral from this funeral-knell."

But, though the clergyman might have given his moral even a keener point, he did not fail to despatch an attendant to inquire into the mystery and stop those sounds so dismally appropriate to such a marriage. A brief space elapsed, during which the silence was broken only by whispers and a few suppressed titterings among the wedding-party and the spectators, who after the first shock were disposed to draw an ill-natured merriment from the affair. The young have less charity for aged follies than the old for those of youth. The widow's glance was observed to wander for an instant toward a window of the church, as if searching for the time-worn marble that she had dedicated to her first husband; then her eyelids dropped over their faded orbs and her thoughts were drawn irresistibly to another grave. Two buried men with a voice at her ear and a cry afar off were calling her to lie down beside them. Perhaps, with momentary truth of feeling, she thought how much happier had been her fate if, after years of bliss, the bell were now tolling for her funeral and she were followed to the grave by the old affection of her earliest lover, long her husband. But why had she returned to him when their cold hearts shrank from each other's embrace?

Still the death-bell tolled so mournfully that the sunshine seemed to fade in the air. A whisper, communicated from those who stood nearest the windows, now spread through the church: a hearse with a train of several coaches was creeping along the street, conveying some dead man to the churchyard, while the bride awaited a living one at the altar. Immediately after, the footsteps of the bridegroom and his friends were heard at the door. The widow looked down the aisle and clenched the arm of one of her bridemaids in her bony hand with such unconscious violence that the fair girl trembled.

"You frighten me, my dear madam," cried she. "For heaven's sake, what is the matter?"

"Nothing, my dear—nothing," said the widow; then, whispering close to her ear, "There is a foolish fancy that I cannot get rid of. I am expecting my bridegroom to come into the church with my two first husbands for groomsmen."

"Look! look!" screamed the bridemaid. "What is here? The funeral!"

As she spoke a dark procession paced into the church. First came an old man and woman, like chief mourners at a funeral, attired from head to foot in the deepest black, all but their pale features and hoary hair, he leaning on a staff and supporting her decrepit form with his nerveless arm. Behind appeared another and another pair, as aged, as black and mournful as the first. As they drew near the widow recognized in every face some trait of former friends long forgotten, but now returning as if from their old graves to warn her to prepare a shroud, or, with purpose almost as unwelcome, to exhibit their wrinkles and infirmity and claim her as their companion by the tokens of her own decay. Many a merry night had she danced with them in youth, and now in joyless age she felt that some withered partner should request her hand and all unite in a dance of death to the music of the funeral-bell.

While these aged mourners were passing up the aisle it was observed that from pew to pew the spectators shuddered with irrepressible awe as some object hitherto concealed by the intervening figures came full in sight. Many turned away their faces; others kept a fixed and rigid stare, and a young girl giggled hysterically and fainted with the laughter on her lips. When the spectral procession approached the altar, each couple separated and slowly diverged, till in the centre appeared a form that had been worthily ushered in with all this gloomy pomp, the death-knell and the funeral. It was the bridegroom in his shroud.

No garb but that of the grave could have befitted such a death-like aspect. The eyes, indeed, had the wild gleam of a sepulchral lamp; all else was fixed in the stern calmness which old men wear in the coffin. The corpse stood motionless, but addressed the widow in accents that seemed to melt into the clang of the bell, which fell heavily on the air while he spoke.

"Come, my bride!" said those pale lips. "The hearse is ready; the sexton stands waiting for us at the door of the tomb. Let us be married, and then to our coffins!"

How shall the widow's horror be represented? It gave her the ghastliness of a dead man's bride. Her youthful friends stood apart, shuddering at the mourners, the shrouded bridegroom and herself; the whole scene expressed by the strongest imagery the vain struggle of the gilded vanities of this world when opposed to age, infirmity, sorrow and death.

The awestruck silence was first broken by the clergyman.

"Mr. Ellenwood," said he, soothingly, yet with somewhat of authority, "you are not well. Your mind has been agitated by the unusual circumstances in which you are placed. The ceremony must be deferred. As an old friend, let me entreat you to return home."

"Home—yes; but not without my bride," answered he, in the same hollow accents. "You deem this mockery—perhaps madness. Had I bedizened my aged and broken frame with scarlet and embroidery, had I forced my withered lips to smile at my dead heart, that might have been mockery or madness; but now let young and old declare which of us has come hither without a wedding-garment— the bridegroom or the bride."

He stepped forward at a ghostly pace and stood beside the widow, contrasting the awful simplicity of his shroud with the glare and glitter in which she had arrayed herself for this unhappy scene. None that beheld them could deny the terrible strength of the moral which his disordered intellect had contrived to draw.

"Cruel! cruel!" groaned the heartstricken bride.

"Cruel?" repeated he; then, losing his deathlike composure in a wild bitterness, "Heaven judge which of us has been cruel to the other! In youth you deprived me of my happiness, my hopes, my aims; you took away all the substance of my life and made it a dream without reality enough even to grieve at—with only a pervading gloom, through which I walked wearily and cared not whither. But after forty years, when I have built my tomb and would not give up the thought of resting there—no, not for such a life as we once pictured—you call me to the altar. At your summons I am here. But other husbands have enjoyed your youth, your beauty, your warmth of heart and all that could be termed your life. What is there for me but your decay and death? And therefore I have bidden these funeral-friends, and bespoken the sexton's deepest knell, and am come in my shroud to wed you as with a burial-service, that we may join our hands at the door of the sepulchre and enter it together."

It was not frenzy, it was not merely the drunkenness of strong emotion in a heart unused to it, that now wrought upon the bride. The stern lesson of the day had done its work; her worldliness was gone. She seized the bridegroom's hand.

"Yes!" cried she; "let us wed even at the door of the sepulchre. My life is gone in vanity and emptiness, but at its close there is one true feeling. It has made me what I was in youth: it makes me worthy of you. Time is no more for both of us. Let us wed for eternity."

With a long and deep regard the bridegroom looked into her eyes, while a tear was gathering in his own. How strange that gush of human feeling from the frozen bosom of a corpse! He wiped away the tear, even with his shroud.

"Beloved of my youth," said he, "I have been wild. The despair of my whole lifetime had returned at once and maddened me. Forgive and be forgiven. Yes; it is evening with us now, and we have realized none of our morning dreams of happiness. But let us join our hands before the altar as lovers whom adverse circumstances have separated through life, yet who meet again as they are leaving it and find their earthly affection changed into something holy as religion. And what is time to the married of eternity?"

Amid the tears of many and a swell of exalted sentiment in those who felt aright was solemnized the union of two immortal souls. The train of withered mourners, the hoary bridegroom in his shroud, the pale features of the aged bride and the death-bell tolling through the whole till its deep voice overpowered the marriage-words,—all marked the funeral of earthly hopes. But as the ceremony proceeded, the organ, as if stirred by the sympathies of this impressive scene, poured forth an anthem, first mingling with the dismal knell, then rising to a loftier strain, till the soul looked down upon its woe. And when the awful rite was finished and with cold hand in cold hand the married of eternity withdrew, the organ's peal of solemn triumph drowned the wedding-knell.

WHEEL OF FORTUNE.

PART II

WHEEL OF FORTUNE

THE DARKLING THRUSH

BY

THOMAS HARDY

I leant upon a coppice gate
    When Frost was spectre-grey,
And Winter's dregs made desolate
    The weakening eye of day.
The tangled bine-stems scored the sky
    Like strings of broken lyres,
And all mankind that haunted nigh
    Had sought their household fires.

The land's sharp features seemed to be
    The Century's corpse outleant,
His crypt the cloudy canopy,
    The wind his death-lament.
The ancient pulse of germ and birth
    Was shrunken hard and dry,
And every spirit upon earth
    Seemed fervourless as I.

At once a voice arose among
    The bleak twigs overhead
In a full-hearted evensong

Of joy illimited;
An aged thrush, frail, gaunt, and small,
　　　In blast-beruffled plume,
Had chosen thus to fling his soul
　　　Upon the growing gloom.

So little cause for carolings
　　　Of such ecstatic sound
Was written on terrestrial things
　　　Afar or nigh around,
That I could think there trembled through
　　　His happy good-night air
Some blessed Hope, whereof he knew
　　　And I was unaware.

THE OLD NURSE'S STORY

BY

ELIZABETH GASKELL

You know, my dears, that your mother was an orphan, and an only child; and I daresay you have heard that your grandfather was a clergyman up in Westmoreland, where I come from. I was just a girl in the village school, when, one day, your grandmother came in to ask the mistress if there was any scholar there who would do for a nurse-maid; and mighty proud I was, I can tell ye, when the mistress called me up, and spoke of me being a good girl at my needle, and a steady, honest girl, and one whose parents were very respectable, though they might be poor. I thought I should like nothing better than to serve the pretty young lady, who was blushing as deep as I was, as she spoke of the coming baby, and what I should have to do with it. However, I see you don't care so much for this part of my story, as for what you think is to come, so I'll tell you at once. I was engaged and settled at the parsonage before Miss Rosamond (that was the baby, who is now your mother) was born. To be sure, I had little enough to do with her when she came, for she was never out of her mother's arms, and slept by her all night long; and proud enough was I sometimes when missis trusted her to me. There never was such a baby before or since, though you've all of you been fine enough in your turns; but for sweet, winning ways, you've none of you come up to your mother. She took after her mother, who was a real lady born; a Miss Furnivall, a grand-daughter of Lord Furnivall's, in Northumberland. I believe she had neither brother nor sister, and had been brought up in my lord's family till she had married your grandfather, who was just a curate, son to a shopkeeper in Carlisle—but a clever, fine gentleman as ever was—and one who was a right-down hard worker in his parish, which was very wide, and scattered all abroad over the Westmoreland Fells. When your mother, little Miss Rosamond, was about four or five years old, both her parents died in a fortnight—one after the other. Ah! that was a sad time. My pretty young mistress and me was looking for another baby, when my master came home from one of his long rides, wet and tired, and took the fever he died of; and then she never held up her head again, but just lived to see her dead baby, and have it laid on her breast, before she sighed away her life. My mistress had asked me, on her death-bed, never to leave Miss Rosamond; but if she had never spoken a word, I would have gone with the little child to the end of the world.

The next thing, and before we had well stilled our sobs, the executors and guardians came to settle the affairs. They were my poor young mistress's own cousin, Lord Furnivall, and Mr. Esthwaite, my master's brother, a shopkeeper in Manchester; not so well to do then as he was afterwards, and with a large family rising about him. Well! I don't know if it were their settling, or because of a letter my mistress wrote on her death-bed to her cousin, my lord; but somehow it was settled that Miss Rosamond and me were to go to Furnivall Manor House, in Northumberland, and my lord spoke as if it had been her mother's wish that she should live with his family, and as if he had no objections, for that one or two more or less could make no difference in so grand a household. So, though that was not the way in which I should have wished the coming of my bright and pretty pet to have been looked at—who was like a sunbeam in any family, be it never so grand—I was well pleased that all the folks in the Dale should stare and admire, when they heard I was going to be young lady's maid at my Lord Furnivall's at Furnivall Manor.

But I made a mistake in thinking we were to go and live where my lord did. It turned out that the family had left Furnivall Manor House fifty years or more. I could not hear that my poor young mistress had never been there, though she had been brought up in the family; and I was sorry for that, for I should have liked Miss Rosamond's youth to have passed where her mother's had been.

My lord's gentleman, from whom I asked as many questions as I durst, said that the Manor House was at the foot of the Cumberland Fells, and a very grand place; that an old Miss Furnivall, a great-aunt of my lord's, lived there, with only a few servants; but that it was a very healthy place, and my lord had thought that it would suit Miss Rosamond very well for a few years, and that her being there might perhaps amuse his old aunt.

I was bidden by my lord to have Miss Rosamond's things ready by a certain day. He was a stern, proud man, as they say all the Lords Furnivall were; and he never spoke a word more than was necessary. Folk did say he had loved my young mistress; but that, because she knew that his father would object, she would never listen to him, and married Mr. Esthwaite; but I don't know. He never married, at any rate. But he never took much notice of Miss Rosamond; which I thought he might have done if he had cared for her dead mother. He sent his gentleman with us to the Manor House, telling him to join him at Newcastle that same evening; so there was no great length of time for him to make us known to all the strangers before he, too, shook us off; and we were left, two lonely young things (I was not eighteen) in the great old Manor House. It seems like yesterday that we drove there. We had left our own dear parsonage very early, and we had both cried as if our

41

hearts would break, though we were travelling in my lord's carriage, which I thought so much of once. And now it was long past noon on a September day, and we stopped to change horses for the last time at a little smoky town, all full of colliers and miners. Miss Rosamond had fallen asleep, but Mr. Henry told me to waken her, that she might see the park and the Manor House as we drove up. I thought it rather a pity; but I did what he bade me, for fear he should complain of me to my lord. We had left all signs of a town, or even a village, and were then inside the gates of a large wild park—not like the parks here in the south, but with rocks, and the noise of running water, and gnarled thorn-trees, and old oaks, all white and peeled with age.

The road went up about two miles, and then we saw a great and stately house, with many trees close around it, so close that in some places their branches dragged against the walls when the wind blew; and some hung broken down; for no one seemed to take much charge of the place;—to lop the wood, or to keep the moss-covered carriage-way in order. Only in front of the house all was clear. The great oval drive was without a weed; and neither tree nor creeper was allowed to grow over the long, many-windowed front; at both sides of which a wing protected, which were each the ends of other side fronts; for the house, although it was so desolate, was even grander than I expected. Behind it rose the Fells; which seemed unenclosed and bare enough; and on the left hand of the house, as you stood facing it, was a little, old-fashioned flower-garden, as I found out afterwards. A door opened out upon it from the west front; it had been scooped out of the thick, dark wood for some old Lady Furnivall; but the branches of the great forest-trees had grown and overshadowed it again, and there were very few flowers that would live there at that time.

When we drove up to the great front entrance, and went into the hall, I thought we would be lost—it was so large, and vast and grand. There was a chandelier all of bronze, hung down from the middle of the ceiling; and I had never seen one before, and looked at it all in amaze. Then, at one end of the hall, was a great fire-place, as large as the sides of the houses in my country, with massy andirons and dogs to hold the wood; and by it were heavy, old-fashioned sofas. At the opposite end of the hall, to the left as you went in—on the western side—was an organ built into the wall, and so large that it filled up the best part of that end. Beyond it, on the same side, was a door; and opposite, on each side of the fire-place, were also doors leading to the east front; but those I never went through as long as I stayed in the house, so I can't tell you what lay beyond.

The afternoon was closing in, and the hall, which had no fire lighted in it, looked dark and gloomy, but we did not stay there a moment. The old servant, who had opened the door for us, bowed to Mr. Henry, and took us in through the door at the further side of the great organ, and led us through several smaller halls and passages into the west drawing-room, where he said that Miss Furnivall was sitting. Poor little Miss Rosamond held very tight to me, as if she were scared and lost in that great place; and as for myself, I was not much better. The west drawing-room was very cheerful-looking, with a warm fire in it, and plenty of good, comfort-able furniture about. Miss Furnivall was an old lady not far from eighty, I should think, but I do not know. She was thin and tall, and had a face as full of fine wrinkles as if they had been drawn all over it with a needle's point. Her eyes were very watchful, to make up, I suppose, for her being so deaf as to be obliged to use a trumpet. Sitting with her, working at the same great piece of tapestry, was Mrs. Stark, her maid and companion, and almost as old as she was. She had lived with Miss Furnivall ever since they both were young, and now she seemed more like a friend than a servant; she looked so cold, and grey, and stony, as if she had never loved or cared for any one; and I don't suppose she did care for any one, except her mistress; and, owing to the great deafness of the latter, Mrs. Stark treated her very much as if she were a child. Mr. Henry gave some message from my lord, and then he bowed good-by to us all,—taking no notice of my sweet little Miss Rosamond's outstretched hand—and left us standing there, being looked at by the two old ladies through their spectacles.

I was right glad when they rung for the old footman who had shown us in at first, and told him to take us to our rooms. So we went out of that great drawing-room and into another sitting-room, and out of that, and then up a great flight of stairs, and along a broad gallery—which was something like a library, having books all down one side, and windows and writing-tables all down the other— till we came to our rooms, which I was not sorry to hear were just over the kitchens; for I began to think I should be lost in that wilderness of a house. There was an old nursery, that had been used for all the little lords and ladies long ago, with a pleasant fire burning in the grate, and the kettle boiling on the hob, and tea-things spread out on the table; and out of that room was the night-nursery, with a little crib for Miss Rosamond close to my bed. And old James called up Dorothy, his wife, to bid us welcome; and both he and she were so hospitable and kind, that by-and-by Miss Rosamond and me felt quite at home; and by the time tea was over, she was sitting on Dorothy's knee, and chattering away as fast as her little tongue could go. I soon found out that Dorothy was from Westmoreland, and that bound her and me together, as it were; and I would never wish to meet with kinder people than were old James and his wife. James had lived pretty nearly all his life in my lord's family, and thought there was no one so grand as they. He even looked down a little on his wife; because, till he had married her, she had never lived in any but a farmer's household. But he was very fond of her, as well he might be. They had one servant

44

under them, to do all the rough work. Agnes they called her; and she and me, and James and Dorothy, with Miss Furnivall and Mrs. Stark, made up the family; always remembering my sweet little Miss Rosamond! I used to wonder what they had done before she came, they thought so much of her now. Kitchen and drawing-room, it was all the same. The hard, sad Miss Furnivall, and the cold Mrs. Stark, looked pleased when she came fluttering in like a bird, playing and pranking hither and thither, with a continual murmur, and pretty prattle of gladness. I am sure, they were sorry many a time when she flitted away into the kitchen, though they were too proud to ask her to stay with them, and were a little surprised at her taste; though to be sure, as Mrs. Stark said, it was not to be wondered at, remembering what stock her father had come of. The great, old rambling house was a famous place for little Miss Rosamond. She made expeditions all over it, with me at her heels; all, except the east wing, which was never opened, and whither we never thought of going. But in the western and northern part was many a pleasant room; full of things that were curiosities to us, though they might not have been to people who had seen more. The windows were darkened by the sweeping boughs of the trees, and the ivy which had overgrown them; but, in the green gloom, we could manage to see old china jars and carved ivory boxes, and great heavy books, and, above all, the old pictures!

Once, I remember, my darling would have Dorothy go with us to tell us who they all were; for they were all portraits of some of my lord's family, though Dorothy could not tell us the names of every one. We had gone through most of the rooms, when we came to the old state drawing-room over the hall, and there was a picture of Miss Furnivall; or, as she was called in those days, Miss Grace, for she was the younger sister. Such a beauty she must have been! but with such a set, proud look, and such scorn looking out of her handsome eyes, with her eyebrows just a little raised, as if she

45

wondered how anyone could have the impertinence to look at her, and her lip curled at us, as we stood there gazing. She had a dress on, the like of which I had never seen before, but it was all the fashion when she was young; a hat of some soft white stuff like beaver, pulled a little over her brows, and a beautiful plume of feathers sweeping round it on one side; and her gown of blue satin was open in front to a quilted white stomacher.

'Well, to be sure!' said I, when I had gazed my fill. 'Flesh is grass, they do say; but who would have thought that Miss Furnivall had been such an out-and-out beauty, to see her now.'

'Yes,' said Dorothy. 'Folks change sadly. But if what my master's father used to say was true, Miss Furnivall, the elder sister, was handsomer than Miss Grace. Her picture is here somewhere; but, if I show it you, you must never let on, even to James, that you have seen it. Can the little lady hold her tongue, think you?' asked she.

I was not so sure, for she was such a little sweet, bold, open-spoken child, so I set her to hide herself; and then I helped Dorothy to turn a great picture, that leaned with its face towards the wall, and was not hung up as the others were. To be sure, it beat Miss Grace for beauty; and, I think, for scornful pride, too, though in that matter it might be hard to choose. I could have looked at it an hour, but Dorothy seemed half frightened at having shown it to me, and hurried it back again, and bade me run and find Miss Rosamond, for that there were some ugly places about the house, where she should like ill for the child to go. I was a brave, high-spirited girl, and thought little of what the old woman said, for I liked hide-and-seek as well as any child in the parish; so off I ran to find my little one.

As winter drew on, and the days grew shorter, I was sometimes almost certain that I heard a noise as if someone was playing on the great organ in the hall. I did not hear it every evening; but, certainly, I did very often, usually when I was sitting with Miss Rosamond, after I had put her to bed, and keeping quite still and silent in the bedroom. Then I used to hear it booming and swelling away in the distance. The first night, when I went down to my supper, I asked Dorothy who had been playing music, and James said very shortly that I was a gowk to take the wind soughing among the trees for music; but I saw Dorothy look at him very fearfully, and Bessy, the kitchen-maid, said something beneath her breath, and went quite white. I saw they did not like my question, so I held my peace till I was with Dorothy alone, when I knew I could get a good deal out of her. So, the next day, I watched my time, and I coaxed and asked her who it was that played the organ; for I knew that it was the organ and not the wind well enough, for all I had kept silence before James. But Dorothy had had her lesson, I'll warrant, and never a word could I get from her. So then I tried Bessy, though I had always held my head rather above her, as I was evened to James and Dorothy, and she was little better than their servant. So she said I must never, never tell; and if ever I told, I was never to say *she* had told me; but it was a very strange noise, and she had heard it many a time, but most of all on winter nights, and before storms; and folks did say it was the old lord playing on the great organ in the hall, just as he used to do when he was alive; but who the old lord was, or why he played, and why he played on stormy winter evenings in particular, she either could not or would not tell me. Well! I told you I had a brave heart; and I thought it was rather pleasant to have that grand music rolling about the house, let who would be the player; for now it rose above the great gusts of wind, and wailed and triumphed just like a living creature, and then it fell to a softness most complete, only it was always music, and tunes, so it was nonsense to call it the wind. I thought at first, that it might be Miss Furnivall who played, unknown to Bessy; but one day, when I was in the hall by myself,

47

I opened the organ and peeped all about it and around it, as I had done to the organ in Crosthwaite church once before, and I saw it was all broken and destroyed inside, though it looked so brave and fine; and then, though it was noon-day, my flesh began to creep a little, and I shut it up, and run away pretty quickly to my own bright nursery; and I did not like hearing the music for some time after that, any more than James and Dorothy did. All this time Miss Rosamond was making herself more and more beloved. The old ladies liked her to dine with them at their early dinner. James stood behind Miss Furnivall's chair, and I behind Miss Rosamond's all in state; and after dinner, she would play about in a corner of the great drawing-room as still as any mouse, while Miss Furnivall slept, and I had my dinner in the kitchen. But she was glad enough to come to me in the nursery afterwards; for, as she said, Miss Furnivall was so sad, and Mrs. Stark so dull; but she and I were merry enough; and by-and-by, I got not to care for that weird rolling music, which did one no harm, if we did not know where it came from.

That winter was very cold. In the middle of October the frosts began, and lasted many, many weeks. I remember one day, at dinner, Miss Furnivall lifted up her sad, heavy eyes, and said to Mrs. Stark, 'I am afraid we shall have a terrible winter,' in a strange kind of meaning way. But Mrs. Stark pretended not to hear, and talked very loud of something else. My little lady and I did not care for the frost; not we! As long as it was dry, we climbed up the steep brows behind the house, and went up on the Fells, which were bleak and bare enough, and there we ran races in the fresh, sharp air; and once we came down by a new path, that took us past the two old gnarled holly-trees, which grew about half-way down by the east side of the house. But the days grew shorter and shorter, and the old lord, if it was he, played away, more and more stormily and sadly, on the great organ. One Sunday afternoon—it must have been towards the end of November—I asked Dorothy to take charge of little missy when she came out of the drawing-room, after Miss Furnivall had had her nap; for it was too cold to take her with me to church, and yet I wanted to go. And Dorothy was glad enough to promise, and was so fond of the child, that all seemed well; and Bessy and I set off very briskly, though the sky hung heavy and black over the white earth, as if the night had never fully gone away, and the air, though still, was very biting and keen.

'We shall have a fall of snow,' said Bessy to me. And sure enough, even while we were in church, it came down thick, in great large flakes,—so thick, it almost darkened the windows. It had stopped snowing before we came out, but it lay soft, thick and deep beneath our feet, as we tramped home. Before we got to the hall, the moon rose, and I think it was lighter then—what with the moon, and what with the white dazzling snow—than it had been when we went to church, between two and three o'clock. I have not told you that Miss Furnivall and Mrs. Stark never went to church; they used to read the prayers together, in their quiet, gloomy way; they seemed to feel the Sunday very long without their tapestry-work to be busy at. So when I went to Dorothy in the kitchen, to fetch Miss Rosamond and take her upstairs with me, I did not much wonder when the old woman told me that the ladies had kept the child with them, and that she had never come to the kitchen, as I had bidden her, when she was tired of behaving pretty in the drawing-room. So I took off my things and went to find her, and bring her to her supper in the nursery. But when I went into the best drawing-room, there sat the two old ladies, very still and quiet, dropping out a word now and then, but looking as if nothing so bright and merry as Miss Rosamond had ever been near them. Still I thought she might be hiding from me; it was one of her pretty ways,—and that she had persuaded them to look as if they knew nothing about her; so I went softly peeping under this sofa, and behind that chair, making believe I was sadly frightened at not finding her.

'What's the matter, Hester?' said Mrs. Stark, sharply. I don't know if Miss Furnivall had seen me, for, as I told you, she was very deaf, and she sat quite still, idly staring into the fire, with her hopeless face. 'I'm only looking for my little Rosy Posy,' replied I, still thinking that the child was there, and near me, though I could not see her.

'Miss Rosamond is not here,' said Mrs. Stark. 'She went away, more than an hour ago, to find Dorothy.' And she, too, turned and went on looking into the fire.

My heart sank at this, and I began to wish I had never left my darling. I went back to Dorothy and told her. James was gone out for the day, but she, and me, and Bessy took lights, and went up into the nursery first; and then we roamed over the great, large house, calling and entreating Miss Rosamond to come out of her hiding-place, and not frighten us to death in that way. But there was no answer; no sound.

'Oh!' said I, at last, 'can she have got into the east wing and hidden there?'

But Dorothy said it was not possible, for that she herself had never been in there; that the doors were always locked, and my lord's steward had the keys, she believed; at any rate, neither she nor James had ever seen them: so I said I would go back, and see if, after all, she was not hidden in the drawing-room, unknown to the old ladies; and if I found her there, I said, I would whip her well for the fright she had given me; but I never meant to do it. Well, I went back to the west drawing-room, and I told Mrs. Stark we could not find her anywhere, and asked for leave to look all about the furniture there, for I thought now that she might have fallen asleep in some warm, hidden corner; but no! we looked—Miss Furnivall got up and looked, trembling all over—and she was nowhere there; then we set off again, every one in the house, and looked in all the places we had searched before, but we could not find her. Miss Furnivall shivered and shook so much, that Mrs. Stark took her back into the warm drawing-room; but not before they had made me promise to bring her to them when she was found. Well-a-day! I began to think she never would be found, when I bethought me to look into the great front court, all covered with snow. I was upstairs when I looked out; but, it was such clear moonlight, I could see, quite plain, two little footprints, which might be traced from the hall-door and round the corner of the east wing. I don't know how I got down, but I tugged open the great stiff hall-door, and, throwing the skirt of my gown over my head for a cloak, I ran out. I turned the east corner, and there a black shadow fell on the snow; but when I came again into the moonlight, there were the little foot-marks going up—up to the Fells. It was bitter cold; so cold, that the air almost took the skin off my face as I ran; but I ran on crying to think how my poor little darling must be perished and frightened. I was within sight of the holly-trees, when I saw a shepherd coming down the hill, bearing something in his arms wrapped in his maud. He shouted to me, and asked me if I had lost a bairn; and, when I could not speak for crying, he bore towards me, and I saw my wee bairnie, lying still, and white, and stiff in his arms, as if she had been dead. He told me he had been up the Fells to gather in his sheep, before the deep cold of night came on, and that under the holly-trees (black marks on the hill-side, where no other bush was for miles around) he had found my little lady—my lamb—my queen—my darling—stiff and cold in the terrible sleep which is frost-begotten. Oh! the joy and the tears of having her in my arms once again! for I would not let him carry her; but took her, maud and all, into my own arms, and held her near my own warm neck and heart, and felt the life stealing slowly back again into her little gentle limbs.

But she was still insensible when we reached the hall, and I had no breath for speech. We went in by the kitchen-door.

'Bring me the warming-pan,' said I; and I carried her upstairs and began undressing her by the nursery fire, which Bessy had kept up. I called my little lammie all the sweet and playful names I could think of,—even while my eyes were blinded by my tears; and at last, oh! at length she opened her large blue eyes. Then I put her into her warm bed, and sent Dorothy down to tell Miss Furnivall that all was well; and I made up my mind to sit by my darling's bedside the live-long night. She fell away into a soft sleep as soon as her pretty head had touched the pillow, and I watched by her till morning light; when she wakened up bright and clear—or so I thought at first—and, my dears, so I think now.

She said, that she had fancied that she should like to go to Dorothy, for that both the old ladies were asleep, and it was very dull in the drawing-room; and that, as she was going through the west lobby, she saw the snow through the high window falling— falling—soft and steady; but she wanted to see it lying pretty and white on the ground; so she made her way into the great hall; and then, going to the window, she saw it bright and soft upon the drive; but while she stood there, she saw a little girl, not so old as she was, 'but so pretty,' said my darling, 'and this little girl beckoned to me to come out; and oh, she was so pretty and so sweet, I could not choose but go.' And then this other little girl had taken her by the hand, and side by side the two had gone round the east corner.

'Now you are a naughty little girl, and telling stories,' said I. 'What would your good mamma, that is in heaven, and never told a story in her life, say to her little Rosamond, if she heard her—and I daresay she does—telling stories!'

'Indeed, Hester,' sobbed out my child, 'I'm telling you true. Indeed I am.'

'Don't tell me!' said I, very stern. 'I tracked you by your foot-marks through the snow; there were only yours to be seen: and if you had had a little girl to go hand-in-hand with you up the hill, don't you think the footprints would have gone along with yours?'

'I can't help it, dear, dear Hester,' said she, crying, 'if they did not; I never looked at her feet, but she held my hand fast and tight in her little one, and it was very, very cold. She took me up the Fell-path, up to the holly-trees; and there I saw a lady weeping and crying; but when she saw me, she hushed her weeping, and smiled very proud and grand, and took me on her knee, and began to lull me to sleep; and that's all, Hester—but that is true; and my dear mamma knows it is,' said she, crying. So I thought the child was in a fever, and pretended to believe her, as she went over her story—over and over again, and always the same. At last Dorothy knocked at the door with Miss Rosamond's breakfast; and she told me the old ladies were down in the eating parlour, and that they wanted to speak to me. They had both been into the night-nursery the evening before, but it was after Miss Rosamond was asleep; so they had only looked at her—not asked me any questions.

'I shall catch it,' thought I to myself, as I went along the north gallery. 'And yet,' I thought, taking courage, 'it was in their charge I left her; and it's they that's to blame for letting her steal away unknown and unwatched.' So I went in boldly, and told my story. I told it all to Miss Furnivall, shouting it close to her ear; but when I came to the mention of the other little girl out in the snow, coaxing and tempting her out, and willing her up to the grand and beautiful lady by the holly-tree, she threw her arms up—her old and withered arms—and cried aloud, 'Oh! Heaven forgive! Have mercy!'

Mrs. Stark took hold of her; roughly enough, I thought; but she was past Mrs. Stark's management, and spoke to me, in a kind of wild warning and authority.

'Hester! keep her from that child! It will lure her to her death! That evil child! Tell her it is a wicked, naughty child.' Then, Mrs. Stark hurried me out of the room; where, indeed, I was glad enough to go; but Miss Furnivall kept shrieking out, 'Oh, have mercy! Wilt Thou never forgive! It is many a long year ago—'

I was very uneasy in my mind after that. I durst never leave Miss Rosamond, night or day, for fear lest she might slip off again, after some fancy or other; and all the more, because I thought I could make out that Miss Furnivall was crazy, from their odd ways about her; and I was afraid lest something of the same kind (which might be in the family, you know) hung over my darling. And the great frost never ceased all this time; and, whenever it was a more stormy night than usual, between the gusts, and through the wind, we heard the old lord playing on the great organ. But, old lord, or not, wherever Miss Rosamond went, there I followed; for my love for her, pretty, helpless orphan, was stronger than my fear for the grand and terrible sound. Besides, it rested with me to keep her cheerful and merry, as beseemed her age. So we played together, and wandered together, here and there, and everywhere; for I never dared to lose sight of her again in that large and rambling house. And so it happened, that one afternoon, not long before Christmas-day, we were playing together on the billiard-table in the great hall (not that we knew the right way of playing, but she liked to roll the smooth ivory balls with her pretty hands, and I liked to do whatever she did); and, by-and-by, without our noticing it, it grew dusk indoors, though it was still light in the open air, and I was thinking of taking her back into the nursery, when, all of a sudden, she cried out,

'Look, Hester! look! there is my poor little girl out in the snow!'

I turned towards the long narrow windows, and there, sure enough, I saw a little girl, less than my Miss Rosamond—dressed all unfit to be out-of-doors such a bitter night—crying, and beating against the window-panes, as if she wanted to be let in. She seemed to sob and wail, till Miss Rosamond could bear it no longer, and was flying to the door to open it, when, all of a sudden, and close upon us, the great organ pealed out so loud and thundering, it fairly made me tremble; and all the more, when I remembered me that, even in the stillness of that dead-cold weather, I had heard no sound of little battering hands upon the windowglass, although the phantom child had seemed to put forth all its force; and, although I had seen it wail and cry, no faintest touch of sound had fallen upon my ears. Whether I remembered all this at the very moment, I do not know; the great organ sound had so stunned me into terror; but this I know, I caught up Miss Rosamond before she got the hall-door opened, and clutched her, and carried her away, kicking and screaming, into the large, bright kitchen, where Dorothy and Agnes were busy with their mince-pies.

'What is the matter with my sweet one?' cried Dorothy, as I bore in Miss Rosamond, who was sobbing as if her heart would break.

'She won't let me open the door for my little girl to come in; and she'll die if she is out on the Fells all night. Cruel, naughty Hester,' she said, slapping me; but she might have struck harder, for I had seen a look of ghastly terror on Dorothy's face, which made my very blood run cold.

'Shut the back-kitchen door fast, and bolt it well,' said she to Agnes. She said no more; she gave me raisins and almonds to quiet Miss Rosamond; but she sobbed about the little girl in the snow, and would not touch any of the good things. I was thankful when she cried herself to sleep in bed. Then I stole down to the kitchen, and told Dorothy I had made up my mind. I would carry my darling back to my father's house in Applethwaite; where, if we lived humbly, we lived at peace. I said I had been frightened enough with the old lord's organ-playing; but now that I had seen for myself this little moaning child, all decked out as no child in the neighbourhood could be, beating and battering to get in, yet always without any sound or noise—with the dark wound on its right shoulder; and that Miss Rosamond had known it again for the phantom that had nearly lured her to her death (which Dorothy knew was true); I would stand it no longer.

I saw Dorothy change colour once or twice. When I had done, she told me she did not think I could take Miss Rosamond with me, for that she was my lord's ward, and I had no right over her; and she asked me would I leave the child that I was so fond of just for sounds and sights that could do me no harm; and that they had all had to get used to in their turns? I was all in a hot, trembling passion; and I said it was very well for her to talk; that knew what these sights and noises betokened, and that had, perhaps, had something to do with the spectre child while it was alive. And I taunted her so, that she told me all she knew at last; and then I wished I had never been told, for it only made me more afraid than ever.

She said she had heard the tale from old neighbours that were alive when she was first married; when folks used to come to the hall sometimes, before it had got such a bad name on the country side: it might not be true, or it might, what she had been told.

The old lord was Miss Furnivall's father—Miss Grace, as Dorothy called her, for Miss Maude was the elder, and Miss Furnivall by rights. The old lord was eaten up with pride. Such a proud man was never seen or heard of; and his daughters were like him. No one was good enough to wed them, although they had choice enough; for they were the great beauties of their day, as I had seen by their portraits, where they hung in the state drawing-room. But, as the old saying is, 'Pride will have a fall;' and these two haughty beauties fell in love with the same man, and he no better than a foreign musician, whom their father had down from London to play music with him at the Manor House. For, above all things, next to his pride, the old lord loved music. He could play on nearly every instrument that ever was heard of, and it was a strange thing it did not soften him; but he was a fierce dour old man, and had broken his poor wife's heart with his cruelty, they said. He was mad after music, and would pay any money for it. So he got this foreigner to come; who made such beautiful music, that they said the very birds on the trees stopped their singing to listen. And, by degrees, this foreign gentleman got such a hold over the old lord, that nothing would serve him but that he must come every year; and it was he that had the great organ brought from Holland, and built up in the hall, where it stood now. He taught the old lord to play on it; but many and many a time, when Lord Furnivall was thinking of nothing but his fine organ, and his finer music, the dark foreigner was walking abroad in the woods with one of the young ladies; now Miss Maude, and then Miss Grace.

Miss Maude won the day and carried off the prize, such as it was; and he and she were married, all unknown to any one; and before he made his next yearly visit, she had been confined of a little girl at a farm-house on the Moors, while her father and Miss Grace thought she was away at Doncaster Races. But though she was a wife and a mother, she was not a bit softened, but as haughty and as passionate as ever; and perhaps more so, for she was jealous of Miss Grace, to whom her foreign husband paid a deal of court— by way of blinding her—as he told his wife. But Miss Grace triumphed over Miss Maude, and Miss Maude grew fiercer and fiercer, both with her husband and with her sister; and the former— who could easily shake off what was disagreeable, and hide himself in foreign countries—went away a month before his usual time that summer, and half-threatened that he would never come back again. Meanwhile, the little girl was left at the farm-house, and her mother used to have her horse saddled and gallop wildly over the hills to see her once every week, at the very least; for where she loved she loved, and where she hated she hated. And the old lord went on playing—playing on his organ; and the servants thought the sweet music he made had soothed down his awful temper, of which (Dorothy said) some terrible tales could be told. He grew infirm too, and had to walk with a crutch; and his son—that was the present Lord Furnivall's father—was with the army in America, and the other son at sea; so Miss Maude had it pretty much her own way, and she and Miss Grace grew colder and bitterer to each other every day; till at last they hardly ever spoke, except when the old lord was by. The foreign musician came again the next summer, but it was for the last time; for they led him such a life with their jealousy and their passions, that he grew weary, and went away, and never was heard of again. And Miss Maude, who had always meant to have her marriage acknowledged when her father should be dead, was left now a deserted wife, whom nobody knew to have been married, with a child that she dared not own, although she loved it to distraction; living with a father whom she feared, and a sister whom she hated. When the next summer passed over, and the dark foreigner never came, both Miss Maude and Miss Grace grew gloomy and sad; they had a haggard look about them, though they looked handsome as ever. But, by-and-by, Maude brightened; for her father grew more and more infirm, and more than ever carried away by his music; and she and Miss Grace lived almost entirely apart, having separate rooms, the one on the west side, Miss Maude on the east—those very rooms which were now shut up. So she thought she might have her little girl with her, and no one need ever know except those who dared not speak about it, and were bound to believe that it was, as she said, a cottager's child she had taken a fancy to. All this, Dorothy said, was pretty well known; but what came afterwards no one knew, except Miss Grace and Mrs. Stark, who was even then her maid, and much more of a friend to her than ever her sister had been. But the servants supposed, from words that were dropped, that Miss Maude had triumphed over Miss Grace, and told her that all the time the dark foreigner had been mocking her with pretended love—he was her own husband. The colour left Miss Grace's cheek and lips that very day for ever, and she was heard to say many a time that sooner or later she would have her revenge; and Mrs. Stark was for ever spying about the east rooms.

One fearful night, just after the New Year had come in, when the snow was lying thick and deep; and the flakes were still falling—fast enough to blind any one who might be out and abroad—there was a great and violent noise heard, and the old lord's voice above all, cursing and swearing awfully, and the cries of a little child, and the proud defiance of a fierce woman, and the sound of a blow, and a dead stillness, and moans and wailings dying away on the hill-side! Then the old lord summoned all his servants, and told them, with terrible oaths, and words more terrible, that his daughter had disgraced herself, and that he had turned her out of doors—her, and her child—and that if ever they gave her help, or food, or shelter, he prayed that they might never enter heaven. And, all the while, Miss Grace stood by him, white and still as any stone; and, when he had ended, she heaved a great sigh, as much as to say her work was done, and her end was accomplished. But the old lord never touched his organ again, and died within the year; and no wonder! for, on the morrow of that wild and fearful night, the shepherds, coming down the Fell side, found Miss Maude sitting, all crazy and smiling, under the holly-trees, nursing a dead child, with a terrible mark on its right shoulder. 'But that was not what killed it,' said Dorothy: 'it was the frost and the cold. Every wild creature was in its hole, and every beast in its fold, while the child and its mother were turned out to wander on the Fells! And now you know all! and I wonder if you are less frightened now?'

I was more frightened than ever; but I said I was not. I wished Miss Rosamond and myself well out of that dreadful house for ever; but I would not leave her, and I dared not take her away. But oh, how I watched her, and guarded her! We bolted the doors, and shut the window-shutters fast, an hour or more before dark, rather than leave them open five minutes too late. But my little lady still heard the weird child crying and mourning; and not all we could do or say could keep her from wanting to go to her, and let her in from the cruel wind and the snow. All this time I kept away from Miss Furnivall and Mrs. Stark, as much as ever I could; for I feared them—I knew no good could be about them, with their grey, hard faces, and their dreamy eyes, looking back into the ghastly years that were gone. But, even in my fear, I had a kind of pity for Miss Furnivall, at least. Those gone down to the pit can hardly have a more hopeless look than that which was ever on her face. At last I even got so sorry for her—who never said a word but what was quite forced from her—that I prayed for her; and I taught Miss Rosamond to pray for one who had done a deadly sin; but often when she came to those words, she would listen, and start up from her knees, and say, 'I hear my little girl plaining and crying very sad—oh, let her in, or she will die!'

One night—just after New Year's Day had come at last, and the long winter had taken a turn, as I hoped—I heard the west drawing-room bell ring three times, which was the signal for me. I would not leave Miss Rosamond alone, for all she was asleep—for the old lord had been playing wilder than ever—and I feared lest my darling should waken to hear the spectre child; see her, I knew she could not. I had fastened the windows too well for that. So I took her out of her bed, and wrapped her up in such outer clothes as were most handy, and carried her down to the drawing-room, where the old ladies sat at their tapestry-work as usual. They looked up when I came in, and Mrs. Stark asked, quite astounded, 'Why did I bring

Miss Rosamond there, out of her warm bed?' I had begun to whisper, 'Because I was afraid of her being tempted out while I was away, by the wild child in the snow,' when she stopped me short (with a glance at Miss Furnivall), and said Miss Furnivall wanted me to undo some work she had done wrong, and which neither of them could see to unpick. So I laid my pretty dear on the sofa, and sat down on a stool by them, and hardened my heart against them, as I heard the wind rising and howling.

Miss Rosamond slept on sound, for all the wind blew so Miss Furnivall said never a word, nor looked round when the gusts shook the windows. All at once she started up to her full height, and put up one hand, as if to bid us to listen.

'I hear voices!' said she. 'I hear terrible screams—I hear my father's voice!'

Just at that moment my darling wakened with a sudden start: 'My little girl is crying, oh, how she is crying!' and she tried to get up and go to her, but she got her feet entangled in the blanket, and I caught her up; for my flesh had begun to creep at these noises, which they heard while we could catch no sound. In a minute or two the noises came, and gathered fast, and filled our ears; we, too, heard voices and screams, and no longer heard the winter's wind that raged abroad. Mrs. Stark looked at me, and I at her, but we dared not speak. Suddenly Miss Furnivall went towards the door, out into the ante-room, through the west lobby, and opened the door into the great hall. Mrs. Stark followed, and I durst not be left, though my heart almost stopped beating for fear. I wrapped my darling tight in my arms, and went out with them. In the hall the screams were louder than ever; they seemed to come from the east wing—nearer and nearer—close on the other side of the locked-up doors—close behind them. Then I noticed that the great bronze chandelier seemed all alight, though the hall was dim, and that a fire was blazing in the vast hearth-place, though it gave no heat; and I shuddered up with terror, and folded my darling closer to me. But as I did so the east door shook, and she, suddenly struggling to get free from me, cried, 'Hester! I must go. My little girl is there! I hear her; she is coming! Hester, I must go!'

I held her tight with all my strength; with a set will, I held her. If I had died, my hands would have grasped her still, I was so resolved in my mind. Miss Furnivall stood listening, and paid no regard to my darling, who had got down to the ground, and whom I, upon my knees now, was holding with both my arms clasped round her neck; she still striving and crying to get free.

All at once, the east door gave way with a thundering crash, as if torn open in a violent passion, and there came into that broad and mysterious light, the figure of a tall old man, with grey hair and gleaming eyes. He drove before him, with many a relentless gesture of abhorrence, a stern and beautiful woman, with a little child clinging to her dress.

'Oh, Hester! Hester!' cried Miss Rosamond; 'it's the lady! the lady below the holly-trees; and my little girl is with her. Hester! Hester! let me go to her; they are drawing me to them. I feel them—I feel them. I must go!'

Again she was almost convulsed by her efforts to get away; but I held her tighter and tighter, till I feared I should do her a hurt; but rather that than let her go towards those terrible phantoms. They passed along towards the great hall-door, where the winds howled and ravened for their prey; but before they reached that, the lady turned; and I could see that she defied the old man with a fierce and proud defiance; but then she quailed—and then she threw up her arms wildly and piteously to save her child—her little child—from a blow from his uplifted crutch.

And Miss Rosamond was torn as by a power stronger than mine and writhed in my arms, and sobbed (for by this time the poor darling was growing faint).

'They want me to go with them on to the Fells—they are drawing me to them. Oh, my little girl! I would come, but cruel, wicked Hester holds me very tight.' But when she saw the uplifted crutch, she swooned away, and I thanked God for it. Just at this moment— when the tall old man, his hair streaming as in the blast of a furnace, was going to strike the little shrinking child—Miss Furnivall, the old woman by my side, cried out, 'Oh father! father! spare the little innocent child!' But just then I saw—we all saw—another phantom shape itself, and grow clear out of the blue and misty light that filled the hall; we had not seen her till now, for it was another lady who stood by the old man, with a look of relentless hate and triumphant scorn. That figure was very beautiful to look upon, with a soft, white hat drawn down over the proud brows, and a red and curling lip. It was dressed in an open robe of blue satin. I had seen that figure before. It was the likeness of Miss Furnivall in her youth; and the terrible phantoms moved on, regardless of old Miss Furnivall's wild entreaty,—and the uplifted crutch fell on the right shoulder of the little child, and the younger sister looked on, stony, and deadly serene. But at that moment, the dim lights, and the fire that gave no heat, went out of themselves, and Miss Furnivall lay at our feet stricken down by the palsy—death-stricken.

Yes! she was carried to her bed that night never to rise again. She lay with her face to the wall, muttering low, but muttering always: 'Alas! alas! what is done in youth can never be undone in age! What is done in youth can never be undone in age!'

III

THE TOWER.

PART III

THE TOWER

THE CASTLE OF OTRANTO

BY
HORACE WALPOLE

CHAPTER I.

Manfred, Prince of Otranto, had one son and one daughter: the latter, a most beautiful virgin, aged eighteen, was called Matilda. Conrad, the son, was three years younger, a homely youth, sickly, and of no promising disposition; yet he was the darling of his father, who never showed any symptoms of affection to Matilda. Manfred had contracted a marriage for his son with the Marquis of Vicenza's daughter, Isabella; and she had already been delivered by her guardians into the hands of Manfred, that he might celebrate the wedding as soon as Conrad's infirm state of health would permit.

Manfred's impatience for this ceremonial was remarked by his family and neighbours. The former, indeed, apprehending the severity of their Prince's disposition, did not dare to utter their surmises on this precipitation. Hippolita, his wife, an amiable lady, did sometimes venture to represent the danger of marrying their only son so early, considering his great youth, and greater infirmities; but she never received any other answer than reflections on her own sterility, who had given him but one heir. His tenants and subjects were less cautious in their discourses. They attributed this hasty wedding to the Prince's dread of seeing accomplished an ancient prophecy, which was said to have pronounced that the castle and lordship of Otranto "should pass from the present family, whenever the real owner should be grown too large to inhabit it." It was difficult to make any sense of this prophecy; and still less easy to conceive what it had to do with the marriage in question. Yet these mysteries, or contradictions, did not make the populace adhere the less to their opinion.

Young Conrad's birthday was fixed for his espousals. The company was assembled in the chapel of the Castle, and everything ready for beginning the divine office, when Conrad himself was missing. Manfred, impatient of the least delay, and who had not observed his son retire, despatched one of his attendants to summon the young Prince. The servant, who had not stayed long enough to have crossed the court to Conrad's apartment, came running back breathless, in a frantic manner, his eyes staring, and foaming at the mouth. He said nothing, but pointed to the court.

The company were struck with terror and amazement. The Princess Hippolita, without knowing what was the matter, but anxious for her son, swooned away. Manfred, less apprehensive than enraged at the procrastination of the nuptials, and at the folly of his domestic, asked imperiously what was the matter? The fellow made no answer, but continued pointing towards the courtyard; and at last, after repeated questions put to him, cried out, "Oh! the helmet! the helmet!"

In the meantime, some of the company had run into the court, from whence was heard a confused noise of shrieks, horror, and surprise. Manfred, who began to be alarmed at not seeing his son, went himself to get information of what occasioned this strange confusion. Matilda remained endeavouring to assist her mother, and Isabella stayed for the same purpose, and to avoid showing any impatience for the bridegroom, for whom, in truth, she had conceived little affection.

The first thing that struck Manfred's eyes was a group of his servants endeavouring to raise something that appeared to him a mountain of sable plumes. He gazed without believing his sight.

"What are ye doing?" cried Manfred, wrathfully; "where is my son?"

A volley of voices replied, "Oh! my Lord! the Prince! the Prince! the helmet! the helmet!"

Shocked with these lamentable sounds, and dreading he knew not what, he advanced hastily,—but what a sight for a father's eyes!—he beheld his child dashed to pieces, and almost buried under an enormous helmet, an hundred times more large than any casque ever made for human being, and shaded with a proportionable quantity of black feathers.

The horror of the spectacle, the ignorance of all around how this misfortune had happened, and above all, the tremendous phenomenon before him, took away the Prince's speech. Yet his silence lasted longer than even grief could occasion. He fixed his eyes on what he wished in vain to believe a vision; and seemed less attentive to his loss, than buried in meditation on the stupendous object that had occasioned it. He touched, he examined the fatal casque; nor could even the bleeding mangled remains of the young Prince divert the eyes of Manfred from the portent before him.

All who had known his partial fondness for young Conrad, were as much surprised at their Prince's insensibility, as thunderstruck themselves at the miracle of the helmet. They conveyed the disfigured corpse into the hall, without receiving the least direction from Manfred. As little was he attentive to the ladies who remained in the chapel. On the contrary, without mentioning the unhappy princesses, his wife and daughter, the first sounds that dropped from Manfred's lips were, "Take care of the Lady Isabella."

The domestics, without observing the singularity of this direction, were guided by their affection to their mistress, to consider it as peculiarly addressed to her situation, and flew to her assistance. They conveyed her to her chamber more dead than alive, and indifferent to all the strange circumstances she heard, except the death of her son.

Matilda, who doted on her mother, smothered her own grief and amazement, and thought of nothing but assisting and comforting her afflicted parent. Isabella, who had been treated by Hippolita like a daughter, and who returned that tenderness with equal duty and affection, was scarce less assiduous about the Princess; at the same time endeavouring to partake and lessen the weight of sorrow which she saw Matilda strove to suppress, for whom she had conceived the warmest sympathy of friendship. Yet her own situation could not help finding its place in her thoughts. She felt no concern for the death of young Conrad, except commiseration; and she was not sorry to be delivered from a marriage which had promised her little felicity, either from her destined bridegroom, or from the severe temper of Manfred, who, though he had distinguished her by great indulgence, had imprinted her mind with terror, from his causeless rigour to such amiable princesses as Hippolita and Matilda.

While the ladies were conveying the wretched mother to her bed, Manfred remained in the court, gazing on the ominous casque, and regardless of the crowd which the strangeness of the event had now assembled around him. The few words he articulated, tended solely to inquiries, whether any man knew from whence it could have come? Nobody could give him the least information. However, as it seemed to be the sole object of his curiosity, it soon became so to the rest of the spectators, whose conjectures were as absurd and improbable, as the catastrophe itself was unprecedented. In the midst of their senseless guesses, a young peasant, whom rumour had drawn thither from a neighbouring village, observed that the miraculous helmet was exactly like that on the figure in black marble of Alfonso the Good, one of their former princes, in the church of St. Nicholas.

"Villain! What sayest thou?" cried Manfred, starting from his trance in a tempest of rage, and seizing the young man by the collar; "how darest thou utter such treason? Thy life shall pay for it."

The spectators, who as little comprehended the cause of the Prince's fury as all the rest they had seen, were at a loss to unravel this new circumstance. The young peasant himself was still more astonished, not conceiving how he had offended the Prince. Yet recollecting himself, with a mixture of grace and humility, he disengaged himself from Manfred's grip, and then with an obeisance, which discovered more jealousy of innocence than dismay, he asked, with respect, of what he was guilty? Manfred, more enraged at the vigour, however decently exerted, with which the young man had shaken off his hold, than appeased by his submission, ordered his attendants to seize him, and, if he had not been withheld by his friends whom he had invited to the nuptials, would have poignarded the peasant in their arms.

During this altercation, some of the vulgar spectators had run to the great church, which stood near the castle, and came back open-mouthed, declaring that the helmet was missing from Alfonso's statue. Manfred, at this news, grew perfectly frantic; and, as if he sought a subject on which to vent the tempest within him, he rushed again on the young peasant, crying—

"Villain! Monster! Sorcerer! 'tis thou hast done this! 'tis thou hast slain my son!"

The mob, who wanted some object within the scope of their capacities, on whom they might discharge their bewildered reasoning, caught the words from the mouth of their lord, and re-echoed—

"Ay, ay; 'tis he, 'tis he: he has stolen the helmet from good Alfonso's tomb, and dashed out the brains of our young Prince with it," never reflecting how enormous the disproportion was between the marble helmet that had been in the church, and that of steel before their eyes; nor how impossible it was for a youth seemingly not twenty, to wield a piece of armour of so prodigious a weight.

The folly of these ejaculations brought Manfred to himself: yet whether provoked at the peasant having observed the resemblance between the two helmets, and thereby led to the farther discovery of the absence of that in the church, or wishing to bury any such rumour under so impertinent a supposition, he gravely pronounced that the young man was certainly a necromancer, and that till the Church could take cognisance of the affair, he would have the Magician, whom they had thus detected, kept prisoner under the helmet itself, which he ordered his attendants to raise, and place the young man under it; declaring he should be kept there without food, with which his own infernal art might furnish him.

It was in vain for the youth to represent against this preposterous sentence: in vain did Manfred's friends endeavour to divert him from this savage and ill-grounded resolution. The generality were charmed with their lord's decision, which, to their apprehensions, carried great appearance of justice, as the Magician was to be punished by the very instrument with which he had offended: nor were they struck with the least compunction at the probability of the youth being starved, for they firmly believed that, by his diabolic skill, he could easily supply himself with nutriment.

Manfred thus saw his commands even cheerfully obeyed; and appointing a guard with strict orders to prevent any food being conveyed to the prisoner, he dismissed his friends and attendants, and retired to his own chamber, after locking the gates of the castle, in which he suffered none but his domestics to remain.

In the meantime, the care and zeal of the young Ladies had brought the Princess Hippolita to herself, who amidst the transports of her own sorrow frequently demanded news of her lord, would have dismissed her attendants to watch over him, and at last enjoined Matilda to leave her, and visit and comfort her father. Matilda, who wanted no affectionate duty to Manfred, though she trembled at his austerity, obeyed the orders of Hippolita, whom she tenderly recommended to Isabella; and inquiring of the domestics for her father, was informed that he was retired to his chamber, and had commanded that nobody should have admittance to him. Concluding that he was immersed in sorrow for the death of her brother, and fearing to renew his tears by the sight of his sole remaining child, she hesitated whether she should break in upon his affliction; yet solicitude for him, backed by the commands of her mother, encouraged her to venture disobeying the orders he had given; a fault she had never been guilty of before.

The gentle timidity of her nature made her pause for some minutes at his door. She heard him traverse his chamber backwards, and forwards with disordered steps; a mood which increased her apprehensions. She was, however, just going to beg admittance, when Manfred suddenly opened the door; and as it was now twilight, concurring with the disorder of his mind, he did not distinguish the person, but asked angrily, who it was? Matilda replied, trembling—

"My dearest father, it is I, your daughter."

Manfred, stepping back hastily, cried, "Begone! I do not want a daughter;" and flinging back abruptly, clapped the door against the terrified Matilda.

She was too well acquainted with her father's impetuosity to venture a second intrusion. When she had a little recovered the shock of so bitter a reception, she wiped away her tears to prevent the additional stab that the knowledge of it would give to Hippolita, who questioned her in the most anxious terms on the health of Manfred, and how he bore his loss. Matilda assured her he was well, and supported his misfortune with manly fortitude.

"But will he not let me see him?" said Hippolita mournfully; "will he not permit me to blend my tears with his, and shed a mother's sorrows in the bosom of her Lord? Or do you deceive me, Matilda? I know how Manfred doted on his son: is not the stroke too heavy for him? has he not sunk under it? You do not answer me—alas! I dread the worst!—Raise me, my maidens; I will, I will see my Lord. Bear me to him instantly: he is dearer to me even than my children."

Matilda made signs to Isabella to prevent Hippolita's rising; and both those lovely young women were using their gentle violence to stop and calm the Princess, when a servant, on the part of Manfred, arrived and told Isabella that his Lord demanded to speak with her.

"With me!" cried Isabella.

"Go," said Hippolita, relieved by a message from her Lord: "Manfred cannot support the sight of his own family. He thinks you less disordered than we are, and dreads the shock of my grief. Console him, dear Isabella, and tell him I will smother my own anguish rather than add to his."

As it was now evening the servant who conducted Isabella bore a torch before her. When they came to Manfred, who was walking impatiently about the gallery, he started, and said hastily—

"Take away that light, and begone."

Then shutting the door impetuously, he flung himself upon a bench against the wall, and bade Isabella sit by him. She obeyed trembling.

"I sent for you, Lady," said he—and then stopped under great appearance of confusion.

"My Lord!"

"Yes, I sent for you on a matter of great moment," resumed he. "Dry your tears, young Lady—you have lost your bridegroom. Yes, cruel fate! and I have lost the hopes of my race! But Conrad was not worthy of your beauty."

"How, my Lord!" said Isabella; "sure you do not suspect me of not feeling the concern I ought: my duty and affection would have always—"

"Think no more of him," interrupted Manfred; "he was a sickly, puny child, and Heaven has perhaps taken him away, that I might not trust the honours of my house on so frail a foundation. The line of Manfred calls for numerous supports. My foolish fondness for that boy blinded the eyes of my prudence—but it is better as it is. I hope, in a few years, to have reason to rejoice at the death of Conrad."

Words cannot paint the astonishment of Isabella. At first she apprehended that grief had disordered Manfred's understanding. Her next thought suggested that this strange discourse was designed to ensnare her: she feared that Manfred had perceived her indifference for his son: and in consequence of that idea she replied—

"Good my Lord, do not doubt my tenderness: my heart would have accompanied my hand. Conrad would have engrossed all my care; and wherever fate shall dispose of me, I shall always cherish his memory, and regard your Highness and the virtuous Hippolita as my parents."

"Curse on Hippolita!" cried Manfred. "Forget her from this moment, as I do. In short, Lady, you have missed a husband undeserving of your charms: they shall now be better disposed of. Instead of a sickly boy, you shall have a husband in the prime of his age, who will know how to value your beauties, and who may expect a numerous offspring."

"Alas, my Lord!" said Isabella, "my mind is too sadly engrossed by the recent catastrophe in your family to think of another marriage. If ever my father returns, and it shall be his pleasure, I shall obey, as I did when I consented to give my hand to your son: but until his return, permit me to remain under your hospitable roof, and employ the melancholy hours in assuaging yours, Hippolita's, and the fair Matilda's affliction."

"I desired you once before," said Manfred angrily, "not to name that woman: from this hour she must be a stranger to you, as she must be to me. In short, Isabella, since I cannot give you my son, I offer you myself."

"Heavens!" cried Isabella, waking from her delusion, "what do I hear? You! my Lord! You! My father-in-law! the father of Conrad! the husband of the virtuous and tender Hippolita!"

"I tell you," said Manfred imperiously, "Hippolita is no longer my wife; I divorce her from this hour. Too long has she cursed me by her unfruitfulness. My fate depends on having sons, and this night I trust will give a new date to my hopes."

At those words he seized the cold hand of Isabella, who was half dead with fright and horror. She shrieked, and started from him, Manfred rose to pursue her, when the moon, which was now up, and gleamed in at the opposite casement, presented to his sight the plumes of the fatal helmet, which rose to the height of the windows, waving backwards and forwards in a tempestuous manner, and accompanied with a hollow and rustling sound. Isabella, who gathered courage from her situation, and who dreaded nothing so much as Manfred's pursuit of his declaration, cried—

"Look, my Lord! see, Heaven itself declares against your impious intentions!"

"Heaven nor Hell shall impede my designs," said Manfred, advancing again to seize the Princess.

At that instant the portrait of his grandfather, which hung over the bench where they had been sitting, uttered a deep sigh, and heaved its breast.

Isabella, whose back was turned to the picture, saw not the motion, nor knew whence the sound came, but started, and said—

"Hark, my Lord! What sound was that?" and at the same time made towards the door.

Manfred, distracted between the flight of Isabella, who had now reached the stairs, and yet unable to keep his eyes from the picture, which began to move, had, however, advanced some steps after her, still looking backwards on the portrait, when he saw it quit its panel, and descend on the floor with a grave and melancholy air.

"Do I dream?" cried Manfred, returning; "or are the devils themselves in league against me? Speak, internal spectre! Or, if thou art my grandsire, why dost thou too conspire against thy wretched descendant, who too dearly pays for—" Ere he could finish the sentence, the vision sighed again, and made a sign to Manfred to follow him.

"Lead on!" cried Manfred; "I will follow thee to the gulf of perdition."

The spectre marched sedately, but dejected, to the end of the gallery, and turned into a chamber on the right hand. Manfred accompanied him at a little distance, full of anxiety and horror, but resolved. As he would have entered the chamber, the door was clapped to with violence by an invisible hand. The Prince, collecting courage from this delay, would have forcibly burst open the door with his foot, but found that it resisted his utmost efforts.

"Since Hell will not satisfy my curiosity," said Manfred, "I will use the human means in my power for preserving my race; Isabella shall not escape me."

The lady, whose resolution had given way to terror the moment she had quitted Manfred, continued her flight to the bottom of the principal staircase. There she stopped, not knowing whither to direct her steps, nor how to escape from the impetuosity of the Prince. The gates of the castle, she knew, were locked, and guards placed in the court. Should she, as her heart prompted her, go and prepare Hippolita for the cruel destiny that awaited her, she did not doubt but Manfred would seek her there, and that his violence would incite him to double the injury he meditated, without leaving room for them to avoid the impetuosity of his passions. Delay might give him time to reflect on the horrid measures he had conceived, or produce some circumstance in her favour, if she could—for that night, at least—avoid his odious purpose. Yet where conceal herself? How avoid the pursuit he would infallibly make throughout the castle?

As these thoughts passed rapidly through her mind, she recollected a subterraneous passage which led from the vaults of the castle to the church of St. Nicholas. Could she reach the altar before she was overtaken, she knew even Manfred's violence would not dare to profane the sacredness of the place; and she determined, if no other means of deliverance offered, to shut herself up for ever among the holy virgins whose convent was contiguous to the cathedral. In this resolution, she seized a lamp that burned at the foot of the staircase, and hurried towards the secret passage.

The lower part of the castle was hollowed into several intricate cloisters; and it was not easy for one under so much anxiety to find the door that opened into the cavern. An awful silence reigned throughout those subterraneous regions, except now and then some blasts of wind that shook the doors she had passed, and which, grating on the rusty hinges, were re-echoed through that long labyrinth of darkness. Every murmur struck her with new terror; yet more she dreaded to hear the wrathful voice of Manfred urging his domestics to pursue her.

She trod as softly as impatience would give her leave, yet frequently stopped and listened to hear if she was followed. In one of those moments she thought she heard a sigh. She shuddered, and recoiled a few paces. In a moment she thought she heard the step of some person. Her blood curdled; she concluded it was Manfred. Every suggestion that horror could inspire rushed into her mind. She condemned her rash flight, which had thus exposed her to his rage in a place where her cries were not likely to draw anybody to her assistance. Yet the sound seemed not to come from behind. If Manfred knew where she was, he must have followed her. She was still in one of the cloisters, and the steps she had heard were too distinct to proceed from the way she had come. Cheered with this reflection, and hoping to find a friend in whoever was not the Prince, she was going to advance, when a door that stood ajar, at some distance to the left, was opened gently: but ere her lamp, which she held up, could discover who opened it, the person retreated precipitately on seeing the light.

Isabella, whom every incident was sufficient to dismay, hesitated whether she should proceed. Her dread of Manfred soon outweighed every other terror. The very circumstance of the person avoiding her gave her a sort of courage. It could only be, she thought, some domestic belonging to the castle. Her gentleness had never raised her an enemy, and conscious innocence made her hope that, unless sent by the Prince's order to seek her, his servants would rather assist than prevent her flight. Fortifying herself with these reflections, and believing by what she could observe that she was near the mouth of the subterraneous cavern, she approached the door that had been opened; but a sudden gust of wind that met her at the door extinguished her lamp, and left her in total darkness.

Words cannot paint the horror of the Princess's situation. Alone in so dismal a place, her mind imprinted with all the terrible events of the day, hopeless of escaping, expecting every moment the arrival of Manfred, and far from tranquil on knowing she was within reach of somebody, she knew not whom, who for some cause seemed concealed thereabouts; all these thoughts crowded on her distracted mind, and she was ready to sink under her apprehensions. She addressed herself to every saint in heaven, and inwardly implored their assistance. For a considerable time she remained in an agony of despair.

At last, as softly as was possible, she felt for the door, and having found it, entered trembling into the vault from whence she had heard the sigh and steps. It gave her a kind of momentary joy to perceive an imperfect ray of clouded moonshine gleam from the roof of the vault, which seemed to be fallen in, and from whence hung a fragment of earth or building, she could not distinguish which, that appeared to have been crushed inwards. She advanced eagerly towards this chasm, when she discerned a human form standing close against the wall.

She shrieked, believing it the ghost of her betrothed Conrad.

THE FALL OF
THE HOUSE OF USHER

BY

EDGAR ALLEN POE

Son cœur est un luth suspendu;
Sitôt qu'on le touche il résonne.

—De Béranger.

D uring the whole of a dull, dark, and soundless day in the autumn of the year, when the clouds hung oppressively low in the heavens, I had been passing alone, on horse-back, through a singularly dreary tract of country, and at length found myself, as the shades of the evening drew on, within view of the melancholy House of Usher. I know not how it was—but, with the first glimpse of the building, a sense of insufferable gloom pervaded my spirit. I say insufferable; for the feeling was unrelieved by any of that half-pleasurable, because poetic, sentiment, with which the mind usually receives even the sternest natural images of the desolate or terrible. I looked upon the scene before me—upon the mere house, and the simple landscape features of the domain—upon the bleak walls—upon the vacant eye-like windows—upon a few rank sedges—and upon a few white trunks of decayed trees—with an utter depression of soul which I can compare to no earthly sensation more properly than to the after-dream of the reveller

upon opium—the bitter lapse into every-day life—the hideous dropping off of the veil. There was an iciness, a sinking, a sickening of
the heart—an unredeemed dreariness of thought which no goading
of the imagination could torture into aught of the sublime. What
was it—I paused to think—what was it that so unnerved me in the
contemplation of the House of Usher? It was a mystery all insoluble;
nor could I grapple with the shadowy fancies that crowded upon
me as I pondered. I was forced to fall back upon the unsatisfactory
conclusion, that while, beyond doubt, there *are* combinations of
very simple natural objects which have the power of thus affecting
us, still the analysis of this power lies among considerations beyond
our depth. It was possible, I reflected, that a mere different arrangement of the particulars of the scene, of the details of the picture,
would be sufficient to modify, or perhaps to annihilate its capacity
for sorrowful impression; and, acting upon this idea, I reined my
horse to the precipitous brink of a black and lurid tarn that lay in
unruffled lustre by the dwelling, and gazed down—but with a
shudder even more thrilling than before—upon the remodelled and
inverted images of the gray sedge, and the ghastly tree-stems, and
the vacant and eye-like windows.

Nevertheless, in this mansion of gloom I now proposed to myself
a sojourn of some weeks. Its proprietor, Roderick Usher, had been
one of my boon companions in boyhood; but many years had elapsed
since our last meeting. A letter, however, had lately reached me in
a distant part of the country—a letter from him—which, in its
wildly importunate nature, had admitted of no other than a
personal reply. The MS. gave evidence of nervous agitation. The
writer spoke of acute bodily illness—of a mental disorder which
oppressed him—and of an earnest desire to see me, as his best and
indeed his only personal friend, with a view of attempting, by the
cheerfulness of my society, some alleviation of his malady. It was
the manner in which all this, and much more, was said—it was the

apparent *heart* that went with his request—which allowed me no room for hesitation; and I accordingly obeyed forthwith what I still considered a very singular summons.

Although, as boys, we had been even intimate associates, yet I really knew little of my friend. His reserve had been always excessive and habitual. I was aware, however, that his very ancient family had been noted, time out of mind, for a peculiar sensibility of temperament, displaying itself, through long ages, in many works of exalted art, and manifested, of late, in repeated deeds of munificent yet unobtrusive charity, as well as in a passionate devotion to the intricacies, perhaps even more than to the orthodox and easily recognizable beauties, of musical science. I had learned, too, the very remarkable fact, that the stem of the Usher race, all time-honored as it was, had put forth, at no period, any enduring branch; in other words, that the entire family lay in the direct line of descent, and had always, with very trifling and very temporary variation, so lain. It was this deficiency, I considered, while running over in thought the perfect keeping of the character of the premises with the accredited character of the people, and while speculating upon the possible influence which the one, in the long lapse of centuries, might have exercised upon the other—it was this deficiency, perhaps, of collateral issue, and the consequent undeviating transmission, from sire to son, of the patrimony with the name, which had, at length, so identified the two as to merge the original title of the estate in the quaint and equivocal appellation of the "House of Usher"—an appellation which seemed to include, in the minds of the peasantry who used it, both the family and the family mansion.

I have said that the sole effect of my somewhat childish experiment—that of looking down within the tarn—had been to deepen the first singular impression. There can be no doubt that the consciousness of the rapid increase of my superstition—for why should I not so term it?—served mainly to accelerate the increase itself. Such, I have long known, is the paradoxical law of all sentiments having terror as a basis. And it might have been for this reason only, that, when I again uplifted my eyes to the house itself, from its image in the pool, there grew in my mind a strange fancy—a fancy so ridiculous, indeed, that I but mention it to show the vivid force of the sensations which oppressed me. I had so worked upon my imagination as really to believe that about the whole mansion and domain there hung an atmosphere peculiar to themselves and their immediate vicinity—an atmosphere which had no affinity with the air of heaven, but which had reeked up from the decayed trees, and the gray wall, and the silent tarn—a pestilent and mystic vapor, dull, sluggish, faintly discernible, and leaden-hued.

Shaking off from my spirit what *must* have been a dream, I scanned more narrowly the real aspect of the building. Its principal feature seemed to be that of an excessive antiquity. The discoloration of ages had been great. Minute fungi overspread the whole exterior, hanging in a fine tangled web-work from the eaves. Yet all this was apart from any extraordinary dilapidation. No portion of the masonry had fallen; and there appeared to be a wild inconsistency between its still perfect adaptation of parts, and the crumbling condition of the individual stones. In this there was much that reminded me of the specious totality of old wood-work which has rotted for long years in some neglected vault, with no disturbance from the breath of the external air. Beyond this indication of extensive decay, however, the fabric gave little token of instability. Perhaps the eye of a scrutinizing observer might have discovered a barely perceptible fissure, which, extending from the roof of the building in front, made its way down the wall in a zigzag direction, until it became lost in the sullen waters of the tarn.

Noticing these things, I rode over a short causeway to the house. A servant in waiting took my horse, and I entered the Gothic archway of the hall. A valet, of stealthy step, thence conducted me, in silence, through many dark and intricate passages in my progress to the *studio* of his master. Much that I encountered on the way contributed, I know not how, to heighten the vague sentiments of which I have already spoken. While the objects around me—while the carvings of the ceilings, the sombre tapestries of the walls, the ebony blackness of the floors, and the phantasmagoric armorial trophies which rattled as I strode, were but matters to which, or to such as which, I had been accustomed from my infancy—while I hesitated not to acknowledge how familiar was all this—I still wondered to find how unfamiliar were the fancies which ordinary images were stirring up. On one of the staircases, I met the physician of the family. His countenance, I thought, wore a mingled expression of low cunning and perplexity. He accosted me with trepidation and passed on. The valet now threw open a door and ushered me into the presence of his master.

The room in which I found myself was very large and lofty. The windows were long, narrow, and pointed, and at so vast a distance from the black oaken floor as to be altogether inaccessible from within. Feeble gleams of encrimsoned light made their way through the trellised panes, and served to render sufficiently distinct the more prominent objects around; the eye, however, struggled in vain to reach the remoter angles of the chamber, or the recesses of the vaulted and fretted ceiling. Dark draperies hung upon the walls. The general furniture was profuse, comfortless, antique, and tattered. Many books and musical instruments lay scattered about, but failed to give any vitality to the scene. I felt that I breathed an atmosphere of sorrow. An air of stern, deep, and irredeemable gloom hung over and pervaded all.

Upon my entrance, Usher rose from a sofa on which he had been lying at full length, and greeted me with a vivacious warmth which had much in it, I at first thought, of an overdone cordiality—of the constrained effort of the *ennuyé* man of the world. A glance, however, at his countenance convinced me of his perfect sincerity. We sat down; and for some moments, while he spoke not, I gazed upon him with a feeling half of pity, half of awe. Surely, man had never before so terribly altered, in so brief a period, as had Roderick Usher! It was with difficulty that I could bring myself to admit the identity of the man being before me with the companion of my early boyhood. Yet the character of his face had been at all times remarkable. A cadaverousness of complexion; an eye large, liquid, and luminous beyond comparison; lips somewhat thin and very pallid, but of a surpassingly beautiful curve; a nose of a delicate Hebrew model, but with a breadth of nostril unusual in similar formations; a finely moulded chin, speaking, in its want of prominence, of a want of moral energy; hair of a more than web-like softness and tenuity;—these features, with an inordinate expansion above the regions of the temple, made up altogether a countenance not easily to be forgotten. And now in the mere exaggeration of the prevailing character of these features, and of the expression they were wont to convey, lay so much of change that I doubted to whom I spoke. The now ghastly pallor of the skin, and the now miraculous lustre of the eye, above all things startled and even awed me. The silken hair, too, had been suffered to grow all unheeded, and as, in its wild gossamer texture, it floated rather than fell about the face, I could not, even with effort, connect its Arabesque expression with any idea of simple humanity.

In the manner of my friend I was at once struck with an incoherence—an inconsistency; and I soon found this to arise from a series of feeble and futile struggles to overcome an habitual trepidancy—an excessive nervous agitation. For something of this nature I had indeed been prepared, no less by his letter, than by reminiscences of certain boyish traits, and by conclusions deduced from his peculiar physical conformation and temperament. His action was alternately vivacious and sullen. His voice varied rapidly from a tremulous indecision (when the animal spirits seemed utterly in abeyance) to that species of energetic concision—that abrupt, weighty, unhurried, and hollow-sounding enunciation—that leaden, self-balanced and perfectly modulated guttural utterance, which may be observed in the lost drunkard, or the irreclaimable eater of opium, during the periods of his most intense excitement.

It was thus that he spoke of the object of my visit, of his earnest desire to see me, and of the solace he expected me to afford him. He entered, at some length, into what he conceived to be the nature of his malady. It was, he said, a constitutional and a family evil, and one for which he despaired to find a remedy—a mere nervous affection, he immediately added, which would undoubtedly soon pass off. It displayed itself in a host of unnatural sensations. Some of these, as he detailed them, interested and bewildered me; although, perhaps, the terms and the general manner of the narration had their weight. He suffered much from a morbid acuteness of the senses; the most insipid food was alone endurable; he could wear only garments of certain texture; the odors of all flowers were oppressive; his eyes were tortured by even a faint light; and there were but peculiar sounds, and these from stringed instruments, which did not inspire him with horror.

To an anomalous species of terror I found him a bounden slave. "I shall perish," said he, "I *must* perish in this deplorable folly. Thus, thus, and not otherwise, shall I be lost. I dread the events of the future, not in themselves, but in their results. I shudder at the thought of any, even the most trivial, incident, which may operate upon this intolerable agitation of soul. I have, indeed, no abhorrence of danger, except in its absolute effect—in terror. In this unnerved, in this pitiable, condition I feel that the period will sooner or later arrive when I must abandon life and reason together, in some struggle with the grim phantasm, FEAR."

I learned, moreover, at intervals, and through broken and equivocal hints, another singular feature of his mental condition. He
was enchained by certain superstitious impressions in regard to the
dwelling which he tenanted, and whence, for many years, he had
never ventured forth—in regard to an influence whose suppositi-
tious force was conveyed in terms too shadowy here to be
re-stated—an influence which some peculiarities in the mere form
and substance of his family mansion had, by dint of long sufferance,
he said, obtained over his spirit—an effect which the *physique* of
the gray walls and turrets, and of the dim tarn into which they all
looked down, had, at length, brought about upon the *morale* of his
existence.

He admitted, however, although with hesitation, that much of
the peculiar gloom which thus afflicted him could be traced to a
more natural and far more palpable origin—to the severe and
long-continued illness—indeed to the evidently approaching dissolution—of a tenderly beloved sister, his sole companion for long
years, his last and only relative on earth. "Her decease," he said,
with a bitterness which I can never forget, "would leave him (him
the hopeless and the frail) the last of the ancient race of the Ushers."
While he spoke, the lady Madeline (for so was she called) passed
slowly through a remote portion of the apartment, and, without
having noticed my presence, disappeared. I regarded her with an
utter astonishment not unmingled with dread; and yet I found it
impossible to account for such feelings. A sensation of stupor
oppressed me as my eyes followed her retreating steps. When a
door, at length, closed upon her, my glance sought instinctively and
eagerly the countenance of the brother; but he had buried his face
in his hands, and I could only perceive that a far more than ordinary
wanness had overspread the emaciated fingers through which
trickled many passionate tears.

The disease of the lady Madeline had long baffled the skill of her physicians. A settled apathy, a gradual wasting away of the person, and frequent although transient affections of a partially cataleptical character were the unusual diagnosis. Hitherto she had steadily borne up against the pressure of her malady, and had not betaken herself finally to bed; but on the closing in of the evening of my arrival at the house, she succumbed (as her brother told me at night with inexpressible agitation) to the prostrating power of the destroyer; and I learned that the glimpse I had obtained of her person would thus probably be the last I should obtain—that the lady, at least while living, would be seen by me no more.

For several days ensuing, her name was unmentioned by either Usher or myself; and during this period I was busied in earnest endeavors to alleviate the melancholy of my friend. We painted and read together, or I listened, as if in a dream, to the wild improvisations of his speaking guitar. And thus, as a closer and still closer intimacy admitted me more unreservedly into the recesses of his spirit, the more bitterly did I perceive the futility of all attempt at cheering a mind from which darkness, as if an inherent positive quality, poured forth upon all objects of the moral and physical universe in one unceasing radiation of gloom.

I shall ever bear about me a memory of the many solemn hours I thus spent alone with the master of the House of Usher. Yet I should fail in any attempt to convey an idea of the exact character of the studies, or of the occupations, in which he involved me, or led me the way. An excited and highly distempered ideality threw a sulphureous lustre over all. His long improvised dirges will ring forever in my ears. Among other things, I hold painfully in mind a certain singular perversion and amplification of the wild air of the last waltz of Von Weber. From the paintings over which his elaborate fancy brooded, and which grew, touch by touch, into vagueness at which I shuddered the more thrillingly, because I shuddered knowing not why—from these paintings (vivid as their images now are before me) I would in vain endeavor to educe more than a small portion which should lie within the compass of merely written words. By the utter simplicity, by the nakedness of his designs, he arrested and overawed attention. If ever mortal painted an idea, that mortal was Roderick Usher. For me at least, in the circumstances then surrounding me, there arose out of the pure abstractions which the hypochondriac contrived to throw upon his canvas, an intensity of intolerable awe, no shadow of which felt I ever yet in the contemplation of the certainly glowing yet too concrete reveries of Fuseli.

One of the phantasmagoric conceptions of my friend, partaking not so rigidly of the spirit of abstraction, may be shadowed forth, although feebly, in words. A small picture presented the interior of an immensely long and rectangular vault or tunnel, with low walls, smooth, white, and without interruption or device. Certain accessory points of the design served well to convey the idea that this excavation lay at an exceeding depth below the surface of the earth. No outlet was observed in any portion of its vast extent, and no torch or other artificial source of light was discernible; yet a flood of intense rays rolled throughout, and bathed the whole in a ghastly and inappropriate splendor.

I have just spoken of that morbid condition of the auditory nerve which rendered all music intolerable to the sufferer, with the exception of certain effects of stringed instruments. It was, perhaps, the narrow limits to which he thus confined himself upon the guitar which gave birth, in great measure, to the fantastic character of the performances. But the fervid *facility* of his *impromptus* could not be so accounted for. They must have been, and were, in the notes, as well as in the words of his wild fantasias (for he not unfrequently accompanied himself with rhymed verbal improvisations), the result of that intense mental collectedness and concentration to which I have previously alluded as observable only in particular moments of the highest artificial excitement. The words of one of these rhapsodies I have easily remembered. I was, perhaps, the more forcibly impressed with it as he gave it, because, in the under or mystic current of its meaning, I fancied that I perceived, and for the first time, a full consciousness on the part of Usher of the tottering of his lofty reason upon her throne. The verses, which were entitled "The Haunted Palace," ran very nearly, if not accurately, thus:—

I.
In the greenest of our valleys,
      By good angels tenanted,
Once a fair and stately palace—
      Radiant palace—reared its head.
In the monarch Thought's dominion—
      It stood there!
Never seraph spread a pinion
      Over fabric half so fair.

II. Banners yellow, glorious, golden,
      On its roof did float and flow;
(This—all this—was in the olden
      Time long ago);
And every gentle air that dallied,
      In that sweet day,
Along the ramparts plumed and pallid,
      A winged odor went away.

III.
Wanderers in that happy valley
      Through two luminous windows saw
Spirits moving musically

To a lute's well-tunèd law;
Round about a throne, where sitting
    (Porphyrogene!)
In state his glory well befitting,
    The ruler of the realm was seen.

IV.

And all with pearl and ruby glowing
    Was the fair palace door,
Through which came flowing, flowing, flowing
    And sparkling evermore,
A troop of Echoes whose sweet duty
    Was but to sing,
In voices of surpassing beauty,
    The wit and wisdom of their king.

III.

Wanderers in that happy valley
    Through two luminous windows saw
Spirits moving musically
    To a lute's well-tunèd law;
Round about a throne, where sitting
    (Porphyrogene!)
In state his glory well befitting,
    The ruler of the realm was seen.

IV.

And all with pearl and ruby glowing
    Was the fair palace door,
Through which came flowing, flowing, flowing
    And sparkling evermore,
A troop of Echoes whose sweet duty

       Was but to sing,
In voices of surpassing beauty,
       The wit and wisdom of their king.

V.

But evil things, in robes of sorrow,
       Assailed the monarch's high estate;
(Ah, let us mourn, for never morrow
       Shall dawn upon him, desolate!)
And, round about his home, the glory
       That blushed and bloomed
Is but a dim-remembered story
       Of the old time entombed.

VI.

And travellers now within that valley,
       Through the red-litten windows see
Vast forms that move fantastically
       To a discordant melody;
While, like a rapid ghastly river,
       Through the pale door,
A hideous throng rush out forever,
       And laugh—but smile no more.

I well remember that suggestions arising from this ballad, led us into a train of thought wherein there became manifest an opinion of Usher's which I mention not so much on account of its novelty (for other men* have thought thus), as on account of the pertinacity with which he maintained it. This opinion, in its general form, was that of the sentience of all vegetable things. But, in his disordered fancy, the idea had assumed a more daring character, and trespassed, under certain conditions, upon the kingdom of inorganization. I lack words to express the full extent, or the earnest *abandon* of his persuasion. The belief, however, was connected (as I have previously hinted) with the gray stones of the home of his forefathers. The conditions of the sentience had been here, he imagined, fulfilled in the method of collocation of these stones—in the order of their arrangement, as well as in that of the many *fungi* which overspread them, and of the decayed trees which stood around—above all, in the long undisturbed endurance of this arrangement, and in its reduplication in the still waters of the tarn. Its evidence—the evidence of the sentience—was to be seen, he said, (and I here started as he spoke), in the gradual yet certain condensation of an atmosphere of their own about the waters and the walls. The result was discoverable, he added, in that silent yet importunate and terrible influence which for centuries had moulded the destinies of his family, and which made *him* what I now saw him—what he was. Such opinions need no comment, and I will make none.

Our books—the books which, for years, had formed no small portion of the mental existence of the invalid—were, as might be supposed, in strict keeping with this character of phantasm. We pored together over such works as the "Ververt et Chartreuse" of Gresset; the "Belphegor" of Machiavelli; the "Heaven and Hell" of Swedenborg; the "Subterranean Voyage of Nicholas Klimm" by Holberg; the "Chiromancy" of Robert Flud, of Jean D'Indaginé, and of De la Chambre; the "Journey into the Blue Distance" of Tieck; and the "City of the Sun" of Campanella. One favorite volume was a small octavo edition of the "Directorium Inquisitorium," by the Dominican Eymeric de Gironne; and there were passages in Pomponius Mela, about the old African Satyrs and Œgipans, over which Usher would sit dreaming for hours. His chief delight, however, was found in the perusal of an exceedingly rare and curious book in quarto Gothic—the manual of a forgotten church—the *Vigiliæ Mortuorum Secundum Chorum Ecclesiæ Maguntinæ.*

I could not help thinking of the wild ritual of this work, and of its probable influence upon the hypochondriac, when, one evening, having informed me abruptly that the lady Madeline was no more, he stated his intention of preserving her corpse for a fortnight (previously to its final interment), in one of the numerous vaults within the main walls of the building. The worldly reason, however, assigned for this singular proceeding, was one which I did not feel at liberty to dispute. The brother had been led to his resolution (so he told me) by consideration of the unusual character of the malady of the deceased, of certain obtrusive and eager inquiries on the part of her medical men, and of the remote and exposed situation of the burial-ground of the family. I will not deny that when I called to mind the sinister countenance of the person whom I met upon the staircase, on the day of my arrival at the house, I had no desire to oppose what I regarded as at best but a harmless, and by no means an unnatural, precaution.

At the request of Usher, I personally aided him in the arrangements for the temporary entombment. The body having been encoffined, we two alone bore it to its rest. The vault in which we placed it (and which had been so long unopened that our torches, half smothered in its oppressive atmosphere, gave us little opportunity for investigation) was small, damp, and entirely without means of admission for light; lying, at great depth, immediately beneath that portion of the building in which was my own sleeping apartment. It had been used, apparently, in remote feudal times, for the worst purposes of a donjon-keep, and, in later days, as a place of deposit for powder, or some other highly combustible substance, as a portion of its floor, and the whole interior of a long archway through which we reached it, were carefully sheathed with copper. The door, of massive iron, had been, also, similarly protected. Its immense weight caused an unusually sharp, grating sound, as it moved upon its hinges.

Having deposited our mournful burden upon tressels within this region of horror, we partially turned aside the yet unscrewed lid of the coffin, and looked upon the face of the tenant. A striking similitude between the brother and sister now first arrested my attention; and Usher, divining, perhaps, my thoughts, murmured out some few words from which I learned that the deceased and himself had been twins, and that sympathies of a scarcely intelligible nature had always existed between them. Our glances, however, rested not long upon the dead—for we could not regard her unawed. The disease which had thus entombed the lady in the maturity of youth, had left, as usual in all maladies of a strictly cataleptical character, the mockery of a faint blush upon the bosom and the face, and that suspiciously lingering smile upon the lip which is so terrible in death. We replaced and screwed down the lid, and, having secured the door of iron, made our way, with toil, into the scarcely less gloomy apartments of the upper portion of the house.

And now, some days of bitter grief having elapsed, an observable change came over the features of the mental disorder of my friend. His ordinary manner had vanished. His ordinary occupations were neglected or forgotten. He roamed from chamber to chamber with hurried, unequal, and objectless step. The pallor of his countenance had assumed, if possible, a more ghastly hue—but the luminousness of his eye had utterly gone out. The once occasional huskiness of his tone was heard no more; and a tremulous quaver, as if of extreme terror, habitually characterized his utterance. There were times, indeed, when I thought his unceasingly agitated mind was laboring with some oppressive secret, to divulge which he struggled for the necessary courage. At times, again, I was obliged to resolve all into the mere inexplicable vagaries of madness, for I beheld him gazing upon vacancy for long hours, in an attitude of the profoundest attention, as if listening to some imaginary sound. It was no wonder that his condition terrified—that it infected me. I felt creeping upon me, by slow yet certain degrees, the wild influences of his own fantastic yet impressive superstitions.

It was, especially, upon retiring to bed late in the night of the seventh or eighth day after the placing of the lady Madeline within the donjon, that I experienced the full power of such feelings. Sleep came not near my couch—while the hours waned and waned away. I struggled to reason off the nervousness which had dominion over me. I endeavored to believe that much, if not all of what I felt, was due to the bewildering influence of the gloomy furniture of the room—of the dark and tattered draperies, which, tortured into motion by the breath of a rising tempest, swayed fitfully to and fro upon the walls, and rustled uneasily about the decorations of the bed. But my efforts were fruitless. An irrepressible tremor gradually pervaded my frame; and, at length, there sat upon my very heart an incubus of utterly causeless alarm. Shaking this off with a gasp and a struggle, I uplifted myself upon the pillows, and, peering earnestly within the intense darkness of the chamber, hearkened—I know not why, except that an instinctive spirit prompted me—to certain low and indefinite sounds which came, through the pauses of the storm, at long intervals, I knew not whence. Overpowered by an intense sentiment of horror, unaccountable yet unendurable, I threw on my clothes with haste (for I felt that I should sleep no more during the night), and endeavored to arouse myself from the pitiable condition into which I had fallen, by pacing rapidly to and fro through the apartment.

I had taken but few turns in this manner, when a light step on an adjoining staircase arrested my attention. I presently recognized it as that of Usher. In an instant afterward he rapped, with a gentle touch, at my door, and entered, bearing a lamp. His countenance was, as usual, cadaverously wan—but, moreover, there was a species of mad hilarity in his eyes—an evidently restrained *hysteria* in his whole demeanor. His air appalled me—but anything was preferable to the solitude which I had so long endured, and I even welcomed his presence as a relief.

"And you have not seen it?" he said abruptly, after having stared about him for some moments in silence—"you have not then seen it?—but, stay! you shall." Thus speaking, and having carefully shaded his lamp, he hurried to one of the casements, and threw it freely open to the storm.

The impetuous fury of the entering gust nearly lifted us from our feet. It was, indeed, a tempestuous yet sternly beautiful night, and one wildly singular in its terror and its beauty. A whirlwind had apparently collected its force in our vicinity; for there were frequent and violent alterations in the direction of the wind; and the exceeding density of the clouds (which hung so low as to press upon the turrets of the house) did not prevent our perceiving the life-like velocity with which they flew careering from all points against each other, without passing away into the distance. I say that even their exceeding density did not prevent our perceiving this—yet we had no glimpse of the moon or stars, nor was there any flashing forth of the lightning. But the under surfaces of the huge masses of agitated vapor, as well as all terrestrial objects immediately around us, were glowing in the unnatural light of a faintly luminous and distinctly visible gaseous exhalation which hung about and enshrouded the mansion.

"You must not—you shall not behold this!" said I, shuddering, to Usher, as I led him, with a gentle violence, from the window to a seat. "These appearances, which bewilder you, are merely electrical phenomena not uncommon—or it may be that they have their ghastly origin in the rank miasma of the tarn. Let us close this casement;—the air is chilling and dangerous to your frame. Here is one of your favorite romances. I will read, and you shall listen:—and so we will pass away this terrible night together."

The antique volume which I had taken up was the "Mad Trist"

of Sir Launcelot Canning; but I had called it a favorite of Usher's more in sad jest than in earnest; for, in truth, there is little in its uncouth and unimaginative prolixity which could have had interest for the lofty and spiritual ideality of my friend. It was, however, the only book immediately at hand; and I indulged a vague hope that the excitement which now agitated the hypochondriac, might find relief (for the history of mental disorder is full of similar anomalies) even in the extremeness of the folly which I should read. Could I have judged, indeed, by the wild overstrained air of vivacity with which he hearkened, or apparently hearkened, to the words of the tale, I might well have congratulated myself upon the success of my design.

I had arrived at that well-known portion of the story where Ethelred, the hero of the Trist, having sought in vain for peaceable admission into the dwelling of the hermit, proceeds to make good an entrance by force. Here, it will be remembered, the words of the narrative run thus:

"And Ethelred, who was by nature of a doughty heart, and who was now mighty withal, on account of the powerfulness of the wine which he had drunken, waited no longer to hold parley with the hermit, who, in sooth, was of an obstinate and maliceful turn, but, feeling the rain upon his shoulders, and fearing the rising of the tempest, uplifted his mace outright, and, with blows, made quickly room in the plankings of the door for his gauntleted hand; and now pulling therewith sturdily, he so cracked, and ripped, and tore all asunder, that the noise of the dry and hollow-sounding wood alarumed and reverberated throughout the forest."

At the termination of this sentence I started and, for a moment, paused; for it appeared to me (although I at once concluded that my excited fancy had deceived me)—it appeared to me that, from some very remote portion of the mansion, there came, indistinctly to my ears, what might have been, in its exact similarity of character, the echo (but a stifled and dull one certainly) of the very cracking and ripping sound which Sir Launcelot had so particularly described. It was, beyond doubt, the coincidence alone which had arrested my attention; for, amid the rattling of the sashes of the casements, and the ordinary commingled noises of the still increasing storm, the sound, in itself, had nothing, surely, which should have interested or disturbed me. I continued the story:

"But the good champion Ethelred, now entering within the door, was sore enraged and amazed to perceive no signal of the maliceful hermit; but, in the stead thereof, a dragon of a scaly and prodigious demeanor, and of a fiery tongue, which sat in guard before a palace of gold, with a floor of silver; and upon the wall there hung a shield of shining brass with this legend enwritten—

Who entereth herein, a conqueror hath bin;
Who slayeth the dragon, the shield he shall win.

And Ethelred uplifted his mace, and struck upon the head of the dragon, which fell before him, and gave up his pesty breath, with a shriek so horrid and harsh, and withal so piercing, that Ethelred had fain to close his ears with his hands against the dreadful noise of it, the like whereof was never before heard."

Here again I paused abruptly, and now with a feeling of wild amazement—for there could be no doubt whatever that, in this instance, I did actually hear (although from what direction it proceeded I found it impossible to say) a low and apparently distant, but harsh, protracted, and most unusual screaming or grating sound—the exact counterpart of what my fancy had already conjured up for the dragon's unnatural shriek as described by the romancer.

Oppressed, as I certainly was, upon the occurrence of this second and most extraordinary coincidence, by a thousand conflicting sensations, in which wonder and extreme terror were predominant, I still retained sufficient presence of mind to avoid exciting, by any observation, the sensitive nervousness of my companion. I was by no means certain that he had noticed the sounds in question; although, assuredly, a strange alteration had, during the last few minutes, taken place in his demeanor. From a position fronting my own, he had gradually brought round his chair, so as to sit with his face to the door of the chamber; and thus I could but partially perceive his features, although I saw that his lips trembled as if he were murmuring inaudibly. His head had dropped upon his breast— yet I knew that he was not asleep, from the wide and rigid opening of the eye as I caught a glance of it in profile. The motion of his body, too, was at variance with this idea—for he rocked from side to side with a gentle yet constant and uniform sway. Having rapidly taken notice of all this, I resumed the narrative of Sir Launcelot, which thus proceeded:

"And now, the champion, having escaped from the terrible fury of the dragon, bethinking himself of the brazen shield, and of the breaking up of the enchantment which was upon it, removed the carcass from out of the way before him, and approached valorously over the silver pavement of the castle to where the shield was upon the wall; which in sooth tarried not for his full coming, but fell down at his feet upon the silver floor, with a mighty great and terrible ringing sound."

No sooner had these syllables passed my lips, than—as if a shield of brass had indeed, at the moment, fallen heavily upon a floor of silver—I became aware of a distinct, hollow, metallic, and clangorous, yet apparently muffled, reverberation. Completely unnerved, I leaped to my feet; but the measured rocking movement of Usher was undisturbed. I rushed to the chair in which he sat. His eyes were bent fixedly before him, and throughout his whole counten-ance there reigned a stony rigidity. But, as I placed my hand upon his shoulder, there came a strong shudder over his whole person; a sickly smile quivered about his lips; and I saw that he spoke in a low, hurried, and gibbering murmur, as if unconscious of my presence. Bending closely over him, I at length drank in the hideous import of his words.

"Not hear it?—yes, I hear it, and *have* heard it. Long—long—long—many minutes, many hours, many days, have I heard it—yet I dared not—oh, pity me, miserable wretch that I am!—I dared not—I *dared* not speak! *We have put her living in the tomb!* Said I not that my senses were acute? I *now* tell you that I heard her first feeble movements in the hollow coffin. I heard them—many, many days ago—yet I dared not—*I dared not speak!* And now—to-night—Ethelred—ha! ha!—the breaking of the hermit's door, and the death-cry of the dragon, and the clangor of the shield!—say, rather, the rending of her coffin, and the grating of the iron hinges of her prison, and her struggles within the coppered archway of the vault! Oh! whither shall I fly? Will she not be here anon? Is she not hurrying to upbraid me for my haste? Have I not heard her footstep on the stair? Do I not distinguish that heavy and horrible beating of her heart? Madman!"—here he sprang furiously to his feet, and shrieked out his syllables, as if in the effort he were giving up his soul—*"Madman! I tell you that she now stands without the door!"*

As if in the superhuman energy of his utterance there had been found the potency of a spell, the huge antique panels to which the speaker pointed threw slowly back, upon the instant, their ponderous and ebony jaws. It was the work of the rushing gust—but then without those doors there *did* stand the lofty and enshrouded figure of the lady Madeline of Usher. There was blood upon her white robes, and the evidence of some bitter struggle upon every portion of her emaciated frame. For a moment she remained trembling and reeling to and fro upon the threshold—then, with a low moaning cry, fell heavily inward upon the person of her brother, and in her violent and now final death-agonies, bore him to the floor a corpse, and a victim to the terrors he had anticipated.

From that chamber, and from that mansion, I fled aghast. The storm was still abroad in all its wrath as I found myself crossing the old causeway. Suddenly there shot along the path a wild light, and I turned to see whence a gleam so unusual could have issued; for the vast house and its shadows were alone behind me. The radiance was that of the full, setting, and blood-red moon which now shone vividly through that once barely-discernible fissure of which I have before spoken as extending from the roof of the building, in a zigzag direction, to the base. While I gazed, this fissure rapidly widened—there came a fierce breath of the whirlwind—the entire orb of the satellite burst at once upon my sight—my brain reeled as I saw the mighty walls rushing asunder—there was a long tumultuous shouting sound like the voice of a thousand waters—and the deep and dank tarn at my feet closed sullenly and silently over the fragments of the *"House of Usher."*

NORTHANGER ABBEY

The night was stormy; the wind had been rising at intervals the whole afternoon; and by the time the party broke up, it blew and rained violently. Catherine, as she crossed the hall, listened to the tempest with sensations of awe; and, when she heard it rage round a corner of the ancient building and close with sudden fury a distant door, felt for the first time that she was really in an abbey. Yes, these were characteristic sounds; they brought to her recollection a countless variety of dreadful situations and horrid scenes, which such buildings had witnessed, and such storms ushered in; and most heartily did she rejoice in the happier circumstances attending her entrance within walls so solemn! She had nothing to dread from midnight assassins or drunken gallants. Henry had certainly been only in jest in what he had told her that morning. In a house so furnished, and so guarded, she could have nothing to explore or to suffer, and might go to her bedroom as securely as if it had been her own chamber at Fullerton. Thus wisely fortifying her mind, as she proceeded upstairs, she was enabled, especially on perceiving that Miss Tilney slept only two doors from her, to enter her room with a tolerably stout heart; and her spirits were immediately assisted by the cheerful blaze of a wood fire. "How much better is this," said she, as she walked to the fender—"how much better to find a fire ready lit, than to have to wait shivering in the cold till all the family are in bed, as so many poor girls have been obliged to do, and then to have a faithful old servant frightening one by coming in with a faggot! How glad I am that Northanger is what it is! If it had been like some other places, I do not know that, in such a night as this, I could have answered for my courage: but now, to be sure, there is nothing to alarm one."

She looked round the room. The window curtains seemed in motion. It could be nothing but the violence of the wind penetrating through the divisions of the shutters; and she stepped boldly forward, carelessly humming a tune, to assure herself of its being so, peeped courageously behind each curtain, saw nothing on either low window seat to scare her, and on placing a hand against the shutter, felt the strongest conviction of the wind's force. A glance at the old chest, as she turned away from this examination, was not without its use; she scorned the causeless fears of an idle fancy, and began with a most happy indifference to prepare herself for bed. "She should take her time; she should not hurry herself; she did not care if she were the last person up in the house. But she would not make up her fire; that would seem cowardly, as if she wished for the protection of light after she were in bed." The fire therefore died away, and Catherine, having spent the best part of an hour in her arrangements, was beginning to think of stepping into bed, when, on giving a parting glance round the room, she was struck by the appearance of a high, old-fashioned black cabinet, which, though in a situation conspicuous enough, had never caught her notice before. Henry's words, his description of the ebony cabinet which was to escape her observation at first, immediately rushed across her; and though there could be nothing really in it, there was something whimsical, it was certainly a very remarkable coincidence! She took her candle and looked closely at the cabinet. It was not absolutely ebony and gold; but it was japan, black and yellow japan of the handsomest kind; and as she held her candle, the yellow had very much the effect of gold. The key was in the door, and she had a strange fancy to look into it; not, however, with the smallest expectation of finding anything, but it was so very odd, after what Henry had said. In short, she could not sleep till she had examined it. So, placing the candle with great caution on a chair, she seized the key with a very tremulous hand and tried to turn it; but it resisted her utmost strength. Alarmed, but not discouraged, she tried it another way; a bolt flew, and she believed herself successful; but how strangely mysterious! The door was still immovable. She paused a moment in breathless wonder. The wind roared down the chimney, the rain beat in torrents against the windows, and everything seemed to speak the awfulness of her situation. To retire to bed, however, unsatisfied on such a point, would be vain, since sleep must be impossible with the conscious-ness of a cabinet so mysteriously closed in her immediate vicinity. Again, therefore, she applied herself to the key, and after moving it in every possible way for some instants with the determined celerity of hope's last effort, the door suddenly yielded to her hand: her heart leaped with exultation at such a victory, and having thrown open each folding door, the second being secured only by bolts of less wonderful construction than the lock, though in that her eye could not discern anything unusual, a double range of small drawers appeared in view, with some larger drawers above and below them; and in the centre, a small door, closed also with a lock and key, secured in all probability a cavity of importance.

Catherine's heart beat quick, but her courage did not fail her. With a cheek flushed by hope, and an eye straining with curiosity, her fingers grasped the handle of a drawer and drew it forth. It was entirely empty. With less alarm and greater eagerness she seized a second, a third, a fourth; each was equally empty. Not one was left unsearched, and in not one was anything found. Well read in the art of concealing a treasure, the possibility of false linings to the drawers did not escape her, and she felt round each with anxious acuteness in vain. The place in the middle alone remained now unexplored; and though she had "never from the first had the smallest idea of finding anything in any part of the cabinet, and was not in the least disappointed at her ill success thus far, it would be foolish not to examine it thoroughly while she was about it." It was some time however before she could unfasten the door, the same difficulty occurring in the management of this inner lock as of the outer; but at length it did open; and not vain, as hitherto, was her search; her quick eyes directly fell on a roll of paper pushed back into the further part of the cavity, apparently for concealment, and her feelings at that moment were indescribable. Her heart fluttered, her knees trembled, and her cheeks grew pale. She seized, with an unsteady hand, the precious manuscript, for half a glance sufficed to ascertain written characters; and while she acknowledged with awful sensations this striking exemplification of what Henry had foretold, resolved instantly to peruse every line before she attempted to rest.

The dimness of the light her candle emitted made her turn to it with alarm; but there was no danger of its sudden extinction; it had yet some hours to burn; and that she might not have any greater difficulty in distinguishing the writing than what its ancient date might occasion, she hastily snuffed it. Alas! It was snuffed and extinguished in one. A lamp could not have expired with more awful effect. Catherine, for a few moments, was motionless with horror. It was done completely; not a remnant of light in the wick could give hope to the rekindling breath. Darkness impenetrable and immovable filled the room. A violent gust of wind, rising with sudden fury, added fresh horror to the moment. Catherine trembled from head to foot. In the pause which succeeded, a sound like receding footsteps and the closing of a distant door struck on her affrighted ear. Human nature could support no more. A cold sweat stood on her forehead, the manuscript fell from her hand, and groping her way to the bed, she jumped hastily in, and sought some suspension of agony by creeping far underneath the clothes. To close her eyes in sleep that night, she felt must be entirely out of the question. With a curiosity so justly awakened, and feelings in every way so agitated, repose must be absolutely impossible. The storm too abroad so dreadful! She had not been used to feel alarm from wind, but now every blast seemed fraught with awful intelligence. The manuscript so wonderfully found, so wonderfully accomplishing the morning's prediction, how was it to be accounted for? What could it contain? To whom could it relate? By what means could it have been so long concealed? And how singularly strange that it should fall to her lot to discover it! Till she had made herself mistress of its contents, however, she could have neither repose nor comfort; and with the sun's first rays she was determined to peruse it. But many were the tedious hours which must yet intervene. She shuddered, tossed about in her bed, and envied every quiet sleeper. The storm still raged, and various were the noises, more terrific even than the wind, which struck at intervals on her startled ear. The very curtains of her bed seemed at one moment in motion, and at another the lock of her door was agitated, as if by the attempt of somebody to enter. Hollow murmurs seemed to creep along the gallery, and more than once her blood was chilled by the sound of distant moans. Hour after hour passed away, and the wearied Catherine had heard three proclaimed by all the clocks in the house before the tempest subsided or she unknowingly fell fast asleep.

THE YELLOW WALLPAPER

BY

CHARLOTTE PERKINS GILMAN

I t is very seldom that mere ordinary people like John and myself secure ancestral halls for the summer.

A colonial mansion, a hereditary estate, I would say a haunted house, and reach the height of romantic felicity—but that would be asking too much of fate!

Still I will proudly declare that there is something queer about it.

Else, why should it be let so cheaply? And why have stood so long untenanted?

John laughs at me, of course, but one expects that in marriage.

John is practical in the extreme. He has no patience with faith, an intense horror of superstition, and he scoffs openly at any talk of things not to be felt and seen and put down in figures.

John is a physician, and *perhaps*—(I would not say it to a living soul, of course, but this is dead paper and a great relief to my mind)—*perhaps* that is one reason I do not get well faster.

You see, he does not believe I am sick!

And what can one do?

If a physician of high standing, and one's own husband, assures friends and relatives that there is really nothing the matter with one but temporary nervous depression—a slight hysterical tendency—what is one to do?

My brother is also a physician, and also of high standing, and he says the same thing.

So I take phosphates or phosphites—whichever it is, and tonics, and journeys, and air, and exercise, and am absolutely forbidden to "work" until I am well again.

Personally, I disagree with their ideas.

Personally, I believe that congenial work, with excitement and change, would do me good.

But what is one to do?

I did write for a while in spite of them; but it *does* exhaust me a good deal—having to be so sly about it, or else meet with heavy opposition.

I sometimes fancy that in my condition if I had less opposition and more society and stimulus—but John says the very worst thing I can do is to think about my condition, and I confess it always makes me feel bad.

So I will let it alone and talk about the house.

The most beautiful place! It is quite alone, standing well back from the road, quite three miles from the village. It makes me think of English places that you read about, for there are hedges and walls and gates that lock, and lots of separate little houses for the gardeners and people.

There is a *delicious* garden! I never saw such a garden—large and shady, full of box-bordered paths, and lined with long grape-covered arbors with seats under them.

There were greenhouses, too, but they are all broken now.

There was some legal trouble, I believe, something about the heirs and co-heirs; anyhow, the place has been empty for years.

That spoils my ghostliness, I am afraid; but I don't care—there is something strange about the house—I can feel it.

I even said so to John one moonlight evening, but he said what I felt was a *draught*, and shut the window.

I get unreasonably angry with John sometimes. I'm sure I never used to be so sensitive. I think it is due to this nervous condition.

But John says if I feel so I shall neglect proper self-control; so I take pains to control myself,—before him, at least,—and that makes me very tired.

I don't like our room a bit. I wanted one downstairs that opened on the piazza and had roses all over the window, and such pretty old-fashioned chintz hangings! but John would not hear of it.

He said there was only one window and not room for two beds, and no near room for him if he took another.

He is very careful and loving, and hardly lets me stir without special direction.

I have a schedule prescription for each hour in the day; he takes all care from me, and so I feel basely ungrateful not to value it more.

He said we came here solely on my account, that I was to have perfect rest and all the air I could get. "Your exercise depends on your strength, my dear," said he, "and your food somewhat on your appetite; but air you can absorb all the time." So we took the nursery, at the top of the house.

It is a big, airy room, the whole floor nearly, with windows that look all ways, and air and sunshine galore. It was nursery first and then playground and gymnasium, I should judge; for the windows are barred for little children, and there are rings and things in the walls.

The paint and paper look as if a boys' school had used it. It is stripped off—the paper—in great patches all around the head of my bed, about as far as I can reach, and in a great place on the other side of the room low down. I never saw a worse paper in my life.

One of those sprawling flamboyant patterns committing every artistic sin.

It is dull enough to confuse the eye in following, pronounced enough to constantly irritate, and provoke study, and when you follow the lame, uncertain curves for a little distance they suddenly commit suicide—plunge off at outrageous angles, destroy themselves in unheard-of contradictions.

The color is repellant, almost revolting; a smouldering, unclean yellow, strangely faded by the slow-turning sunlight.

It is a dull yet lurid orange in some places, a sickly sulphur tint in others.

No wonder the children hated it! I should hate it myself if I had to live in this room long.

There comes John, and I must put this away,—he hates to have me write a word.

We have been here two weeks, and I haven't felt like writing before, since that first day.

I am sitting by the window now, up in this atrocious nursery, and there is nothing to hinder my writing as much as I please, save lack of strength.

John is away all day, and even some nights when his cases are serious.

I am glad my case is not serious!

But these nervous troubles are dreadfully depressing.

John does not know how much I really suffer. He knows there is no *reason* to suffer, and that satisfies him.

Of course it is only nervousness. It does weigh on me so not to do my duty in any way!

I meant to be such a help to John, such a real rest and comfort, and here I am a comparative burden already!

Nobody would believe what an effort it is to do what little I am able—to dress and entertain, and order things.

It is fortunate Mary is so good with the baby. Such a dear baby! And yet I *cannot* be with him, it makes me so nervous.

I suppose John never was nervous in his life. He laughs at me so about this wallpaper!

At first he meant to repaper the room, but afterwards he said that I was letting it get the better of me, and that nothing was worse for a nervous patient than to give way to such fancies.

He said that after the wallpaper was changed it would be the heavy bedstead, and then the barred windows, and then that gate at the head of the stairs, and so on.

"You know the place is doing you good," he said, "and really, dear, I don't care to renovate the house just for a three months' rental."

"Then do let us go downstairs," I said, "there are such pretty rooms there."

Then he took me in his arms and called me a blessed little goose, and said he would go down to the cellar if I wished, and have it whitewashed into the bargain.

But he is right enough about the beds and windows and things.

It is as airy and comfortable a room as any one need wish, and, of course, I would not be so silly as to make him uncomfortable just for a whim.

I'm really getting quite fond of the big room, all but that horrid paper.

Out of one window I can see the garden, those mysterious deep-shaded arbors, the riotous old-fashioned flowers, and bushes and gnarly trees.

Out of another I get a lovely view of the bay and a little private wharf belonging to the estate. There is a beautiful shaded lane that runs down there from the house. I always fancy I see people walking in these numerous paths and arbors, but John has cautioned me not to give way to fancy in the least. He says that with my imaginative power and habit of story-making a nervous weakness like mine is sure to lead to all manner of excited fancies, and that I ought to use my will and good sense to check the tendency. So I try.

I think sometimes that if I were only well enough to write a little it would relieve the press of ideas and rest me.

But I find I get pretty tired when I try.

It is so discouraging not to have any advice and companionship about my work. When I get really well John says we will ask Cousin Henry and Julia down for a long visit; but he says he would as soon put fire-works in my pillow-case as to let me have those stimulating people about now.

I wish I could get well faster.

But I must not think about that. This paper looks to me as if it *knew* what a vicious influence it had!

There is a recurrent spot where the pattern lolls like a broken neck and two bulbous eyes stare at you upside-down.

I get positively angry with the impertinence of it and the ever-lastingness. Up and down and sideways they crawl, and those absurd, unblinking eyes are everywhere. There is one place where two breadths didn't match, and the eyes go all up and down the line, one a little higher than the other.

I never saw so much expression in an inanimate thing before, and we all know how much expression they have! I used to lie awake as a child and get more entertainment and terror out of blank walls and plain furniture than most children could find in a toy-store.

I remember what a kindly wink the knobs of our big old bureau used to have, and there was one chair that always seemed like a strong friend.

I used to feel that if any of the other things looked too fierce I could always hop into that chair and be safe.

The furniture in this room is no worse than inharmonious, however, for we had to bring it all from downstairs. I suppose when this was used as a playroom they had to take the nursery things out, and no wonder! I never saw such ravages as the children have made here.

The wallpaper, as I said before, is torn off in spots, and it sticketh closer than a brother—they must have had perseverance as well as hatred.

Then the floor is scratched and gouged and splintered, the plaster itself is dug out here and there, and this great heavy bed, which is all we found in the room, looks as if it had been through the wars.

But I don't mind it a bit—only the paper.

There comes John's sister. Such a dear girl as she is, and so careful of me! I must not let her find me writing.

She is a perfect, and enthusiastic housekeeper, and hopes for no better profession. I verily believe she thinks it is the writing which made me sick!

But I can write when she is out, and see her a long way off from these windows.

There is one that commands the road, a lovely, shaded, winding road, and one that just looks off over the country. A lovely country, too, full of great elms and velvet meadows.

This wallpaper has a kind of sub-pattern in a different shade, a particularly irritating one, for you can only see it in certain lights, and not clearly then.

But in the places where it isn't faded, and where the sun is just so, I can see a strange, provoking, formless sort of figure, that seems to sulk about behind that silly and conspicuous front design.

There's sister on the stairs!

Well, the Fourth of July is over! The people are gone and I am tired out. John thought it might do me good to see a little company, so we just had mother and Nellie and the children down for a week.

Of course I didn't do a thing. Jennie sees to everything now.

But it tired me all the same.

John says if I don't pick up faster he shall send me to Weir Mitchell in the fall.

But I don't want to go there at all. I had a friend who was in his hands once, and she says he is just like John and my brother, only more so!

Besides, it is such an undertaking to go so far.

I don't feel as if it was worth while to turn my hand over for anything, and I'm getting dreadfully fretful and querulous.

I cry at nothing, and cry most of the time.

Of course I don't when John is here, or anybody else, but when I am alone.

And I am alone a good deal just now. John is kept in town very often by serious cases, and Jennie is good and lets me alone when I want her to.

So I walk a little in the garden or down that lovely lane, sit on the porch under the roses, and lie down up here a good deal.

I'm getting really fond of the room in spite of the wallpaper. Perhaps *because* of the wallpaper.

It dwells in my mind so!

I lie here on this great immovable bed—it is nailed down, I believe—and follow that pattern about by the hour. It is as good as gymnastics, I assure you. I start, we'll say, at the bottom, down in the corner over there where it has not been touched, and I determine for the thousandth time that I *will* follow that pointless pattern to some sort of a conclusion.

I know a little of the principle of design, and I know this thing was not arranged on any laws of radiation, or alternation, or repetition, or symmetry, or anything else that I ever heard of.

It is repeated, of course, by the breadths, but not otherwise.

Looked at in one way each breadth stands alone, the bloated curves and flourishes—a kind of "debased Romanesque" with *delirium tremens*—go waddling up and down in isolated columns of fatuity.

But, on the other hand, they connect diagonally, and the sprawling outlines run off in great slanting waves of optic horror, like a lot of wallowing seaweeds in full chase.

The whole thing goes horizontally, too, at least it seems so, and I exhaust myself in trying to distinguish the order of its going in that direction.

They have used a horizontal breadth for a frieze, and that adds wonderfully to the confusion.

There is one end of the room where it is almost intact, and there, when the cross-lights fade and the low sun shines directly upon it, I can almost fancy radiation after all,—the interminable grotesques seem to form around a common centre and rush off in headlong plunges of equal distraction.

It makes me tired to follow it. I will take a nap, I guess.

I don't know why I should write this.

I don't want to.

I don't feel able.

And I know John would think it absurd. But I *must* say what I feel and think in some way—it is such a relief!

But the effort is getting to be greater than the relief.

Half the time now I am awfully lazy, and lie down ever so much.

John says I musn't lose my strength, and has me take cod-liver oil and lots of tonics and things, to say nothing of ale and wine and rare meat.

Dear John! He loves me very dearly, and hates to have me sick. I tried to have a real earnest reasonable talk with him the other day, and tell him how I wish he would let me go and make a visit to Cousin Henry and Julia.

But he said I wasn't able to go, nor able to stand it after I got there; and I did not make out a very good case for myself, for I was crying before I had finished.

It is getting to be a great effort for me to think straight. Just this nervous weakness, I suppose.

And dear John gathered me up in his arms, and just carried me upstairs and laid me on the bed, and sat by me and read to me till it tired my head.

He said I was his darling and his comfort and all he had, and that I must take care of myself for his sake, and keep well.

He says no one but myself can help me out of it, that I must use my will and self-control and not let any silly fancies run away with me.

There's one comfort, the baby is well and happy, and does not have to occupy this nursery with the horrid wallpaper.

If we had not used it that blessed child would have! What a fortunate escape! Why, I wouldn't have a child of mine, an impressionable little thing, live in such a room for worlds.

I never thought of it before, but it is lucky that John kept me here after all. I can stand it so much easier than a baby, you see.

Of course I never mention it to them any more,—I am too wise,—but I keep watch of it all the same.

There are things in that paper that nobody knows but me, or ever will.

Behind that outside pattern the dim shapes get clearer every day.

It is always the same shape, only very numerous.

And it is like a woman stooping down and creeping about behind that pattern. I don't like it a bit. I wonder—I begin to think—I wish John would take me away from here!

It is so hard to talk with John about my case, because he is so wise, and because he loves me so.

But I tried it last night.

It was moonlight. The moon shines in all around, just as the sun does.

I hate to see it sometimes, it creeps so slowly, and always comes in by one window or another.

John was asleep and I hated to waken him, so I kept still and watched the moonlight on that undulating wallpaper till I felt creepy.

The faint figure behind seemed to shake the pattern, just as if she wanted to get out.

I got up softly and went to feel and see if the paper *did* move, and when I came back John was awake.

"What is it, little girl?" he said. "Don't go walking about like that—you'll get cold."

I though it was a good time to talk, so I told him that I really was not gaining here, and that I wished he would take me away.

"Why darling!" said he, "our lease will be up in three weeks, and I can't see how to leave before.

"The repairs are not done at home, and I cannot possibly leave town just now. Of course if you were in any danger I could and would, but you really are better, dear, whether you can see it or not. I am a doctor, dear, and I know. You are gaining flesh and color, your appetite is better. I feel really much easier about you."

"I don't weigh a bit more," said I, "nor as much; and my appetite may be better in the evening, when you are here, but it is worse in the morning when you are away."

"Bless her little heart!" said he with a big hug; "she shall be as sick as she pleases! But now let's improve the shining hours by going to sleep, and talk about it in the morning!"

"And you won't go away?" I asked gloomily.

"Why, how can I, dear? It is only three weeks more and then we will take a nice little trip of a few days while Jennie is getting the house ready. Really, dear, you are better!"

"Better in body perhaps"—I began, and stopped short, for he sat up straight and looked at me with such a stern, reproachful look that I could not say another word.

"My darling," said he, "I beg of you, for my sake and for our child's sake, as well as for your own, that you will never for one instant let that idea enter your mind! There is nothing so dangerous, so fascinating, to a temperament like yours. It is a false and foolish fancy. Can you not trust me as a physician when I tell you so?"

So of course I said no more on that score, and we went to sleep before long. He thought I was asleep first, but I wasn't,—I lay there for hours trying to decide whether that front pattern and the back pattern really did move together or separately.

On a pattern like this, by daylight, there is a lack of sequence, a defiance of law, that is a constant irritant to a normal mind.

The color is hideous enough, and unreliable enough, and infuriating enough, but the pattern is torturing.

You think you have mastered it, but just as you get well under way in following, it turns a back somersault and there you are. It slaps you in the face, knocks you down, and tramples upon you. It is like a bad dream.

The outside pattern is a florid arabesque, reminding one of a fungus. If you can imagine a toadstool in joints, an interminable string of toadstools, budding and sprouting in endless convolutions,—why, that is something like it.

That is, sometimes!

There is one marked peculiarity about this paper, a thing nobody seems to notice but myself, and that is that it changes as the light changes.

When the sun shoots in through the east window—I always

watch for that first long, straight ray—it changes so quickly that I never can quite believe it.

That is why I watch it always.

By moonlight—the moon shines in all night when there is a moon—I wouldn't know it was the same paper.

At night in any kind of light, in twilight, candlelight, lamplight, and worst of all by moonlight, it becomes bars! The outside pattern I mean, and the woman behind it is as plain as can be.

I didn't realize for a long time what the thing was that showed behind,—that dim sub-pattern,—but now I am quite sure it is a woman.

By daylight she is subdued, quiet. I fancy it is the pattern that keeps her so still. It is so puzzling. It keeps me quiet by the hour.

I lie down ever so much now. John says it is good for me, and to sleep all I can.

Indeed, he started the habit by making me lie down for an hour after each meal.

It is a very bad habit, I am convinced, for, you see, I don't sleep.

And that cultivates deceit, for I don't tell them I'm awake,—oh, no!

The fact is, I am getting a little afraid of John.

He seems very queer sometimes, and even Jennie has an inexplicable look.

It strikes me occasionally, just as a scientific hypothesis, that perhaps it is the paper!

I have watched John when he did not know I was looking, and come into the room suddenly on the most innocent excuses, and I've caught him several times *looking at the paper!* And Jennie too. I caught Jennie with her hand on it once.

She didn't know I was in the room, and when I asked her in a quiet, a very quiet voice, with the most restrained manner possible, what she was doing with the paper she turned around as if she had been caught stealing, and looked quite angry—asked me why I should frighten her so!

Then she said that the paper stained everything it touched, that she had found yellow smooches on all my clothes and John's, and she wished we would be more careful!

Did not that sound innocent? But I know she was studying that pattern, and I am determined that nobody shall find it out but myself!

Life is very much more exciting now than it used to be. You see I have something more to expect, to look forward to, to watch. I really do eat better, and am more quiet than I was.

John is so pleased to see me improve! He laughed a little the other day, and said I seemed to be flourishing in spite of my wallpaper.

I turned it off with a laugh. I had no intention of telling him it was *because* of the wallpaper—he would make fun of me. He might even want to take me away.

I don't want to leave now until I have found it out. There is a week more, and I think that will be enough.

I'm feeling ever so much better! I don't sleep much at night, for it is so interesting to watch developments; but I sleep a good deal in the daytime.

In the daytime it is tiresome and perplexing.

There are always new shoots on the fungus, and new shades of yellow all over it. I cannot keep count of them, though I have tried conscientiously.

It is the strangest yellow, that wallpaper! It makes me think of all the yellow things I ever saw—not beautiful ones like buttercups, but old foul, bad yellow things.

But there is something else about that paper—the smell! I noticed it the moment we came into the room, but with so much air and sun it was not bad. Now we have had a week of fog and rain, and whether the windows are open or not, the smell is here.

It creeps all over the house.

I find it hovering in the dining-room, skulking in the parlor, hiding in the hall, lying in wait for me on the stairs.

It gets into my hair.

Even when I go to ride, if I turn my head suddenly and surprise it—there is that smell!

Such a peculiar odor, too! I have spent hours in trying to analyze it, to find what it smelled like.

It is not bad—at first, and very gentle, but quite the subtlest, most enduring odor I ever met.

In this damp weather it is awful. I wake up in the night and find it hanging over me.

It used to disturb me at first. I thought seriously of burning the house—to reach the smell.

But now I am used to it. The only thing I can think of that it is like is the *color* of the paper! A yellow smell.

There is a very funny mark on this wall, low down, near the mopboard. A streak that runs round the room. It goes behind every piece of furniture, except the bed, a long, straight, even *smooch*, as if it had been rubbed over and over.

I wonder how it was done and who did it, and what they did it for. Round and round and round—round and round and round—it makes me dizzy!

I really have discovered something at last.

Through watching so much at night, when it changes so, I have finally found out.

The front pattern *does* move—and no wonder! The woman behind shakes it!

Sometimes I think there are a great many women behind, and

123

sometimes only one, and she crawls around fast, and her crawling shakes it all over.

Then in the very bright spots she keeps still, and in the very shady spots she just takes hold of the bars and shakes them hard.

And she is all the time trying to climb through. But nobody could climb through that pattern—it strangles so; I think that is why it has so many heads.

They get through, and then the pattern strangles them off and turns them upside-down, and makes their eyes white!

If those heads were covered or taken off it would not be half so bad.

I think that woman gets out in the daytime!

And I'll tell you why—privately—I've seen her!

I can see her out of every one of my windows!

It is the same woman, I know, for she is always creeping, and most women do not creep by daylight.

I see her on that long shaded lane, creeping up and down. I see her in those dark grape arbors, creeping all around the garden.

I see her on that long road under the trees, creeping along, and when a carriage comes she hides under the blackberry vines.

I don't blame her a bit. It must be very humiliating to be caught creeping by daylight!

I always lock the door when I creep by daylight. I can't do it at night, for I know John would suspect something at once.

And John is so queer now, that I don't want to irritate him. I wish he would take another room! Besides, I don't want anybody to get that woman out at night but myself.

I often wonder if I could see her out of all the windows at once.

But, turn as fast as I can, I can only see out of one at one time.

And though I always see her she *may* be able to creep faster than I can turn!

I have watched her sometimes away off in the open country, creeping as fast as a cloud shadow in a high wind.

If only that top pattern could be gotten off from the under one! I mean to try it, little by little.

I have found out another funny thing, but I shan't tell it this time! It does not do to trust people too much.

There are only two more days to get this paper off, and I believe John is beginning to notice. I don't like the look in his eyes.

And I heard him ask Jennie a lot of professional questions about me. She had a very good report to give.

She said I slept a good deal in the daytime.

John knows I don't sleep very well at night, for all I'm so quiet!

He asked me all sorts of questions, too, and pretended to be very loving and kind.

As if I couldn't see through him!

Still, I don't wonder he acts so, sleeping under this paper for three months.

It only interests me, but I feel sure John and Jennie are secretly affected by it.

Hurrah! This is the last day, but it is enough. John is to stay in town over night, and won't be out until this evening.

Jennie wanted to sleep with me—the sly thing! but I told her I should undoubtedly rest better for a night all alone.

That was clever, for really I wasn't alone a bit! As soon as it was moonlight, and that poor thing began to crawl and shake the pattern, I got up and ran to help her.

I pulled and she shook, I shook and she pulled, and before morning we had peeled off yards of that paper.

A strip about as high as my head and half around the room.

And then when the sun came and that awful pattern began to laugh at me I declared I would finish it to-day!

We go away to-morrow, and they are moving all my furniture down again to leave things as they were before.

Jennie looked at the wall in amazement, but I told her merrily that I did it out of pure spite at the vicious thing.

She laughed and said she wouldn't mind doing it herself, but I must not get tired.

How she betrayed herself that time!

But I am here, and no person touches this paper but me—not *alive*!

She tried to get me out of the room—it was too patent! But I said it was so quiet and empty and clean now that I believed I would lie down again and sleep all I could; and not to wake me even for dinner—I would call when I woke.

So now she is gone, and the servants are gone, and the things are gone, and there is nothing left but that great bedstead nailed down, with the canvas mattress we found on it.

We shall sleep downstairs to-night, and take the boat home to-morrow.

I quite enjoy the room, now it is bare again.

How those children did tear about here!

This bedstead is fairly gnawed!

But I must get to work.

I have locked the door and thrown the key down into the front path.

I don't want to go out, and I don't want to have anybody come in, till John comes.

I want to astonish him.

I've got a rope up here that even Jennie did not find. If that woman does get out, and tries to get away, I can tie her!

But I forgot I could not reach far without anything to stand on!

This bed will *not* move!

I tried to lift and push it until I was lame, and then I got so angry I bit off a little piece at one corner—but it hurt my teeth.

Then I peeled off all the paper I could reach standing on the floor. It sticks horribly and the pattern just enjoys it! All those strangled heads and bulbous eyes and waddling fungus growths just shriek with derision!

I am getting angry enough to do something desperate. To jump out of the window would be admirable exercise, but the bars are too strong even to try.

Besides I wouldn't do it. Of course not. I know well enough that a step like that is improper and might be misconstrued.

I don't like to *look* out of the windows even—there are so many of those creeping women, and they creep so fast.

I wonder if they all come out of that wallpaper as I did?

But I am securely fastened now by my well-hidden rope—you don't get *me* out in the road there!

I suppose I shall have to get back behind the pattern when it comes night, and that is hard!

It is so pleasant to be out in this great room and creep around as I please!

I don't want to go outside. I won't, even if Jennie asks me to.

For outside you have to creep on the ground, and everything is green instead of yellow.

But here I can creep smoothly on the floor, and my shoulder just fits in that long smooch around the wall, so I cannot lose my way.

Why, there's John at the door!

It is no use, young man, you can't open it!

How he does call and pound!

Now he's crying for an axe.

It would be a shame to break down that beautiful door!

"John dear!" said I in the gentlest voice, "the key is down by the front steps, under a plantain leaf!"

That silenced him for a few moments.

Then he said—very quietly indeed, "Open the door, my darling!"

"I can't," said I. "The key is down by the front door under a plantain leaf!"

And then I said it again, several times, very gently and slowly, and said it so often that he had to go and see, and he got it, of course, and came in. He stopped short by the door.

"What is the matter?" he cried. "For God's sake, what are you doing!"

I kept on creeping just the same, but I looked at him over my shoulder.

"I've got out at last," said I, "in spite of you and Jane! And I've pulled off most of the paper, so you can't put me back!"

Now why should that man have fainted? But he did, and right across my path by the wall, so that I had to creep over him every time!

IV

THE MAGICIAN.

PART IV

THE MAGICIAN

EXTRACT FROM

FRANKENSTEIN

BY

MARY SHELLEY

I t was on a dreary night of November that I beheld the accom-
plishment of my toils. With an anxiety that almost amounted
to agony, I collected the instruments of life around me, that
I might infuse a spark of being into the lifeless thing that lay at
my feet. It was already one in the morning; the rain pattered dismally
against the panes, and my candle was nearly burnt out, when, by
the glimmer of the half-extinguished light, I saw the dull yellow
eye of the creature open; it breathed hard, and a convulsive motion
agitated its limbs.

How can I describe my emotions at this catastrophe, or how
delineate the wretch whom with such infinite pains and care I
had endeavoured to form? His limbs were in proportion, and I had
selected his features as beautiful. Beautiful! Great God! His yellow
skin scarcely covered the work of muscles and arteries beneath; his
hair was of a lustrous black, and flowing; his teeth of a pearly
whiteness; but these luxuriances only formed a more horrid contrast
with his watery eyes, that seemed almost of the same colour as the
dun-white sockets in which they were set, his shrivelled complexion
and straight black lips.

The different accidents of life are not so changeable as the feelings of human nature. I had worked hard for nearly two years, for the sole purpose of infusing life into an inanimate body. For this I had deprived myself of rest and health. I had desired it with an ardour that far exceeded moderation; but now that I had finished, the beauty of the dream vanished, and breathless horror and disgust filled my heart. Unable to endure the aspect of the being I had created, I rushed out of the room and continued a long time traversing my bed-chamber, unable to compose my mind to sleep. At length lassitude succeeded to the tumult I had before endured, and I threw myself on the bed in my clothes, endeavouring to seek a few moments of forgetfulness. But it was in vain; I slept, indeed, but I was disturbed by the wildest dreams. I thought I saw Elizabeth, in the bloom of health, walking in the streets of Ingolstadt. Delighted and surprised, I embraced her, but as I imprinted the first kiss on her lips, they became livid with the hue of death; her features appeared to change, and I thought that I held the corpse of my dead mother in my arms; a shroud enveloped her form, and I saw the grave-worms crawling in the folds of the flannel. I started from my sleep with horror; a cold dew covered my forehead, my teeth chattered, and every limb became convulsed; when, by the dim and yellow light of the moon, as it forced its way through the window shutters, I beheld the wretch—the miserable monster whom I had created. He held up the curtain of the bed; and his eyes, if eyes they may be called, were fixed on me. His jaws opened, and he muttered some inarticulate sounds, while a grin wrinkled his cheeks. He might have spoken, but I did not hear; one hand was stretched out, seemingly to detain me, but I escaped and rushed downstairs. I took refuge in the courtyard belonging to the house which I inhabited, where I remained during the rest of the night, walking up and down in the greatest agitation, listening attentively, catching and fearing each sound as if it were to announce the approach of the demoniacal corpse to which I had so miserably given life.

Oh! No mortal could support the horror of that countenance. A mummy again endued with animation could not be so hideous as that wretch. I had gazed on him while unfinished; he was ugly then, but when those muscles and joints were rendered capable of motion, it became a thing such as even Dante could not have conceived.

I passed the night wretchedly. Sometimes my pulse beat so quickly and hardly that I felt the palpitation of every artery; at others, I nearly sank to the ground through languor and extreme weakness. Mingled with this horror, I felt the bitterness of disappointment; dreams that had been my food and pleasant rest for so long a space were now become a hell to me; and the change was so rapid, the overthrow so complete!

Morning, dismal and wet, at length dawned and discovered to my sleepless and aching eyes the church of Ingolstadt, its white steeple and clock, which indicated the sixth hour. The porter opened the gates of the court, which had that night been my asylum, and I issued into the streets, pacing them with quick steps, as if I sought to avoid the wretch whom I feared every turning of the street would present to my view. I did not dare return to the apartment which I inhabited, but felt impelled to hurry on, although drenched by the rain which poured from a black and comfortless sky.

THE BODY-SNATCHER

BY
ROBERT LOUIS STEVENSON

E very night in the year, four of us sat in the small parlour of
the George at Debenham—the undertaker, and the landlord,
and Fettes, and myself. Sometimes there would be more;
but blow high, blow low, come rain or snow or frost, we four would
be each planted in his own particular arm-chair. Fettes was an old
drunken Scotchman, a man of education obviously, and a man of
some property, since he lived in idleness. He had come to Debenham
years ago, while still young, and by a mere continuance of living had
grown to be an adopted townsman. His blue camlet cloak was a
local antiquity, like the church-spire. His place in the parlour at the
George, his absence from church, his old, crapulous, disreputable
vices, were all things of course in Debenham. He had some vague
Radical opinions and some fleeting infidelities, which he would now
and again set forth and emphasise with tottering slaps upon the
table. He drank rum—five glasses regularly every evening; and for
the greater portion of his nightly visit to the George sat, with his
glass in his right hand, in a state of melancholy alcoholic saturation.
We called him the Doctor, for he was supposed to have some special
knowledge of medicine, and had been known, upon a pinch, to set
a fracture or reduce a dislocation; but beyond these slight particulars, we had no knowledge of his character and antecedents.

One dark winter night—it had struck nine some time before the landlord joined us—there was a sick man in the George, a great neighbouring proprietor suddenly struck down with apoplexy on his way to Parliament; and the great man's still greater London doctor had been telegraphed to his bedside. It was the first time that such a thing had happened in Debenham, for the railway was but newly open, and we were all proportionately moved by the occurrence.

'He's come,' said the landlord, after he had filled and lighted his pipe.

'He?' said I. 'Who?—not the doctor?'

'Himself,' replied our host.

'What is his name?'

'Doctor Macfarlane,' said the landlord.

Fettes was far through his third tumbler, stupidly fuddled, now nodding over, now staring mazily around him; but at the last word he seemed to awaken, and repeated the name 'Macfarlane' twice, quietly enough the first time, but with sudden emotion at the second.

'Yes,' said the landlord, 'that's his name, Doctor Wolfe Macfarlane.'

Fettes became instantly sober; his eyes awoke, his voice became clear, loud, and steady, his language forcible and earnest. We were all startled by the transformation, as if a man had risen from the dead.

'I beg your pardon,' he said, 'I am afraid I have not been paying much attention to your talk. Who is this Wolfe Macfarlane?' And then, when he had heard the landlord out, 'It cannot be, it cannot be,' he added; 'and yet I would like well to see him face to face.'

'Do you know him, Doctor?' asked the undertaker, with a gasp.

'God forbid!' was the reply. 'And yet the name is a strange one; it were too much to fancy two. Tell me, landlord, is he old?'

'Well,' said the host, 'he's not a young man, to be sure, and his hair is white; but he looks younger than you.'

'He is older, though; years older. But,' with a slap upon the table, 'it's the rum you see in my face—rum and sin. This man, perhaps, may have an easy conscience and a good digestion. Conscience! Hear me speak. You would think I was some good, old, decent Christian, would you not? But no, not I; I never canted. Voltaire might have canted if he'd stood in my shoes; but the brains'—with a rattling fillip on his bald head—'the brains were clear and active, and I saw and made no deductions.'

'If you know this doctor,' I ventured to remark, after a somewhat awful pause, 'I should gather that you do not share the landlord's good opinion.'

Fettes paid no regard to me.

'Yes,' he said, with sudden decision, 'I must see him face to face.'

There was another pause, and then a door was closed rather sharply on the first floor, and a step was heard upon the stair.

'That's the doctor,' cried the landlord. 'Look sharp, and you can catch him.'

It was but two steps from the small parlour to the door of the old George Inn; the wide oak staircase landed almost in the street; there was room for a Turkey rug and nothing more between the threshold and the last round of the descent; but this little space was every evening brilliantly lit up, not only by the light upon the stair and the great signal-lamp below the sign, but by the warm radiance of the bar-room window. The George thus brightly advertised itself to passers-by in the cold street. Fettes walked steadily to the spot, and we, who were hanging behind, beheld the two men meet, as one of them had phrased it, face to face. Dr. Macfarlane was alert and vigorous. His white hair set off his pale and placid, although energetic, countenance. He was richly dressed in the finest of broadcloth and the whitest of linen, with a great gold watch-chain, and studs and spectacles of the same precious material. He wore a broad-folded tie, white and speckled with lilac, and he carried on his arm a comfortable driving-coat of fur. There was no doubt but he became his years, breathing, as he did, of wealth and consideration; and it was a surprising contrast to see our parlour sot—bald, dirty, pimpled, and robed in his old camlet cloak—confront him at the bottom of the stairs.

'Macfarlane!' he said somewhat loudly, more like a herald than a friend.

The great doctor pulled up short on the fourth step, as though the familiarity of the address surprised and somewhat shocked his dignity.

'Toddy Macfarlane!' repeated Fettes.

The London man almost staggered. He stared for the swiftest of seconds at the man before him, glanced behind him with a sort of scare, and then in a startled whisper, 'Fettes!' he said, 'You!'

'Ay,' said the other, 'me! Did you think I was dead too? We are not so easy shut of our acquaintance.'

'Hush, hush!' exclaimed the doctor. 'Hush, hush! this meeting is so unexpected—I can see you are unmanned. I hardly knew you, I confess, at first; but I am overjoyed—overjoyed to have this opportunity. For the present it must be how-d'ye-do and good-bye in one, for my fly is waiting, and I must not fail the train; but you shall—let me see—yes—you shall give me your address, and you can count on early news of me. We must do something for you, Fettes. I fear you are out at elbows; but we must see to that for auld lang syne, as once we sang at suppers.'

'Money!' cried Fettes; 'money from you! The money that I had from you is lying where I cast it in the rain.'

Dr. Macfarlane had talked himself into some measure of superiority and confidence, but the uncommon energy of this refusal cast him back into his first confusion.

A horrible, ugly look came and went across his almost venerable countenance. 'My dear fellow,' he said, 'be it as you please; my last thought is to offend you. I would intrude on none. I will leave you my address, however—'

'I do not wish it—I do not wish to know the roof that shelters you,' interrupted the other. 'I heard your name; I feared it might be you; I wished to know if, after all, there were a God; I know now that there is none. Begone!'

He still stood in the middle of the rug, between the stair and doorway; and the great London physician, in order to escape, would be forced to step to one side. It was plain that he hesitated before the thought of this humiliation. White as he was, there was a dangerous glitter in his spectacles; but while he still paused uncertain, he became aware that the driver of his fly was peering in from the street at this unusual scene and caught a glimpse at the same time of our little body from the parlour, huddled by the corner of the bar. The presence of so many witnesses decided him at once to flee. He crouched together, brushing on the wainscot, and made a dart like a serpent, striking for the door. But his tribulation was not yet entirely at an end, for even as he was passing Fettes clutched him by the arm and these words came in a whisper, and yet painfully distinct, 'Have you seen it again?'

The great rich London doctor cried out aloud with a sharp, throttling cry; he dashed his questioner across the open space, and, with his hands over his head, fled out of the door like a detected thief. Before it had occurred to one of us to make a movement the fly was already rattling toward the station. The scene was over like a dream, but the dream had left proofs and traces of its passage. Next day the servant found the fine gold spectacles broken on the threshold, and that very night we were all standing breathless by the bar-room window, and Fettes at our side, sober, pale, and resolute in look.

'God protect us, Mr. Fettes!' said the landlord, coming first into possession of his customary senses. 'What in the universe is all this? These are strange things you have been saying.'

Fettes turned toward us; he looked us each in succession in the face. 'See if you can hold your tongues,' said he. 'That man Macfarlane is not safe to cross; those that have done so already have repented it too late.'

And then, without so much as finishing his third glass, far less waiting for the other two, he bade us good-bye and went forth, under the lamp of the hotel, into the black night.

We three turned to our places in the parlour, with the big red fire and four clear candles; and as we recapitulated what had passed, the first chill of our surprise soon changed into a glow of curiosity. We sat late; it was the latest session I have known in the old George. Each man, before we parted, had his theory that he was bound to prove; and none of us had any nearer business in this world than to track out the past of our condemned companion, and surprise the secret that he shared with the great London doctor. It is no great boast, but I believe I was a better hand at worming out a story than either of my fellows at the George; and perhaps there is now no other man alive who could narrate to you the following foul and unnatural events.

In his young days Fettes studied medicine in the schools of Edinburgh. He had talent of a kind, the talent that picks up swiftly what it hears and readily retails it for its own. He worked little at home; but he was civil, attentive, and intelligent in the presence of his masters. They soon picked him out as a lad who listened closely and remembered well; nay, strange as it seemed to me when I first heard it, he was in those days well favoured, and pleased by his exterior. There was, at that period, a certain extramural teacher of anatomy, whom I shall here designate by the letter K. His name was subsequently too well known. The man who bore it skulked through the streets of Edinburgh in disguise, while the mob that applauded at the execution of Burke called loudly for the blood of his employer. But Mr. K— was then at the top of his vogue; he enjoyed a popularity due partly to his own talent and address, partly to the incapacity of his rival, the university professor. The students, at least, swore by his name, and Fettes believed himself, and was believed by others, to have laid the foundations of success when he had acquired the favour of this meteorically famous man. Mr. K— was a *bon vivant* as well as an accomplished teacher; he liked a sly illusion no less than a careful preparation. In both capacities Fettes enjoyed and deserved his notice, and by the second year of his attendance he held the half-regular position of second demonstrator or sub-assistant in his class.

In this capacity the charge of the theatre and lecture-room devolved in particular upon his shoulders. He had to answer for the cleanliness of the premises and the conduct of the other students, and it was a part of his duty to supply, receive, and divide the various subjects. It was with a view to this last—at that time very delicate—affair that he was lodged by Mr. K— in the same wynd, and at last in the same building, with the dissecting-rooms. Here, after a night of turbulent pleasures, his hand still tottering, his sight still misty and confused, he would be called out of bed in the black hours before the winter dawn by the unclean and desperate interlopers who supplied the table. He would open the door to these men, since infamous throughout the land. He would help them with their tragic burden, pay them their sordid price, and remain alone, when they were gone, with the unfriendly relics of humanity. From such a scene he would return to snatch another hour or two of slumber, to repair the abuses of the night, and refresh himself for the labours of the day.

Few lads could have been more insensible to the impressions of a life thus passed among the ensigns of mortality. His mind was closed against all general considerations. He was incapable of interest in the fate and fortunes of another, the slave of his own desires and low ambitions. Cold, light, and selfish in the last resort, he had that modicum of prudence, miscalled morality, which keeps a man from inconvenient drunkenness or punishable theft. He coveted, besides, a measure of consideration from his masters and his fellow-pupils, and he had no desire to fail conspicuously in the external parts of life. Thus he made it his pleasure to gain some distinction in his studies, and day after day rendered unimpeachable eye-service to his employer, Mr. K—. For his day of work he indemnified himself by nights of roaring, blackguardly enjoyment; and when that balance had been struck, the organ that he called his conscience declared itself content.

The supply of subjects was a continual trouble to him as well as to his master. In that large and busy class, the raw material of the anatomists kept perpetually running out; and the business thus rendered necessary was not only unpleasant in itself, but threatened dangerous consequences to all who were concerned. It was the policy of Mr. K— to ask no questions in his dealings with the trade. 'They bring the body, and we pay the price,' he used to say, dwelling on the alliteration—'*quid pro quo*.' And, again, and somewhat profanely, 'Ask no questions,' he would tell his assistants, 'for conscience' sake.' There was no understanding that the subjects were provided by the crime of murder. Had that idea been broached to him in words, he would have recoiled in horror; but the lightness of his speech upon so grave a matter was, in itself, an offence against good manners, and a temptation to the men with whom he dealt. Fettes, for instance, had often remarked to himself upon the singular freshness of the bodies. He had been struck again and again by the hang-dog, abominable looks of the ruffians who came to him before the dawn; and putting things together clearly in his private thoughts, he perhaps attributed a meaning too immoral and too categorical to the unguarded counsels of his master. He understood his duty, in short, to have three branches: to take what was brought, to pay the price, and to avert the eye from any evidence of crime.

One November morning this policy of silence was put sharply to the test. He had been awake all night with a racking toothache— pacing his room like a caged beast or throwing himself in fury on his bed—and had fallen at last into that profound, uneasy slumber that so often follows on a night of pain, when he was awakened by the third or fourth angry repetition of the concerted signal. There was a thin, bright moonshine; it was bitter cold, windy, and frosty; the town had not yet awakened, but an indefinable stir already preluded the noise and business of the day. The ghouls had come later than usual, and they seemed more than usually eager to be gone. Fettes, sick with sleep, lighted them upstairs. He heard their grumbling Irish voices through a dream; and as they stripped the sack from their sad merchandise he leaned dozing, with his shoulder propped against the wall; he had to shake himself to find the men their money. As he did so his eyes lighted on the dead face. He started; he took two steps nearer, with the candle raised.

'God Almighty!' he cried. 'That is Jane Galbraith!'

The men answered nothing, but they shuffled nearer the door.

'I know her, I tell you,' he continued. 'She was alive and hearty yesterday. It's impossible she can be dead; it's impossible you should have got this body fairly.'

'Sure, sir, you're mistaken entirely,' said one of the men.

But the other looked Fettes darkly in the eyes, and demanded the money on the spot.

It was impossible to misconceive the threat or to exaggerate the danger. The lad's heart failed him. He stammered some excuses, counted out the sum, and saw his hateful visitors depart. No sooner were they gone than he hastened to confirm his doubts. By a dozen unquestionable marks he identified the girl he had jested with the day before. He saw, with horror, marks upon her body that might well betoken violence. A panic seized him, and he took refuge in his room. There he reflected at length over the discovery that he had made; considered soberly the bearing of Mr. K—'s instructions and the danger to himself of interference in so serious a business, and at last, in sore perplexity, determined to wait for the advice of his immediate superior, the class assistant.

This was a young doctor, Wolfe Macfarlane, a high favourite among all the reckless students, clever, dissipated, and unscrupulous to the last degree. He had travelled and studied abroad. His manners were agreeable and a little forward. He was an authority on the stage, skilful on the ice or the links with skate or golf-club; he dressed with nice audacity, and, to put the finishing touch upon his glory, he kept a gig and a strong trotting-horse. With Fettes he was on terms of intimacy; indeed, their relative positions called for some community of life; and when subjects were scarce the pair would drive far into the country in Macfarlane's gig, visit and desecrate some lonely graveyard, and return before dawn with their booty to the door of the dissecting-room.

On that particular morning Macfarlane arrived somewhat earlier than his wont. Fettes heard him, and met him on the stairs, told him his story, and showed him the cause of his alarm. Macfarlane examined the marks on her body.

'Yes,' he said with a nod, 'it looks fishy.'

'Well, what should I do?' asked Fettes.

'Do?' repeated the other. 'Do you want to do anything? Least said soonest mended, I should say.'

'Some one else might recognise her,' objected Fettes. 'She was as well known as the Castle Rock.'

'We'll hope not,' said Macfarlane, 'and if anybody does—well, you didn't, don't you see, and there's an end. The fact is, this has been going on too long. Stir up the mud, and you'll get K— into the most unholy trouble; you'll be in a shocking box yourself. So will I, if you come to that. I should like to know how any one of us would look, or what the devil we should have to say for ourselves, in any Christian

145

witness-box. For me, you know there's one thing certain—that, practically speaking, all our subjects have been murdered.'

'Macfarlane!' cried Fettes.

'Come now!' sneered the other. 'As if you hadn't suspected it yourself!'

'Suspecting is one thing—'

'And proof another. Yes, I know; and I'm as sorry as you are this should have come here,' tapping the body with his cane. 'The next best thing for me is not to recognise it; and,' he added coolly, 'I don't. You may, if you please. I don't dictate, but I think a man of the world would do as I do; and I may add, I fancy that is what K— would look for at our hands. The question is, Why did he choose us two for his assistants? And I answer, because he didn't want old wives.'

This was the tone of all others to affect the mind of a lad like Fettes. He agreed to imitate Macfarlane. The body of the unfortunate girl was duly dissected, and no one remarked or appeared to recognise her.

One afternoon, when his day's work was over, Fettes dropped into a popular tavern and found Macfarlane sitting with a stranger. This was a small man, very pale and dark, with coal-black eyes. The cut of his features gave a promise of intellect and refinement which was but feebly realised in his manners, for he proved, upon a nearer acquaintance, coarse, vulgar, and stupid. He exercised, however, a very remarkable control over Macfarlane; issued orders like the Great Bashaw; became inflamed at the least discussion or delay, and commented rudely on the servility with which he was obeyed. This most offensive person took a fancy to Fettes on the spot, plied him with drinks, and honoured him with unusual confidences on his past career. If a tenth part of what he confessed were true, he was a very loathsome rogue; and the lad's vanity was tickled by the attention of so experienced a man.

'I'm a pretty bad fellow myself,' the stranger remarked, 'but Macfarlane is the boy—Toddy Macfarlane I call him. Toddy, order your friend another glass.' Or it might be, 'Toddy, you jump up and shut the door.' 'Toddy hates me,' he said again. 'Oh yes, Toddy, you do!'

'Don't you call me that confounded name,' growled Macfarlane.

'Hear him! Did you ever see the lads play knife? He would like to do that all over my body,' remarked the stranger.

'We medicals have a better way than that,' said Fettes. 'When we dislike a dead friend of ours, we dissect him.'

Macfarlane looked up sharply, as though this jest were scarcely to his mind.

The afternoon passed. Gray, for that was the stranger's name, invited Fettes to join them at dinner, ordered a feast so sumptuous that the tavern was thrown into commotion, and when all was done commanded Macfarlane to settle the bill. It was late before they separated; the man Gray was incapably drunk. Macfarlane, sobered by his fury, chewed the cud of the money he had been forced to squander and the slights he had been obliged to swallow. Fettes, with various liquors singing in his head, returned home with devious footsteps and a mind entirely in abeyance. Next day Macfarlane was absent from the class, and Fettes smiled to himself as he imagined him still squiring the intolerable Gray from tavern to tavern. As soon as the hour of liberty had struck he posted from place to place in quest of his last night's companions. He could find them, however, nowhere; so returned early to his rooms, went early to bed, and slept the sleep of the just.

At four in the morning he was awakened by the well-known signal. Descending to the door, he was filled with astonishment to find Macfarlane with his gig, and in the gig one of those long and ghastly packages with which he was so well acquainted.

'What?' he cried. 'Have you been out alone? How did you manage?'

But Macfarlane silenced him roughly, bidding him turn to business. When they had got the body upstairs and laid it on the table, Macfarlane made at first as if he were going away. Then he paused and seemed to hesitate; and then, 'You had better look at the face,' said he, in tones of some constraint. 'You had better,' he repeated, as Fettes only stared at him in wonder.

'But where, and how, and when did you come by it?' cried the other.

'Look at the face,' was the only answer.

Fettes was staggered; strange doubts assailed him. He looked from the young doctor to the body, and then back again. At last, with a start, he did as he was bidden. He had almost expected the sight that met his eyes, and yet the shock was cruel. To see, fixed in the rigidity of death and naked on that coarse layer of sackcloth, the man whom he had left well clad and full of meat and sin upon the threshold of a tavern, awoke, even in the thoughtless Fettes, some of the terrors of the conscience. It was a *cras tibi* which re-echoed in his soul, that two whom he had known should have come to lie upon these icy tables. Yet these were only secondary thoughts. His first concern regarded Wolfe. Unprepared for a challenge so momentous, he knew not how to look his comrade in the face. He durst not meet his eye, and he had neither words nor voice at his command.

It was Macfarlane himself who made the first advance. He came up quietly behind and laid his hand gently but firmly on the other's shoulder.

'Richardson,' said he, 'may have the head.'

Now Richardson was a student who had long been anxious for that portion of the human subject to dissect. There was no answer, and the murderer resumed: 'Talking of business, you must pay me; your accounts, you see, must tally.'

Fettes found a voice, the ghost of his own: 'Pay you!' he cried. 'Pay you for that?'

'Why, yes, of course you must. By all means and on every possible account, you must,' returned the other. 'I dare not give it for nothing, you dare not take it for nothing; it would compromise us both. This is another case like Jane Galbraith's. The more things are wrong the more we must act as if all were right. Where does old K— keep his money?'

'There,' answered Fettes hoarsely, pointing to a cupboard in the corner.

'Give me the key, then,' said the other, calmly, holding out his hand.

There was an instant's hesitation, and the die was cast. Macfarlane could not suppress a nervous twitch, the infinitesimal mark of an immense relief, as he felt the key between his fingers. He opened the cupboard, brought out pen and ink and a paper-book that stood in one compartment, and separated from the funds in a drawer a sum suitable to the occasion.

'Now, look here,' he said, 'there is the payment made—first proof of your good faith: first step to your security. You have now to clinch it by a second. Enter the payment in your book, and then you for your part may defy the devil.'

The next few seconds were for Fettes an agony of thought; but in balancing his terrors it was the most immediate that triumphed. Any future difficulty seemed almost welcome if he could avoid a present quarrel with Macfarlane. He set down the candle which he had been carrying all this time, and with a steady hand entered the date, the nature, and the amount of the transaction.

'And now,' said Macfarlane, 'it's only fair that you should pocket the lucre. I've had my share already. By the bye, when a man of the world falls into a bit of luck, has a few shillings extra in his pocket—I'm ashamed to speak of it, but there's a rule of conduct in the case. No treating, no purchase of expensive class-books, no squaring of old debts; borrow, don't lend.'

'Macfarlane,' began Fettes, still somewhat hoarsely, 'I have put my neck in a halter to oblige you.'

'To oblige me?' cried Wolfe. 'Oh, come! You did, as near as I can see the matter, what you downright had to do in self-defence. Suppose I got into trouble, where would you be? This second little matter flows clearly from the first. Mr. Gray is the continuation of Miss Galbraith. You can't begin and then stop. If you begin, you must keep on beginning; that's the truth. No rest for the wicked.'

A horrible sense of blackness and the treachery of fate seized hold upon the soul of the unhappy student.

'My God!' he cried, 'but what have I done? and when did I begin? To be made a class assistant—in the name of reason, where's the harm in that? Service wanted the position; Service might have got it. Would *he* have been where *I* am now?'

'My dear fellow,' said Macfarlane, 'what a boy you are! What harm *has* come to you? What harm *can* come to you if you hold your tongue? Why, man, do you know what this life is? There are two squads of us—the lions and the lambs. If you're a lamb, you'll come to lie upon these tables like Gray or Jane Galbraith; if you're a lion, you'll live and drive a horse like me, like K—, like all the world with any wit or courage. You're staggered at the first. But look at K—! My dear fellow, you're clever, you have pluck. I like you, and K— likes you. You were born to lead the hunt; and I tell you, on my honour and my experience of life, three days from now you'll laugh at all these scarecrows like a High School boy at a farce.'

And with that Macfarlane took his departure and drove off up the wynd in his gig to get under cover before daylight. Fettes was thus left alone with his regrets. He saw the miserable peril in which he stood involved. He saw, with inexpressible dismay, that there was no limit to his weakness, and that, from concession to concession, he had fallen from the arbiter of Macfarlane's destiny to his paid and helpless accomplice. He would have given the world to have been a little braver at the time, but it did not occur to him that he might still be brave. The secret of Jane Galbraith and the cursed entry in the day-book closed his mouth.

Hours passed; the class began to arrive; the members of the unhappy Gray were dealt out to one and to another, and received without remark. Richardson was made happy with the head; and before the hour of freedom rang Fettes trembled with exultation to perceive how far they had already gone toward safety.

For two days he continued to watch, with increasing joy, the dreadful process of disguise.

On the third day Macfarlane made his appearance. He had been ill, he said; but he made up for lost time by the energy with which he directed the students. To Richardson in particular he extended the most valuable assistance and advice, and that student, encouraged by the praise of the demonstrator, burned high with ambitious hopes, and saw the medal already in his grasp.

Before the week was out Macfarlane's prophecy had been fulfilled. Fettes had outlived his terrors and had forgotten his baseness. He began to plume himself upon his courage, and had so arranged the story in his mind that he could look back on these events with an unhealthy pride. Of his accomplice he saw but little. They met, of course, in the business of the class; they received their orders together from Mr. K—. At times they had a word or two in private, and Macfarlane was from first to last particularly kind and jovial. But it was plain that he avoided any reference to their common secret; and even when Fettes whispered to him that he had cast in his lot with the lions and foresworn the lambs, he only signed to him smilingly to hold his peace.

At length an occasion arose which threw the pair once more

into a closer union. Mr. K— was again short of subjects; pupils were eager, and it was a part of this teacher's pretensions to be always well supplied. At the same time there came the news of a burial in the rustic graveyard of Glencorse. Time has little changed the place in question. It stood then, as now, upon a cross road, out of call of human habitations, and buried fathom deep in the foliage of six cedar trees. The cries of the sheep upon the neighbouring hills, the streamlets upon either hand, one loudly singing among pebbles, the other dripping furtively from pond to pond, the stir of the wind in mountainous old flowering chestnuts, and once in seven days the voice of the bell and the old tunes of the precentor, were the only sounds that disturbed the silence around the rural church. The Resurrection Man—to use a byname of the period—was not to be deterred by any of the sanctities of customary piety. It was part of his trade to despise and desecrate the scrolls and trumpets of old tombs, the paths worn by the feet of worshippers and mourners, and the offerings and the inscriptions of bereaved affection. To rustic neighbourhoods, where love is more than commonly tenacious, and where some bonds of blood or fellowship unite the entire society of a parish, the body-snatcher, far from being repelled by natural respect, was attracted by the ease and safety of the task. To bodies that had been laid in earth, in joyful expectation of a far different awakening, there came that hasty, lamp-lit, terror-haunted resurrection of the spade and mattock. The coffin was forced, the cerements torn, and the melancholy relics, clad in sackcloth, after being rattled for hours on moonless byways, were at length exposed to uttermost indignities before a class of gaping boys.

Somewhat as two vultures may swoop upon a dying lamb, Fettes and Macfarlane were to be let loose upon a grave in that green and quiet resting-place. The wife of a farmer, a woman who had lived for sixty years, and been known for nothing but good butter and a godly conversation, was to be rooted from her grave at midnight and carried, dead and naked, to that far-away city that she had always honoured with her Sunday's best; the place beside her family was to be empty till the crack of doom; her innocent and almost venerable members to be exposed to that last curiosity of the anatomist.

Late one afternoon the pair set forth, well wrapped in cloaks and furnished with a formidable bottle. It rained without remission—a cold, dense, lashing rain. Now and again there blew a puff of wind, but these sheets of falling water kept it down. Bottle and all, it was a sad and silent drive as far as Penicuik, where they were to spend the evening. They stopped once, to hide their implements in a thick bush not far from the churchyard, and once again at the Fisher's Tryst, to have a toast before the kitchen fire and vary their nips of whisky with a glass of ale. When they reached their journey's end the gig was housed, the horse was fed and comforted, and the two young doctors in a private room sat down to the best dinner and the best wine the house afforded. The lights, the fire, the beating rain upon the window, the cold, incongruous work that lay before them, added zest to their enjoyment of the meal. With every glass their cordiality increased. Soon Macfarlane handed a little pile of gold to his companion.

'A compliment,' he said. 'Between friends these little d-d accommodations ought to fly like pipe-lights.'

Fettes pocketed the money, and applauded the sentiment to the echo. 'You are a philosopher,' he cried. 'I was an ass till I knew you. You and K— between you, by the Lord Harry! but you'll make a man of me.'

'Of course we shall,' applauded Macfarlane. 'A man? I tell you, it required a man to back me up the other morning. There are some big, brawling, forty-year-old cowards who would have turned sick at the look of the d-d thing; but not you—you kept your head. I watched you.'

'Well, and why not?' Fettes thus vaunted himself. 'It was no affair of mine. There was nothing to gain on the one side but disturbance, and on the other I could count on your gratitude, don't you see?' And he slapped his pocket till the gold pieces rang.

Macfarlane somehow felt a certain touch of alarm at these unpleasant words. He may have regretted that he had taught his young companion so successfully, but he had no time to interfere, for the other noisily continued in this boastful strain:—

'The great thing is not to be afraid. Now, between you and me, I don't want to hang—that's practical; but for all cant, Macfarlane, I was born with a contempt. Hell, God, Devil, right, wrong, sin, crime, and all the old gallery of curiosities—they may frighten boys, but men of the world, like you and me, despise them. Here's to the memory of Gray!'

It was by this time growing somewhat late. The gig, according to order, was brought round to the door with both lamps brightly shining, and the young men had to pay their bill and take the road. They announced that they were bound for Peebles, and drove in that direction till they were clear of the last houses of the town; then, extinguishing the lamps, returned upon their course, and followed a by-road toward Glencorse. There was no sound but that of their own passage, and the incessant, strident pouring of the rain. It was pitch dark; here and there a white gate or a white stone in the wall guided them for a short space across the night; but for the most part it was at a foot pace, and almost groping, that they picked their way through that resonant blackness to their solemn and isolated destination. In the sunken woods that traverse the neighbourhood of the burying-ground the last glimmer failed them, and it became necessary to kindle a match and re-illumine one of the lanterns of the gig. Thus, under the dripping trees, and environed by huge and moving shadows, they reached the scene of their unhallowed labours.

They were both experienced in such affairs, and powerful with the spade; and they had scarce been twenty minutes at their task before they were rewarded by a dull rattle on the coffin lid. At the same moment Macfarlane, having hurt his hand upon a stone, flung it carelessly above his head. The grave, in which they now stood almost to the shoulders, was close to the edge of the plateau of the graveyard; and the gig lamp had been propped, the better to illuminate their labours, against a tree, and on the immediate verge of the steep bank descending to the stream. Chance had taken a sure aim with the stone. Then came a clang of broken glass; night fell upon them; sounds alternately dull and ringing announced the bounding of the lantern down the bank, and its occasional collision with the trees. A stone or two, which it had dislodged in its descent, rattled behind it into the profundities of the glen; and then silence, like night, resumed its sway; and they might bend their hearing to its utmost pitch, but naught was to be heard except the rain, now marching to the wind, now steadily falling over miles of open country.

They were so nearly at an end of their abhorred task that they judged it wisest to complete it in the dark. The coffin was exhumed and broken open; the body inserted in the dripping sack and carried between them to the gig; one mounted to keep it in its place, and the other, taking the horse by the mouth, groped along by wall and bush until they reached the wider road by the Fisher's Tryst. Here was a faint, diffused radiancy, which they hailed like daylight; by that they pushed the horse to a good pace and began to rattle along merrily in the direction of the town.

They had both been wetted to the skin during their operations, and now, as the gig jumped among the deep ruts, the thing that stood propped between them fell now upon one and now upon the other. At every repetition of the horrid contact each instinctively repelled it with the greater haste; and the process, natural although it was, began to tell upon the nerves of the companions. Macfarlane made some ill-favoured jest about the farmer's wife, but it came hollowly from his lips, and was allowed to drop in silence. Still their unnatural burden bumped from side to side; and now the head would be laid, as if in confidence, upon their shoulders, and now the drenching sack-cloth would flap icily about their faces. A creeping chill began to possess the soul of Fettes. He peered at the bundle, and it seemed somehow larger than at first. All over the country-side, and from every degree of distance, the farm dogs accompanied their passage with tragic ululations; and it grew and grew upon his mind that some unnatural miracle had been accomplished, that some nameless change had befallen the dead body, and that it was in fear of their unholy burden that the dogs were howling.

'For God's sake,' said he, making a great effort to arrive at speech, 'for God's sake, let's have a light!'

Seemingly Macfarlane was affected in the same direction; for, though he made no reply, he stopped the horse, passed the reins to his companion, got down, and proceeded to kindle the remaining lamp. They had by that time got no farther than the cross-road down to Auchenclinny. The rain still poured as though the deluge were returning, and it was no easy matter to make a light in such a world of wet and darkness. When at last the flickering blue flame had been transferred to the wick and began to expand and clarify, and shed a wide circle of misty brightness round the gig, it became possible for the two young men to see each other and the thing they had along with them. The rain had moulded the rough sacking to the outlines of the body underneath; the head was distinct from the trunk, the shoulders plainly modelled; something at once spectral and human riveted their eyes upon the ghastly comrade of their drive.

For some time Macfarlane stood motionless, holding up the

lamp. A nameless dread was swathed, like a wet sheet, about the body, and tightened the white skin upon the face of Fettes; a fear that was meaningless, a horror of what could not be, kept mounting to his brain. Another beat of the watch, and he had spoken. But his comrade forestalled him.

'That is not a woman,' said Macfarlane, in a hushed voice.

'It was a woman when we put her in,' whispered Fettes.

'Hold that lamp,' said the other. 'I must see her face.'

And as Fettes took the lamp his companion untied the fastenings of the sack and drew down the cover from the head. The light fell very clear upon the dark, well-moulded features and smooth-shaven cheeks of a too familiar countenance, often beheld in dreams of both of these young men. A wild yell rang up into the night; each leaped from his own side into the roadway: the lamp fell, broke, and was extinguished; and the horse, terrified by this unusual commotion, bounded and went off toward Edinburgh at a gallop, bearing along with it, sole occupant of the gig, the body of the dead and long-dissected Gray.

THE DREAM WOMAN: A MYSTERY IN FOUR NARRATIVES

BY

WILKIE COLLINS

THE FIRST NARRATIVE

INTRODUCTORY STATEMENT OF THE FACTS BY PERCY FAIRBANK

I

"Hullo, there! Hostler! Hullo-o-o!"

"My dear! why don't you look for the bell?"

"I have looked—there is no bell."

"And nobody in the yard. How very extraordinary! Call again, dear."

"Hostler! Hullo, there! Hostler-r-r!"

My second call echoes through empty space, and rouses nobody—produces, in short, no visible result. I am at the end of my resources—I don't know what to say or what to do next. Here I stand in the solitary inn yard of a strange town, with two horses to hold, and a lady to take care of. By way of adding to my responsibilities, it so happens that one of the horses is dead lame, and that the lady is my wife.

Who am I?—you will ask.

There is plenty of time to answer the question. Nothing happens; and nobody appears to receive us. Let me introduce myself and my wife.

I am Percy Fairbank—English gentleman—age (let us say) forty—no profession—moderate politics—middle height—fair complexion—easy character—plenty of money.

My wife is a French lady. She was Mademoiselle Clotilde Delorge—when I was first presented to her at her father's house in France. I fell in love with her—I really don't know why. It might have been because I was perfectly idle, and had nothing else to do at the time. Or it might have been because all my friends said she was the very last woman whom I ought to think of marrying. On the surface, I must own, there is nothing in common between Mrs. Fairbank and me. She is tall; she is dark; she is nervous, excitable, romantic; in all her opinions she proceeds to extremes. What could such a woman see in me? what could I see in her? I know no more than you do. In some mysterious manner we exactly suit each other. We have been man and wife for ten years, and our only regret is, that we have no children. I don't know what you may think; I call that—upon the whole—a happy marriage.

So much for ourselves. The next question is—what has brought us into the inn yard? and why am I obliged to turn groom, and hold the horses?

We live for the most part in France—at the country house in which my wife and I first met. Occasionally, by way of variety, we pay visits to my friends in England. We are paying one of those visits now. Our host is an old college friend of mine, possessed of a fine estate in Somersetshire; and we have arrived at his house—called Farleigh Hall—toward the close of the hunting season.

On the day of which I am now writing—destined to be a memorable day in our calendar—the hounds meet at Farleigh Hall.

Mrs. Fairbank and I are mounted on two of the best horses in my friend's stables. We are quite unworthy of that distinction; for we know nothing and care nothing about hunting. On the other hand, we delight in riding, and we enjoy the breezy Spring morning and the fair and fertile English landscape surrounding us on every side. While the hunt prospers, we follow the hunt. But when a check occurs—when time passes and patience is sorely tried; when the bewildered dogs run hither and thither, and strong language falls from the lips of exasperated sportsmen—we fail to take any further interest in the proceedings. We turn our horses' heads in the direction of a grassy lane, delightfully shaded by trees. We trot merrily along the lane, and find ourselves on an open common. We gallop across the common, and follow the windings of a second lane. We cross a brook, we pass through a village, we emerge into pastoral solitude among the hills. The horses toss their heads, and neigh to each other, and enjoy it as much as we do. The hunt is forgotten. We are as happy as a couple of children; we are actually singing a French song—when in one moment our merriment comes to an end. My wife's horse sets one of his forefeet on a loose stone, and stumbles. His rider's ready hand saves him from falling. But, at the first attempt he makes to go on, the sad truth shows itself—a tendon is strained; the horse is lame.

What is to be done? We are strangers in a lonely part of the country. Look where we may, we see no signs of a human habitation. There is nothing for it but to take the bridle road up the hill, and try what we can discover on the other side. I transfer the saddles, and mount my wife on my own horse. He is not used to carry a lady; he misses the familiar pressure of a man's legs on either side of him; he fidgets, and starts, and kicks up the dust. I follow on foot, at a respectful distance from his heels, leading the lame horse. Is there a more miserable object on the face of creation than a lame horse? I have seen lame men and lame dogs who were cheerful creatures; but I never yet saw a lame horse who didn't look heart-broken over his own misfortune.

For half an hour my wife capers and curvets sideways along the bridle road. I trudge on behind her; and the heartbroken horse halts behind *me*. Hard by the top of the hill, our melancholy procession passes a Somersetshire peasant at work in a field. I summon the man to approach us; and the man looks at me stolidly, from the middle of the field, without stirring a step. I ask at the top of my voice how far it is to Farleigh Hall. The Somersetshire peasant answers at the top of *his* voice:

"Vourteen mile. Gi' oi a drap o' zyder."

I translate (for my wife's benefit) from the Somersetshire language into the English language. We are fourteen miles from Farleigh Hall; and our friend in the field desires to be rewarded, for giving us that information, with a drop of cider. There is the peasant, painted by himself! Quite a bit of character, my dear! Quite a bit of character!

Mrs. Fairbank doesn't view the study of agricultural human nature with my relish. Her fidgety horse will not allow her a moment's repose; she is beginning to lose her temper.

"We can't go fourteen miles in this way," she says. "Where is the nearest inn? Ask that brute in the field!"

I take a shilling from my pocket and hold it up in the sun. The shilling exercises magnetic virtues. The shilling draws the peasant slowly toward me from the middle of the field. I inform him that we want to put up the horses and to hire a carriage to take us back to Farleigh Hall. Where can we do that? The peasant answers (with his eye on the shilling):

"At Oonderbridge, to be zure." (At Underbridge, to be sure.)

"Is it far to Underbridge?"

The peasant repeats, "Var to Oonderbridge?"—and laughs at the question. "Hoo-hoo-hoo!" (Underbridge is evidently close by—if we could only find it.) "Will you show us the way, my man?" "Will you gi' oi a drap of zyder?" I courteously bend my head, and point to the shilling. The agricultural intelligence exerts itself. The peasant joins our melancholy procession. My wife is a fine woman, but he never once looks at my wife—and, more extraordinary still, he never even looks at the horses. His eyes are with his mind—and his mind is on the shilling.

We reach the top of the hill—and, behold on the other side, nestling in a valley, the shrine of our pilgrimage, the town of Underbridge! Here our guide claims his shilling, and leaves us to find out the inn for ourselves. I am constitutionally a polite man. I say "Good morning" at parting. The guide looks at me with the shilling between his teeth to make sure that it is a good one. "Marnin!" he says savagely—and turns his back on us, as if we had offended him. A curious product, this, of the growth of civilization. If I didn't see a church spire at Underbridge, I might suppose that we had lost ourselves on a savage island.

II

Arriving at the town, we had no difficulty in finding the inn. The town is composed of one desolate street; and midway in that street stands the inn—an ancient stone building sadly out of repair. The painting on the sign-board is obliterated. The shutters over the long range of front windows are all closed. A cock and his hens are the only living creatures at the door. Plainly, this is one of the old inns of the stage-coach period, ruined by the railway. We pass through the open arched doorway, and find no one to welcome us. We advance into the stable yard behind; I assist my wife to dismount—and there we are in the position already disclosed to view at the opening of this narrative. No bell to ring. No human creature to answer when I call. I stand helpless, with the bridles of the horses in my hand. Mrs. Fairbank saunters gracefully down the length of the yard and does—what all women do, when they find themselves in a strange place. She opens every door as she passes it, and peeps in. On my side, I have just recovered my breath, I am on the point of shouting for the hostler for the third and last time, when I hear Mrs. Fairbank suddenly call to me:

"Percy! come here!"

Her voice is eager and agitated. She has opened a last door at the end of the yard, and has started back from some sight which has suddenly met her view. I hitch the horses' bridles on a rusty nail in the wall near me, and join my wife. She has turned pale, and catches me nervously by the arm.

"Good heavens!" she cries; "look at that!"

I look—and what do I see? I see a dingy little stable, containing two stalls. In one stall a horse is munching his corn. In the other a man is lying asleep on the litter.

A worn, withered, woebegone man in a hostler's dress. His hollow wrinkled cheeks, his scanty grizzled hair, his dry yellow skin, tell their own tale of past sorrow or suffering. There is an ominous frown on his eyebrows—there is a painful nervous contraction on the side of his mouth. I hear him breathing convulsively when I first look in; he shudders and sighs in his sleep. It is not a pleasant sight to see, and I turn round instinctively to the bright sunlight in the yard. My wife turns me back again in the direction of the stable door.

"Wait!" she says. "Wait! he may do it again."

"Do what again?"

"He was talking in his sleep, Percy, when I first looked in. He was dreaming some dreadful dream. Hush! he's beginning again."

I look and listen. The man stirs on his miserable bed. The man speaks in a quick, fierce whisper through his clinched teeth. "Wake up! Wake up, there! Murder!"

163

There is an interval of silence. He moves one lean arm slowly until it rests over his throat; he shudders, and turns on his straw; he raises his arm from his throat, and feebly stretches it out; his hand clutches at the straw on the side toward which he has turned; he seems to fancy that he is grasping at the edge of something. I see his lips begin to move again; I step softly into the stable; my wife follows me, with her hand fast clasped in mine. We both bend over him. He is talking once more in his sleep—strange talk, mad talk, this time.

"Light gray eyes" (we hear him say), "and a droop in the left eyelid—flaxen hair, with a gold-yellow streak in it—all right, mother! a fair, white arms with a down on them—little, lady's hand, with a reddish look round the fingernails—the knife—the cursed knife—first on one side, then on the other—aha, you she-devil! where is the knife?"

He stops and grows restless on a sudden. We see him writhing on the straw. He throws up both his hands and gasps hysterically for breath. His eyes open suddenly. For a moment they look at nothing, with a vacant glitter in them—then they close again in deeper sleep. Is he dreaming still? Yes; but the dream seems to have taken a new course. When he speaks next, the tone is altered; the words are few—sadly and imploringly repeated over and over again. "Say you love me! I am so fond of *you*. Say you love me! say you love me!" He sinks into deeper and deeper sleep, faintly repeating those words. They die away on his lips. He speaks no more.

By this time Mrs. Fairbank has got over her terror; she is devoured by curiosity now. The miserable creature on the straw has appealed to the imaginative side of her character. Her illimitable appetite for romance hungers and thirsts for more. She shakes me impatiently by the arm.

"Do you hear? There is a woman at the bottom of it, Percy! There is love and murder in it, Percy! Where are the people of the inn? Go into the yard, and call to them again."

My wife belongs, on her mother's side, to the South of France.

The South of France breeds fine women with hot tempers. I say no more. Married men will understand my position. Single men may need to be told that there are occasions when we must not only love and honor—we must also obey—our wives.

I turn to the door to obey *my* wife, and find myself confronted by a stranger who has stolen on us unawares. The stranger is a tiny, sleepy, rosy old man, with a vacant pudding-face, and a shining bald head. He wears drab breeches and gaiters, and a respectable square-tailed ancient black coat. I feel instinctively that here is the landlord of the inn.

"Good morning, sir," says the rosy old man. "I'm a little hard of hearing. Was it you that was a-calling just now in the yard?"

Before I can answer, my wife interposes. She insists (in a shrill voice, adapted to our host's hardness of hearing) on knowing who that unfortunate person is sleeping on the straw. "Where does he come from? Why does he say such dreadful things in his sleep? Is he married or single? Did he ever fall in love with a murderess? What sort of a looking woman was she? Did she really stab him or not? In short, dear Mr. Landlord, tell us the whole story!"

Dear Mr. Landlord waits drowsily until Mrs. Fairbank has quite done—then delivers himself of his reply as follows:

"His name's Francis Raven. He's an Independent Methodist. He was forty-five year old last birthday. And he's my hostler. That's his story."

My wife's hot southern temper finds its way to her foot, and expresses itself by a stamp on the stable yard.

The landlord turns himself sleepily round, and looks at the horses. "A fine pair of horses, them two in the yard. Do you want to put 'em in my stables?" I reply in the affirmative by a nod. The landlord, bent on making himself agreeable to my wife, addresses her once more. "I'm a-going to wake Francis Raven. He's an Independent Methodist. He was forty-five year old last birthday. And he's my hostler. That's his story."

Having issued this second edition of his interesting narrative, the landlord enters the stable. We follow him to see how he will wake Francis Raven, and what will happen upon that. The stable broom stands in a corner; the landlord takes it—advances toward the sleeping hostler—and coolly stirs the man up with a broom as if he was a wild beast in a cage. Francis Raven starts to his feet with a cry of terror—looks at us wildly, with a horrid glare of suspicion in his eyes—recovers himself the next moment—and suddenly changes into a decent, quiet, respectable serving-man.

"I beg your pardon, ma'am. I beg your pardon, sir."

The tone and manner in which he makes his apologies are both above his apparent station in life. I begin to catch the infection of Mrs. Fairbank's interest in this man. We both follow him out into the yard to see what he will do with the horses. The manner in which he lifts the injured leg of the lame horse tells me at once that he understands his business. Quickly and quietly, he leads the animal into an empty stable; quickly and quietly, he gets a bucket of hot water, and puts the lame horse's leg into it. "The warm water will reduce the swelling, sir. I will bandage the leg afterwards." All that he does is done intelligently; all that he says, he says to the purpose.

Nothing wild, nothing strange about him now. Is this the same man whom we heard talking in his sleep?—the same man who woke with that cry of terror and that horrid suspicion in his eyes? I determine to try him with one or two questions.

III

"Not much to do here," I say to the hostler.

"Very little to do, sir," the hostler replies.

"Anybody staying in the house?"

"The house is quite empty, sir."

"I thought you were all dead. I could make nobody hear me."

"The landlord is very deaf, sir, and the waiter is out on an errand."

"Yes; and *you* were fast asleep in the stable. Do you often take a nap in the daytime?"

The worn face of the hostler faintly flushes. His eyes look away from my eyes for the first time. Mrs. Fairbank furtively pinches my arm. Are we on the eve of a discovery at last? I repeat my question. The man has no civil alternative but to give me an answer. The answer is given in these words:

"I was tired out, sir. You wouldn't have found me asleep in the daytime but for that."

"Tired out, eh? You had been hard at work, I suppose?"

"No, sir."

"What was it, then?"

He hesitates again, and answers unwillingly, "I was up all night."

"Up all night? Anything going on in the town?"

"Nothing going on, sir."

"Anybody ill?"

"Nobody ill, sir."

That reply is the last. Try as I may, I can extract nothing more from him. He turns away and busies himself in attending to the horse's leg. I leave the stable to speak to the landlord about the carriage which is to take us back to Farleigh Hall. Mrs. Fairbank remains with the hostler, and favors me with a look at parting. The look says plainly, "*I* mean to find out why he was up all night. Leave him to Me."

The ordering of the carriage is easily accomplished. The inn possesses one horse and one chaise. The landlord has a story to tell of the horse, and a story to tell of the chaise. They resemble the story of Francis Raven—with this exception, that the horse and chaise belong to no religious persuasion. "The horse will be nine year old next birthday. I've had the shay for four-and-twenty year. Mr. Max, of Underbridge, he bred the horse; and Mr. Pooley, of Yeovil, he built the shay. It's my horse and my shay. And that's *their* story!" Having relieved his mind of these details, the landlord proceeds to put the harness on the horse. By way of assisting him, I drag the chaise into the yard. Just as our preparations are completed, Mrs. Fairbank appears. A moment or two later the hostler follows her out. He has bandaged the horse's leg, and is now ready to drive us to Farleigh Hall. I observe signs of agitation in his face and manner, which suggest that my wife has found her way into his confidence. I put the question to her privately in a corner of the yard. "Well? Have you found out why Francis Raven was up all night?"

Mrs. Fairbank has an eye to dramatic effect. Instead of answering plainly, Yes or No, she suspends the interest and excites the audience by putting a question on her side.

"What is the day of the month, dear?"

"The day of the month is the first of March."

"The first of March, Percy, is Francis Raven's birthday."

I try to look as if I was interested—and don't succeed.

"Francis was born," Mrs. Fairbank proceeds gravely, "at two o'clock in the morning."

I begin to wonder whether my wife's intellect is going the way of the landlord's intellect. "Is that all?" I ask.

"It is *not* all," Mrs. Fairbank answers. "Francis Raven sits up on the morning of his birthday because he is afraid to go to bed."

"And why is he afraid to go to bed?"

"Because he is in peril of his life."

"On his birthday?"

"On his birthday. At two o'clock in the morning. As regularly as the birthday comes round."

There she stops. Has she discovered no more than that? No more thus far. I begin to feel really interested by this time. I ask eagerly what it means? Mrs. Fairbank points mysteriously to the chaise—with Francis Raven (hitherto our hostler, now our

168

coachman) waiting for us to get in. The chaise has a seat for two in front, and a seat for one behind. My wife casts a warning look at me, and places herself on the seat in front.

The necessary consequence of this arrangement is that Mrs. Fairbank sits by the side of the driver during a journey of two hours and more. Need I state the result? It would be an insult to your intelligence to state the result. Let me offer you my place in the chaise. And let Francis Raven tell his terrible story in his own words.

THE SECOND NARRATIVE

THE HOSTLER'S STORY.—TOLD BY HIMSELF

IV

It is now ten years ago since I got my first warning of the great trouble of my life in the Vision of a Dream.

I shall be better able to tell you about it if you will please suppose yourselves to be drinking tea along with us in our little cottage in Cambridgeshire, ten years since.

The time was the close of day, and there were three of us at the table, namely, my mother, myself, and my mother's sister, Mrs. Chance. These two were Scotchwomen by birth, and both were widows. There was no other resemblance between them that I can call to mind. My mother had lived all her life in England, and had no more of the Scotch brogue on her tongue than I have. My aunt Chance had never been out of Scotland until she came to keep house with my mother after her husband's death. And when *she* opened her lips you heard broad Scotch, I can tell you, if you ever heard it yet!

As it fell out, there was a matter of some consequence in debate among us that evening. It was this: whether I should do well or not to take a long journey on foot the next morning.

Now the next morning happened to be the day before my birthday; and the purpose of the journey was to offer myself for a situation as groom at a great house in the neighboring county to ours. The place was reported as likely to fall vacant in about three weeks' time. I was as well fitted to fill it as any other man. In the prosperous days of our family, my father had been manager of a training stable, and he had kept me employed among the horses from my boyhood upward. Please to excuse my troubling you with these small matters. They all fit into my story farther on, as you will soon find out. My poor mother was dead against my leaving home on the morrow.

"You can never walk all the way there and all the way back again by to-morrow night," she says. "The end of it will be that you will sleep away from home on your birthday. You have never done that yet, Francis, since your father's death, I don't like your doing it now. Wait a day longer, my son—only one day."

For my own part, I was weary of being idle, and I couldn't abide the notion of delay. Even one day might make all the difference. Some other man might take time by the forelock, and get the place.

"Consider how long I have been out of work," I says, "and don't ask me to put off the journey. I won't fail you, mother. I'll get back by to-morrow night, if I have to pay my last sixpence for a lift in a cart."

My mother shook her head. "I don't like it, Francis—I don't like it!" There was no moving her from that view. We argued and argued, until we were both at a deadlock. It ended in our agreeing to refer the difference between us to my mother's sister, Mrs. Chance.

While we were trying hard to convince each other, my aunt Chance sat as dumb as a fish, stirring her tea and thinking her own thoughts. When we made our appeal to her, she seemed as it were to wake up. "Ye baith refer it to my puir judgment?" she says, in her broad Scotch. We both answered Yes. Upon that my aunt Chance first cleared the tea-table, and then pulled out from the pocket of her gown a pack of cards.

Don't run away, if you please, with the notion that this was done lightly, with a view to amuse my mother and me. My aunt Chance seriously believed that she could look into the future by telling fortunes on the cards. She did nothing herself without first consulting the cards. She could give no more serious proof of her interest in my welfare than the proof which she was offering now. I don't say it profanely; I only mention the fact—the cards had, in some incomprehensible way, got themselves jumbled up together with her religious convictions. You meet with people nowadays who believe in spirits working by way of tables and chairs. On the same principle (if there *is* any principle in it) my aunt Chance believed in Providence working by way of the cards.

"Whether *you* are right, Francie, or your mither—whether ye will do weel or ill, the morrow, to go or stay—the cairds will tell it. We are a' in the hands of Proavidence. The cairds will tell it."

Hearing this, my mother turned her head aside, with something of a sour look in her face. Her sister's notions about the cards were little better than flat blasphemy to her mind. But she kept her opinion to herself. My aunt Chance, to own the truth, had inherited, through her late husband, a pension of thirty pounds a year. This was an important contribution to our housekeeping, and we poor relations were bound to treat her with a certain respect. As for myself, if my poor father never did anything else for me before he fell into difficulties, he gave me a good education, and raised me (thank God) above superstitions of all sorts. However, a very little amused me in those days; and I waited to have my fortune told, as patiently as if I believed in it too!

My aunt began her hocus pocus by throwing out all the cards

171

in the pack under seven. She shuffled the rest with her left hand for luck; and then she gave them to me to cut. "Wi' yer left hand, Francie. Mind that! Pet your trust in Proavidence—but dinna forget that your luck's in yer left hand!" A long and roundabout shifting of the cards followed, reducing them in number until there were just fifteen of them left, laid out neatly before my aunt in a half circle. The card which happened to lie outermost, at the right-hand end of the circle, was, according to rule in such cases, the card chosen to represent Me. By way of being appropriate to my situation as a poor groom out of employment, the card was—the King of Diamonds.

"I tak' up the King o' Diamants," says my aunt. "I count seven cairds fra' richt to left; and I humbly ask a blessing on what follows." My aunt shut her eyes as if she was saying grace before meat, and held up to me the seventh card. I called the seventh card—the Queen of Spades. My aunt opened her eyes again in a hurry, and cast a sly look my way. "The Queen o' Spades means a dairk woman. Ye'll be thinking in secret, Francie, of a dairk woman?"

When a man has been out of work for more than three months, his mind isn't troubled much with thinking of women—light or dark. I was thinking of the groom's place at the great house, and I tried to say so. My aunt Chance wouldn't listen. She treated my interpretation with contempt. "Hoot-toot! there's the caird in your hand! If ye're no thinking of her the day, ye'll be thinking of her the morrow. Where's the harm of thinking of a dairk woman! I was ance a dairk woman myself, before my hair was gray. Haud yer peace, Francie, and watch the cairds."

I watched the cards as I was told. There were seven left on the table. My aunt removed two from one end of the row and two from the other, and desired me to call the two outermost of the three cards now left on the table. I called the Ace of Clubs and the Ten of Diamonds. My aunt Chance lifted her eyes to the ceiling with a look of devout gratitude which sorely tried my mother's patience.

The Ace of Clubs and the Ten of Diamonds, taken together, signified—first, good news (evidently the news of the groom's place); secondly, a journey that lay before me (pointing plainly to my journey to-morrow!); thirdly and lastly, a sum of money (probably the groom's wages!) waiting to find its way into my pockets. Having told my fortune in these encouraging terms, my aunt declined to carry the experiment any further. "Eh, lad! it's a clean tempting o' Proavidence to ask mair o' the cairds than the cairds have tauld us noo. Gae yer ways to-morrow to the great hoose. A dairk woman will meet ye at the gate; and she'll have a hand in getting ye the groom's place, wi' a' the gratifications and pairquisites appertaining to the same. And, mebbe, when yer poaket's full o' money, ye'll no' be forgetting yer aunt Chance, maintaining her ain unblemished widowhood—wi' Proavidence assisting—on thratty punds a year!"

I promised to remember my aunt Chance (who had the defect, by the way, of being a terribly greedy person after money) on the next happy occasion when my poor empty pockets were to be filled at last. This done, I looked at my mother. She had agreed to take her sister for umpire between us, and her sister had given it in my favor. She raised no more objections. Silently, she got on her feet, and kissed me, and sighed bitterly—and so left the room. My aunt Chance shook her head. "I doubt, Francie, yer puir mither has but a heathen notion of the vairtue of the cairds!"

By daylight the next morning I set forth on my journey. I looked back at the cottage as I opened the garden gate. At one window was my mother, with her handkerchief to her eyes. At the other stood my aunt Chance, holding up the Queen of Spades by way of encouraging me at starting. I waved my hands to both of them in token of farewell, and stepped out briskly into the road. It was then the last day of February. Be pleased to remember, in connection with this, that the first of March was the day, and two o'clock in the morning the hour of my birth.

V

Now you know how I came to leave home. The next thing to tell is, what happened on the journey.

I reached the great house in reasonably good time considering the distance. At the very first trial of it, the prophecy of the cards turned out to be wrong. The person who met me at the lodge gate was not a dark woman—in fact, not a woman at all—but a boy. He directed me on the way to the servants' offices; and there again the cards were all wrong. I encountered, not one woman, but three—and not one of the three was dark. I have stated that I am not superstitious, and I have told the truth. But I must own that I did feel a certain fluttering at the heart when I made my bow to the steward, and told him what business had brought me to the house. His answer completed the discomfiture of aunt Chance's fortune-telling. My ill-luck still pursued me. That very morning another man had applied for the groom's place, and had got it.

I swallowed my disappointment as well as I could, and thanked the steward, and went to the inn in the village to get the rest and food which I sorely needed by this time.

Before starting on my homeward walk I made some inquiries at the inn, and ascertained that I might save a few miles, on my return, by following a new road. Furnished with full instructions, several times repeated, as to the various turnings I was to take, I set forth, and walked on till the evening with only one stoppage for bread and cheese. Just as it was getting toward dark, the rain came on and the wind began to rise; and I found myself, to make matters worse, in a part of the country with which I was entirely unacquainted, though I guessed myself to be some fifteen miles from home. The first house I found to inquire at, was a lonely roadside inn, standing on the outskirts of a thick wood. Solitary as the place looked, it was welcome to a lost man who was also hungry, thirsty, footsore, and wet. The landlord was civil and respectable-looking; and the price he asked for a bed was reasonable enough. I was grieved to disappoint my mother. But there was no conveyance to be had, and I could go no farther afoot that night. My weariness fairly forced me to stop at the inn.

I may say for myself that I am a temperate man. My supper simply consisted of some rashers of bacon, a slice of home-made bread, and a pint of ale. I did not go to bed immediately after this moderate meal, but sat up with the landlord, talking about my bad prospects and my long run of ill-luck, and diverging from these topics to the subjects of horse-flesh and racing. Nothing was said, either by myself, my host, or the few laborers who strayed into the tap-room, which could, in the slightest degree, excite my mind, or set my fancy—which is only a small fancy at the best of times— playing tricks with my common sense.

At a little after eleven the house was closed. I went round with the landlord, and held the candle while the doors and lower windows were being secured. I noticed with surprise the strength of the bolts, bars, and iron-sheathed shutters.

"You see, we are rather lonely here," said the landlord. "We never have had any attempts to break in yet, but it's always as well to be on the safe side. When nobody is sleeping here, I am the only man in the house. My wife and daughter are timid, and the servant girl takes after her missuses. Another glass of ale, before you turn in?—No!—Well, how such a sober man as you comes to be out of a place is more than I can understand for one.—Here's where you're to sleep. You're the only lodger to-night, and I think you'll say my missus has done her best to make you comfortable. You're quite sure you won't have another glass of ale?—Very well. Good night."

It was half-past eleven by the clock in the passage as we went upstairs to the bedroom. The window looked out on the wood at the back of the house.

I locked my door, set my candle on the chest of drawers, and wearily got me ready for bed. The bleak wind was still blowing, and the solemn, surging moan of it in the wood was very dreary to hear through the night silence. Feeling strangely wakeful, I resolved to keep the candle alight until I began to grow sleepy. The truth is, I was not quite myself. I was depressed in mind by my disappointment of the morning; and I was worn out in body by my long walk. Between the two, I own I couldn't face the prospect of lying awake in the darkness, listening to the dismal moan of the wind in the wood.

Sleep stole on me before I was aware of it; my eyes closed, and I fell off to rest, without having so much as thought of extinguishing the candle.

The next thing that I remember was a faint shivering that ran through me from head to foot, and a dreadful sinking pain at my heart, such as I had never felt before. The shivering only disturbed my slumbers—the pain woke me instantly. In one moment I passed from a state of sleep to a state of wakefulness—my eyes wide open— my mind clear on a sudden as if by a miracle. The candle had burned down nearly to the last morsel of tallow, but the unsnuffed wick had just fallen off, and the light was, for the moment, fair and full.

Between the foot of the bed and the closet door, I saw a person in my room. The person was a woman, standing looking at me, with a knife in her hand. It does no credit to my courage to confess it—but the truth *is* the truth. I was struck speechless with terror. There I lay with my eyes on the woman; there the woman stood (with the knife in her hand) with *her* eyes on *me*.

She said not a word as we stared each other in the face; but she moved after a little—moved slowly toward the left-hand side of the bed.

The light fell full on her face. A fair, fine woman, with yellowish flaxen hair, and light gray eyes, with a droop in the left eyelid. I noticed these things and fixed them in my mind, before she was quite round at the side of the bed. Without saying a word; without any change in the stony stillness of her face; without any noise following her footfall, she came closer and closer; stopped at the bed-head; and lifted the knife to stab me. I laid my arm over my throat to save it; but, as I saw the blow coming, I threw my hand across the bed to the right side, and jerked my body over that way, just as the knife came down, like lightning, within a hair's breadth of my shoulder.

My eyes fixed on her arm and her hand—she gave me time to look at them as she slowly drew the knife out of the bed. A white, well-shaped arm, with a pretty down lying lightly over the fair skin. A delicate lady's hand, with a pink flush round the finger nails.

She drew the knife out, and passed back again slowly to the foot of the bed; she stopped there for a moment looking at me; then she came on without saying a word; without any change in the stony stillness of her face; without any noise following her foot-fall—came on to the side of the bed where I now lay.

Getting near me, she lifted the knife again, and I drew myself away to the left side. She struck, as before right into the mattress, with a swift downward action of her arm; and she missed me, as before; by a hair's breadth. This time my eyes wandered from *her* to the knife. It was like the large clasp knives which laboring men use to cut their bread and bacon with. Her delicate little fingers did not hide more than two thirds of the handle; I noticed that it was made of buckhorn, clean and shining as the blade was, and looking like new.

For the second time she drew the knife out of the bed, and suddenly hid it away in the wide sleeve of her gown. That done, she stopped by the bedside watching me. For an instant I saw her standing in that position—then the wick of the spent candle fell over into the socket. The flame dwindled to a little blue point, and the room grew dark.

A moment, or less, if possible, passed so—and then the wick flared up, smokily, for the last time. My eyes were still looking for her over the right-hand side of the bed when the last flash of light came. Look as I might, I could see nothing. The woman with the knife was gone.

I began to get back to myself again. I could feel my heart beating; I could hear the woeful moaning of the wind in the wood; I could leap up in bed, and give the alarm before she escaped from the house. "Murder! Wake up there! Murder!"

Nobody answered to the alarm. I rose and groped my way through the darkness to the door of the room. By that way she must have got in. By that way she must have gone out.

The door of the room was fast locked, exactly as I had left it on going to bed! I looked at the window. Fast locked too!

Hearing a voice outside, I opened the door. There was the landlord, coming toward me along the passage, with his burning candle in one hand, and his gun in the other.

"What is it?" he says, looking at me in no very friendly way.

I could only answer in a whisper, "A woman, with a knife in her hand. In my room. A fair, yellow-haired woman. She jabbed at me with the knife, twice over."

He lifted his candle, and looked at me steadily from head to foot. "She seems to have missed you—twice over."

"I dodged the knife as it came down. It struck the bed each time. Go in, and see."

The landlord took his candle into the bedroom immediately. In less than a minute he came out again into the passage in a violent passion.

"The devil fly away with you and your woman with the knife! There isn't a mark in the bedclothes anywhere. What do you mean by coming into a man's place and frightening his family out of their wits by a dream?"

A dream? The woman who had tried to stab me, not a living human being like myself? I began to shake and shiver. The horrors got hold of me at the bare thought of it.

"I'll leave the house," I said. "Better be out on the road in the rain and dark, than back in that room, after what I've seen in it. Lend me the light to get my clothes by, and tell me what I'm to pay."

The landlord led the way back with his light into the bedroom. "Pay?" says he. "You'll find your score on the slate when you go downstairs. I wouldn't have taken you in for all the money you've got about you, if I had known your dreaming, screeching ways beforehand. Look at the bed—where's the cut of a knife in it? Look at the window—is the lock bursted? Look at the door (which I heard you fasten yourself)—is it broke in? A murdering woman with a knife in my house! You ought to be ashamed of yourself!"

My eyes followed his hand as it pointed first to the bed—then to the window—then to the door. There was no gainsaying it. The bed sheet was as sound as on the day it was made. The window was fast. The door hung on its hinges as steady as ever. I huddled my clothes on without speaking. We went downstairs together. I looked at the clock in the bar-room. The time was twenty minutes past two in the morning. I paid my bill, and the landlord let me out. The rain had ceased; but the night was dark, and the wind was bleaker than ever. Little did the darkness, or the cold, or the doubt about the way home matter to *me*. My mind was away from all these things. My mind was fixed on the vision in the bedroom. What had I seen trying to murder me? The creature of a dream? Or that other creature from the world beyond the grave, whom men call ghost? I could make nothing of it as I walked along in the night; I had made nothing by it by midday—when I stood at last, after many times missing my road, on the doorstep of home.

VI

My mother came out alone to welcome me back. There were no secrets between us two. I told her all that had happened, just as I have told it to you. She kept silence till I had done. And then she put a question to me.

"What time was it, Francis, when you saw the Woman in your Dream?"

I had looked at the clock when I left the inn, and I had noticed that the hands pointed to twenty minutes past two. Allowing for the time consumed in speaking to the landlord, and in getting on my clothes, I answered that I must have first seen the Woman at two o'clock in the morning. In other words, I had not only seen her on my birthday, but at the hour of my birth.

My mother still kept silence. Lost in her own thoughts, she took me by the hand, and led me into the parlor. Her writing-desk was on the table by the fireplace. She opened it, and signed to me to take a chair by her side.

"My son! your memory is a bad one, and mine is fast failing me. Tell me again what the Woman looked like. I want her to be as well known to both of us, years hence, as she is now."

I obeyed; wondering what strange fancy might be working in her mind. I spoke; and she wrote the words as they fell from my lips:

"Light gray eyes, with a droop in the left eyelid. Flaxen hair, with a golden-yellow streak in it. White arms, with a down upon them. Little, lady's hands, with a rosy-red look about the finger nails."

"Did you notice how she was dressed, Francis?"

"No, mother."

"Did you notice the knife?"

"Yes. A large clasp knife, with a buckhorn handle, as good as new."

My mother added the description of the knife. Also the year, month, day of the week, and hour of the day when the Dream-Woman appeared to me at the inn. That done, she locked up the paper in her desk.

"Not a word, Francis, to your aunt. Not a word to any living soul. Keep your Dream a secret between you and me."

The weeks passed, and the months passed. My mother never returned to the subject again. As for me, time, which wears out all things, wore out my remembrance of the Dream. Little by little, the image of the Woman grew dimmer and dimmer. Little by little, she faded out of my mind.

VII

The story of the warning is now told. Judge for yourself if it was a true warning or a false, when you hear what happened to me on my next birthday.

In the Summer time of the year, the Wheel of Fortune turned the right way for me at last. I was smoking my pipe one day, near an old stone quarry at the entrance to our village, when a carriage accident happened, which gave a new turn, as it were, to my lot in life. It was an accident of the commonest kind—not worth mentioning at any length. A lady driving herself; a runaway horse; a cowardly man-servant in attendance, frightened out of his wits; and the stone quarry too near to be agreeable—that is what I saw, all in a few moments, between two whiffs of my pipe. I stopped the horse at the edge of the quarry, and got myself a little hurt by the shaft of the chaise. But that didn't matter. The lady declared I had saved her life; and her husband, coming with her to our cottage the next day, took me into his service then and there. The lady happened to be of a dark complexion; and it may amuse you to hear that my aunt Chance instantly pitched on that circumstance as a means of saving the credit of the cards. Here was the promise of the Queen of Spades performed to the very letter, by means of "a dark woman," just as my aunt had told me. "In the time to come, Francis, beware o' pettin' yer ain blinded intairpretation on the cairds. Ye're ower ready, I trow, to murmur under dispensation of Proavidence that ye canna fathom—like the Eesraelites of auld. I'll say nae mair to ye. Mebbe when the mony's powering into yer poakets, ye'll no forget yer aunt Chance, left like a sparrow on the housetop, wi' a sma' annuitee o' thratty punds a year."

I remained in my situation (at the West-end of London) until the Spring of the New Year. About that time, my master's health failed. The doctors ordered him away to foreign parts, and the establishment was broken up. But the turn in my luck still held good. When I left my place, I left it—thanks to the generosity of my kind master—with a yearly allowance granted to me, in remembrance of the day when I had saved my mistress's life. For the future, I could go back to service or not, as I pleased; my little income was enough to support my mother and myself.

My master and mistress left England toward the end of February. Certain matters of business to do for them detained me in London until the last day of the month. I was only able to leave for our village by the evening train, to keep my birthday with my mother as usual. It was bedtime when I got to the cottage; and I was sorry to find that she was far from well. To make matters worse, she had finished her bottle of medicine on the previous day, and had omitted to get it replenished, as the doctor had strictly directed. He dispensed his own medicines, and I offered to go and knock him up. She refused to let me do this; and, after giving me my supper, sent me away to my bed.

I fell asleep for a little, and woke again. My mother's bed-chamber was next to mine. I heard my aunt Chance's heavy footsteps going to and fro in the room, and, suspecting something wrong, knocked at the door. My mother's pains had returned upon her; there was a serious necessity for relieving her sufferings as speedily as possible, I put on my clothes, and ran off, with the medicine bottle in my hand, to the other end of the village, where the doctor lived. The church clock chimed the quarter to two on my birthday just as I reached his house. One ring of the night bell brought him to his bedroom window to speak to me. He told me to wait, and he would let me in at the surgery door. I noticed, while I was waiting, that the night was wonderfully fair and warm for the time of year. The old stone quarry where the carriage accident had happened was within view. The moon in the clear heavens lit it up almost as bright as day.

In a minute or two the doctor let me into the surgery. I closed the door, noticing that he had left his room very lightly clad. He kindly pardoned my mother's neglect of his directions, and set to work at once at compounding the medicine. We were both intent on the bottle; he filling it, and I holding the light—when we heard the surgery door suddenly opened from the street.

VIII

Who could possibly be up and about in our quiet village at the second hour of the morning?

The person who opened the door appeared within range of the light of the candle. To complete our amazement, the person proved to be a woman! She walked up to the counter, and standing side by side with me, lifted her veil. At the moment when she showed her face, I heard the church clock strike two. She was a stranger to me, and a stranger to the doctor. She was also, beyond all comparison, the most beautiful woman I have ever seen in my life.

"I saw the light under the door," she said. "I want some medicine."

She spoke quite composedly, as if there was nothing at all extraordinary in her being out in the village at two in the morning, and following me into the surgery to ask for medicine! The doctor stared at her as if he suspected his own eyes of deceiving him. "Who are you?" he asked. "How do you come to be wandering about at this time in the morning?"

She paid no heed to his questions. She only told him coolly what she wanted. "I have got a bad toothache. I want a bottle of laudanum."

The doctor recovered himself when she asked for the laudanum. He was on his own ground, you know, when it came to a matter of laudanum; and he spoke to her smartly enough this time.

"Oh, you have got the toothache, have you? Let me look at the tooth."

She shook her head, and laid a two-shilling piece on the counter. "I won't trouble you to look at the tooth," she said. "There is the money. Let me have the laudanum, if you please."

The doctor put the two-shilling piece back again in her hand. "I don't sell laudanum to strangers," he answered. "If you are in any distress of body or mind, that is another matter. I shall be glad to help you."

She put the money back in her pocket. "*You* can't help me," she said, as quietly as ever. "Good morning."

With that, she opened the surgery door to go out again into the street. So far, I had not spoken a word on my side. I had stood with the candle in my hand (not knowing I was holding it)—with my eyes fixed on her, with my mind fixed on her like a man bewitched. Her looks betrayed, even more plainly than her words, her resolution, in one way or another, to destroy herself. When she opened the door, in my alarm at what might happen I found the use of my tongue.

"Stop!" I cried out. "Wait for me. I want to speak to you before you go away." She lifted her eyes with a look of careless surprise and a mocking smile on her lips.

"What can *you* have to say to me?" She stopped, and laughed to herself. "Why not?" she said. "I have got nothing to do, and nowhere to go." She turned back a step, and nodded to me. "You're a strange man—I think I'll humor you—I'll wait outside." The door of the surgery closed on her. She was gone.

I am ashamed to own what happened next. The only excuse for me is that I was really and truly a man bewitched. I turned me round to follow her out, without once thinking of my mother. The doctor stopped me.

"Don't forget the medicine," he said. "And if you will take my advice, don't trouble yourself about that woman. Rouse up the constable. It's his business to look after her—not yours."

I held out my hand for the medicine in silence: I was afraid I should fail in respect if I trusted myself to answer him. He must have seen, as I saw, that she wanted the laudanum to poison herself. He had, to my mind, taken a very heartless view of the matter. I just thanked him when he gave me the medicine—and went out.

She was waiting for me as she had promised; walking slowly to and fro—a tall, graceful, solitary figure in the bright moonbeams. They shed over her fair complexion, her bright golden hair, her large gray eyes, just the light that suited them best. She looked hardly mortal when she first turned to speak to me.

"Well?" she said. "And what do you want?"

In spite of my pride, or my shyness, or my better sense—whichever it might me—all my heart went out to her in a moment. I caught hold of her by the hands, and owned what was in my thoughts, as freely as if I had known her for half a lifetime.

"You mean to destroy yourself," I said. "And I mean to prevent you from doing it. If I follow you about all night, I'll prevent you from doing it."

She laughed. "You saw yourself that he wouldn't sell me the laudanum. Do you really care whether I live or die?" She squeezed my hands gently as she put the question: her eyes searched mine with a languid, lingering look in them that ran through me like fire. My voice died away on my lips; I couldn't answer her.

She understood, without my answering. "You have given me a fancy for living, by speaking kindly to me," she said. "Kindness has a wonderful effect on women, and dogs, and other domestic animals. It is only men who are superior to kindness. Make your mind easy—I promise to take as much care of myself as if I was the happiest woman living! Don't let me keep you here, out of your bed. Which way are you going?"

Miserable wretch that I was, I had forgotten my mother—with the medicine in my hand! "I am going home," I said. "Where are you staying? At the inn?"

She laughed her bitter laugh, and pointed to the stone quarry. "There is my inn for to-night," she said. "When I got tired of walking about, I rested there."

We walked on together, on my way home. I took the liberty of asking her if she had any friends.

"I thought I had one friend left," she said, "or you would never have met me in this place. It turns out I was wrong. My friend's door was closed in my face some hours since; my friend's servants threatened me with the police. I had nowhere else to go, after trying my luck in your neighborhood; and nothing left but my two-shilling piece and these rags on my back. What respectable innkeeper would take *me* into his house? I walked about, wondering how I could find my way out of the world without disfiguring myself, and without suffering much pain. You have no river in these parts. I didn't see my way out of the world, till I heard you ringing at the doctor's house. I got a glimpse at the bottles in the surgery, when he let you in, and I thought of the laudanum directly. What were you doing there? Who is that medicine for? Your wife?"

"I am not married!"

She laughed again. "Not married! If I was a little better dressed there might be a chance for ME. Where do you live? Here?"

We had arrived, by this time, at my mother's door. She held out her hand to say good-by. Houseless and homeless as she was, she never asked me to give her a shelter for the night. It was my proposal that she should rest, under my roof, unknown to my mother and my aunt. Our kitchen was built out at the back of the cottage: she might remain there unseen and unheard until the household was astir in the morning. I led her into the kitchen, and set a chair for her by the dying embers of the fire. I dare say I was to blame—shamefully to blame, if you like. I only wonder what *you* would have done in my place. On your word of honor as a man, would *you* have let that beautiful creature wander back to the shelter of the stone quarry like a stray dog? God help the woman who is foolish enough to trust and love you, if you would have done that!

I left her by the fire, and went to my mother's room.

IX

If you have ever felt the heartache, you will know what I suffered in secret when my mother took my hand, and said, "I am sorry, Francis, that your night's rest has been disturbed through *me*." I gave her the medicine; and I waited by her till the pains abated. My aunt Chance went back to her bed; and my mother and I were left alone. I noticed that her writing-desk, moved from its customary place, was on the bed by her side. She saw me looking at it. "This is your birthday, Francis," she said. "Have you anything to tell me?" I had so completely forgotten my Dream, that I had no notion of what was passing in her mind when she said those words. For a moment there was a guilty fear in me that she suspected something. I turned away my face, and said, "No, mother; I have nothing to tell." She signed to me to stoop down over the pillow and kiss her. "God bless you, my love!" she said; "and many happy returns of the day." She patted my hand, and closed her weary eyes, and, little by little, fell off peaceably into sleep.

I stole downstairs again. I think the good influence of my mother must have followed me down. At any rate, this is true: I stopped with my hand on the closed kitchen door, and said to myself: "Suppose I leave the house, and leave the village, without seeing her or speaking to her more?"

Should I really have fled from temptation in this way, if I had been left to myself to decide? Who can tell? As things were, I was not left to decide. While my doubt was in my mind, she heard me, and opened the kitchen door. My eyes and her eyes met. That ended it.

We were together, unsuspected and undisturbed, for the next two hours. Time enough for her to reveal the secret of her wasted life. Time enough for her to take possession of me as her own, to do with me as she liked. It is needless to dwell here on the misfortunes which had brought her low; they are misfortunes too common to interest anybody.

Her name was Alicia Warlock. She had been born and bred a lady. She had lost her station, her character, and her friends. Virtue shuddered at the sight of her; and Vice had got her for the rest of her days. Shocking and common, as I told you. It made no difference to *me*. I have said it already—I say it again—I was a man bewitched. Is there anything so very wonderful in that? Just remember who I was. Among the honest women in my own station in life, where could I have found the like of *her*? Could *they* walk as she walked? and look as she looked? When *they* gave me a kiss, did their lips linger over it as hers did? Had *they* her skin, her laugh, her foot, her hand, her touch? *She* never had a speck of dirt on her: I tell you her flesh was a perfume. When she embraced me, her arms folded round me like the wings of angels; and her smile covered me softly with its light like the sun in heaven. I leave you to laugh at me, or to cry over me, just as your temper may incline. I am not trying to excuse myself—I am trying to explain. You are gentle-folks; what dazzled and maddened *me*, is everyday experience to *you*. Fallen or not, angel or devil, it came to this—she was a lady; and I was a groom.

Before the house was astir, I got her away (by the workmen's train) to a large manufacturing town in our parts.

Here—with my savings in money to help her—she could get her outfit of decent clothes and her lodging among strangers who asked no questions so long as they were paid. Here—now on one pretense and now on another—I could visit her, and we could both plan together what our future lives were to be. I need not tell you that I stood pledged to make her my wife. A man in my station always marries a woman of her sort.

Do you wonder if I was happy at this time? I should have been perfectly happy but for one little drawback. It was this: I was never quite at my ease in the presence of my promised wife.

I don't mean that I was shy with her, or suspicious of her, or ashamed of her. The uneasiness I am speaking of was caused by a faint doubt in my mind whether I had not seen her somewhere, before the morning when we met at the doctor's house. Over and over again, I found myself wondering whether her face did not remind me of some other face—*what* other I never could tell. This strange feeling, this one question that could never be answered, vexed me to a degree that you would hardly credit. It came between us at the strangest times—oftenest, however, at night, when the candles were lit. You have known what it is to try and remember a forgotten name—and to fail, search as you may, to find it in your mind. That was my case. I failed to find my lost face, just as you failed to find your lost name.

In three weeks we had talked matters over, and had arranged how I was to make a clean breast of it at home. By Alicia's advice,

I was to describe her as having been one of my fellow servants during the time I was employed under my kind master and mistress in London. There was no fear now of my mother taking any harm from the shock of a great surprise. Her health had improved during the three weeks' interval. On the first evening when she was able to take her old place at tea time, I summoned my courage, and told her I was going to be married. The poor soul flung her arms round my neck, and burst out crying for joy. "Oh, Francis!" she says, "I am so glad you will have somebody to comfort you and care for you when I am gone!" As for my aunt Chance, you can antici-pate what *she* did, without being told. Ah, me! If there had really been any prophetic virtue in the cards, what a terrible warning they might have given us that night! It was arranged that I was to bring my promised wife to dinner at the cottage on the next day.

X

I own I was proud of Alicia when I led her into our little parlor at the appointed time. She had never, to my mind, looked so beautiful as she looked that day. I never noticed any other woman's dress—I noticed hers as carefully as if I had been a woman myself! She wore a black silk gown, with plain collar and cuffs, and a modest lavender-colored bonnet, with one white rose in it placed at the side. My mother, dressed in her Sunday best, rose up, all in a flutter, to welcome her daughter-in-law that was to be. She walked forward a few steps, half smiling, half in tears—she looked Alicia full in the face—and suddenly stood still. Her cheeks turned white in an instant; her eyes stared in horror; her hands dropped helplessly at her sides. She staggered back, and fell into the arms of my aunt, standing behind her. It was no swoon—she kept her senses. Her eyes turned slowly from Alicia to me. "Francis," she said, "does that woman's face remind you of nothing?".

Before I could answer, she pointed to her writing-desk on the table at the fireside. "Bring it!" she cried, "bring it!".

At the same moment I felt Alicia's hand on my shoulder, and saw Alicia's face red with anger—and no wonder!

"What does this mean?" she asked. "Does your mother want to insult me?".

I said a few words to quiet her; what they were I don't remember—I was so confused and astonished at the time. Before I had done, I heard my mother behind me.

My aunt had fetched her desk. She had opened it; she had taken a paper from it. Step by step, helping herself along by the wall, she came nearer and nearer, with the paper in her hand. She looked at the paper—she looked in Alicia's face—she lifted the long, loose sleeve of her gown, and examined her hand and arm. I saw fear suddenly take the place of anger in Alicia's eyes. She shook herself free of my mother's grasp. "Mad!" she said to herself, "and Francis never told me!" With those words she ran out of the room.

I was hastening out after her, when my mother signed to me to stop. She read the words written on the paper. While they fell slowly, one by one, from her lips, she pointed toward the open door.

"Light gray eyes, with a droop in the left eyelid. Flaxen hair, with a gold-yellow streak in it. White arms, with a down upon them. Little, lady's hand, with a rosy-red look about the finger nails. The Dream Woman, Francis! The Dream Woman!"

Something darkened the parlor window as those words were spoken. I looked sidelong at the shadow. Alicia Warlock had come back! She was peering in at us over the low window blind. There was the fatal face which had first looked at me in the bedroom of the lonely inn. There, resting on the window blind, was the lovely little hand which had held the murderous knife. I *had* seen her before we met in the village. The Dream Woman! The Dream Woman!

XI

I expect nobody to approve of what I have next to tell of myself. In three weeks from the day when my mother had identified her with the Woman of the Dream, I took Alicia Warlock to church, and made her my wife. I was a man bewitched. Again and again I say it—I was a man bewitched!

During the interval before my marriage, our little household at the cottage was broken up. My mother and my aunt quarreled. My mother, believing in the Dream, entreated me to break off my engagement. My aunt, believing in the cards, urged me to marry.

This difference of opinion produced a dispute between them, in the course of which my aunt Chance—quite unconscious of having any superstitious feelings of her own—actually set out the cards which prophesied happiness to me in my married life, and asked my mother how anybody but "a blinded heathen could be fule enough, after seeing those cairds, to believe in a dream!" This was, naturally, too much for my mother's patience; hard words followed on either side; Mrs. Chance returned in dudgeon to her friends in Scotland. She left me a written statement of my future prospects, as revealed by the cards, and with it an address at which a post-office order would reach her. "The day was not that far off," she remarked, "when Francie might remember what he owed to his aunt Chance, maintaining her ain unbleemished widowhood on thratty punds a year."

Having refused to give her sanction to my marriage, my mother also refused to be present at the wedding, or to visit Alicia afterwards. There was no anger at the bottom of this conduct on her part. Believing as she did in this Dream, she was simply in mortal fear of my wife. I understood this, and I made allowances for her. Not a cross word passed between us. My one happy remembrance now—though I did disobey her in the matter of my marriage—is this: I loved and respected my good mother to the last.

As for my wife, she expressed no regret at the estrangement between her mother-in-law and herself. By common consent, we never spoke on that subject. We settled in the manufacturing town which I have already mentioned, and we kept a lodging-house. My kind master, at my request, granted me a lump sum in place of my annuity. This put us into a good house, decently furnished. For a while things went well enough. I may describe myself at this time of my life as a happy man.

My misfortunes began with a return of the complaint with which my mother had already suffered. The doctor confessed, when I asked him the question, that there was danger to be dreaded this time. Naturally, after hearing this, I was a good deal away at the cottage. Naturally also, I left the business of looking after the house, in my absence, to my wife. Little by little, I found her beginning to alter toward me. While my back was turned, she formed acquaintances with people of the doubtful and dissipated sort. One day, I observed something in her manner which forced the suspicion on me that she had been drinking. Before the week was out, my suspicion was a certainty. From keeping company with drunkards, she had grown to be a drunkard herself.

I did all a man could do to reclaim her. Quite useless! She had never really returned the love I felt for her: I had no influence; I could do nothing. My mother, hearing of this last worse trouble, resolved to try what her influence could do. Ill as she was, I found her one day dressed to go out.

"I am not long for this world, Francis," she said. "I shall not feel easy on my deathbed, unless I have done my best to the last to make you happy. I mean to put my own fears and my own feelings out of the question, and go with you to your wife, and try what I can do to reclaim her. Take me home with you, Francis. Let me do all I can to help my son, before it is too late."

How could I disobey her? We took the railway to the town: it

193

was only half an hour's ride. By one o'clock in the afternoon we reached my house. It was our dinner hour, and Alicia was in the kitchen. I was able to take my mother quietly into the parlor and then to prepare my wife for the visit. She had drunk but little at that early hour; and, luckily, the devil in her was tamed for the time.

She followed me into the parlor, and the meeting passed off better than I had ventured to forecast; with this one drawback, that my mother—though she tried hard to control herself—shrank from looking my wife in the face when she spoke to her. It was a relief to me when Alicia began to prepare the table for dinner.

She laid the cloth, brought in the bread tray, and cut some slices for us from the loaf. Then she returned to the kitchen. At that moment, while I was still anxiously watching my mother, I was startled by seeing the same ghastly change pass over her face which had altered it in the morning when Alicia and she first met. Before I could say a word, she started up with a look of horror.

"Take me back!—home, home again, Francis! Come with me, and never go back more!"

I was afraid to ask for an explanation; I could only sign her to be silent, and help her quickly to the door. As we passed the bread tray on the table, she stopped and pointed to it.

"Did you see what your wife cut your bread with?" she asked.

"No, mother; I was not noticing. What was it?"

"Look!"

I did look. A new clasp knife, with a buckhorn handle, lay with the loaf in the bread tray. I stretched out my hand to possess myself of it. At the same moment, there was a noise in the kitchen, and my mother caught me by the arm.

"The knife of the Dream! Francis, I'm faint with fear—take me away before she comes back!"

I couldn't speak to comfort or even to answer her. Superior as

I was to superstition, the discovery of the knife staggered me. In silence, I helped my mother out of the house; and took her home.

I held out my hand to say good-by. She tried to stop me.

"Don't go back, Francis! don't go back!".

"I must get the knife, mother. I must go back by the next train." I held to that resolution. By the next train I went back.

XII

My wife had, of course, discovered our secret departure from the house. She had been drinking. She was in a fury of passion. The dinner in the kitchen was flung under the grate; the cloth was off the parlor table. Where was the knife?

I was foolish enough to ask for it. She refused to give it to me. In the course of the dispute between us which followed, I discovered that there was a horrible story attached to the knife. It had been used in a murder—years since—and had been so skillfully hidden that the authorities had been unable to produce it at the trial. By help of some of her disreputable friends, my wife had been able to purchase this relic of a bygone crime. Her perverted nature set some horrid unacknowledged value on the knife. Seeing there was no hope of getting it by fair means, I determined to search for it, later in the day, in secret. The search was unsuccessful. Night came on, and I left the house to walk about the streets. You will understand what a broken man I was by this time, when I tell you I was afraid to sleep in the same room with her!

Three weeks passed. Still she refused to give up the knife; and still that fear of sleeping in the same room with her possessed me. I walked about at night, or dozed in the parlor, or sat watching by my mother's bedside. Before the end of the first week in the new month, the worst misfortune of all befell me—my mother died. It wanted then but a short time to my birthday. She had longed to live till that day. I was present at her death. Her last words in this world were addressed to me. "Don't go back, my son—don't go back!"

I was obliged to go back, if it was only to watch my wife. In the last days of my mother's illness she had spitefully added a sting to my grief by declaring she would assert her right to attend the funeral. In spite of all that I could do or say, she held to her word. On the day appointed for the burial she forced herself, inflamed and shameless with drink, into my presence, and swore she would walk in the funeral procession to my mother's grave.

This last insult—after all I had gone through already—was more than I could endure. It maddened me. Try to make allowances for a man beside himself. I struck her.

The instant the blow was dealt, I repented it. She crouched down, silent, in a corner of the room, and eyed me steadily. It was a look that cooled my hot blood in an instant. There was no time now to think of making atonement. I could only risk the worst, and make sure of her till the funeral was over. I locked her into her bedroom.

When I came back, after laying my mother in the grave, I found her sitting by the bedside, very much altered in look and bearing, with a bundle on her lap. She faced me quietly; she spoke with a curious stillness in her voice—strangely and unnaturally composed in look and manner.

"No man has ever struck me yet," she said. "My husband shall have no second opportunity. Set the door open, and let me go."

She passed me, and left the room. I saw her walk away up the street. Was she gone for good?

All that night I watched and waited. No footstep came near the house. The next night, overcome with fatigue, I lay down on the bed in my clothes, with the door locked, the key on the table, and the candle burning. My slumber was not disturbed. The third night, the fourth, the fifth, the sixth, passed, and nothing happened. I lay down on the seventh night, still suspicious of something happening; still in my clothes; still with the door locked, the key on the table, and the candle burning.

My rest was disturbed. I awoke twice, without any sensation of uneasiness. The third time, that horrid shivering of the night at the lonely inn, that awful sinking pain at the heart, came back again, and roused me in an instant. My eyes turned to the left-hand side of the bed. And there stood, looking at me—

The Dream Woman again? No! My wife. The living woman, with the face of the Dream—in the attitude of the Dream—the fair arm up; the knife clasped in the delicate white hand.

I sprang upon her on the instant; but not quickly enough to stop her from hiding the knife. Without a word from me, without a cry from her, I pinioned her in a chair. With one hand I felt up her sleeve; and there, where the Dream Woman had hidden the knife, my wife had hidden it—the knife with the buckhorn handle, that looked like new.

What I felt when I made that discovery I could not realize at the time, and I can't describe now. I took one steady look at her with the knife in my hand. "You meant to kill me?" I said.

"Yes," she answered; "I meant to kill you." She crossed her arms over her bosom, and stared me coolly in the face. "I shall do it yet," she said. "With that knife."

I don't know what possessed me—I swear to you I am no coward; and yet I acted like a coward. The horrors got hold of me. I couldn't look at her—I couldn't speak to her. I left her (with the knife in my hand), and went out into the night.

There was a bleak wind abroad, and the smell of rain was in the air. The church clocks chimed the quarter as I walked beyond the last house in the town. I asked the first policeman I met what hour that was, of which the quarter past had just struck.

The man looked at his watch, and answered, "Two o'clock." Two in the morning. What day of the month was this day that had just begun? I reckoned it up from the date of my mother's funeral. The horrid parallel between the dream and the reality was complete—it was my birthday!

Had I escaped the mortal peril which the dream foretold? or had I only received a second warning? As that doubt crossed my mind I stopped on my way out of the town. The air had revived me—I felt in some degree like my own self again. After a little thinking, I began to see plainly the mistake I had made in leaving my wife free to go where she liked and to do as she pleased.

I turned instantly, and made my way back to the house. It was still dark. I had left the candle burning in the bedchamber. When I looked up to the window of the room now, there was no light in it. I advanced to the house door. On going away, I remembered to have closed it; on trying it now, I found it open.

I waited outside, never losing sight of the house till daylight. Then I ventured indoors—listened, and heard nothing—looked into the kitchen, scullery, parlor, and found nothing—went up at last into the bedroom. It was empty.

A picklock lay on the floor, which told me how she had gained entrance in the night. And that was the one trace I could find of the Dream Woman.

XIII

I waited in the house till the town was astir for the day, and then I went to consult a lawyer. In the confused state of my mind at the time, I had one clear notion of what I meant to do: I was determined to sell my house and leave the neighborhood. There were obstacles in the way which I had not counted on. I was told I had creditors to satisfy before I could leave—I, who had given my wife the money to pay my bills regularly every week! Inquiry showed that she had embezzled every farthing of the money I had intrusted to her. I had no choice but to pay over again.

Placed in this awkward position, my first duty was to set things right, with the help of my lawyer. During my forced sojourn in the town I did two foolish things. And, as a consequence that followed, I heard once more, and heard for the last time, of my wife.

In the first place, having got possession of the knife, I was rash enough to keep it in my pocket. In the second place, having something of importance to say to my lawyer, at a late hour of the evening, I went to his house after dark—alone and on foot. I got there safely enough. Returning, I was seized on from behind by two men, dragged down a passage and robbed—not only of the little money I had about me, but also of the knife. It was the lawyer's opinion (as it was mine) that the thieves were among the disreputable acquaintances formed by my wife, and that they had attacked me at her instigation. To confirm this view I received a letter the next day, without date or address, written in Alicia's hand. The first line informed me that the knife was back again in her possession. The second line reminded me of the day when I struck her. The third line warned me that she would wash out the stain of that blow in my blood, and repeated the words, "I shall do it with the knife!"

These things happened a year ago. The law laid hands on the men who had robbed me; but from that time to this, the law has failed completely to find a trace of my wife.

My story is told. When I had paid the creditors and paid the legal expenses, I had barely five pounds left out of the sale of my house; and I had the world to begin over again. Some months since—drifting here and there—I found my way to Underbridge. The landlord of the inn had known something of my father's family in times past. He gave me (all he had to give) my food, and shelter in the yard. Except on market days, there is nothing to do. In the coming winter the inn is to be shut up, and I shall have to shift for myself. My old master would help me if I applied to him—but I don't like to apply: he has done more for me already than I deserve. Besides, in another year who knows but my troubles may all be at an end? Next winter will bring me nigh to my next birthday, and my next birthday may be the day of my death. Yes! it's true I sat up all last night; and I heard two in the morning strike: and nothing happened. Still, allowing for that, the time to come is a time I don't trust. My wife has got the knife—my wife is looking for me. I am above superstition, mind! I don't say I believe in dreams; I only say, Alicia Warlock is looking for me. It is possible I may be wrong. It is possible I may be right. Who can tell?

THE THIRD NARRATIVE

THE STORY CONTINUED BY PERCY FAIRBANK

XIV

We took leave of Francis Raven at the door of Farleigh Hall, with the understanding that he might expect to hear from us again.

The same night Mrs. Fairbank and I had a discussion in the sanctuary of our own room. The topic was "The Hostler's Story"; and the question in dispute between us turned on the measure of charitable duty that we owed to the hostler himself.

The view I took of the man's narrative was of the purely matter-of-fact kind. Francis Raven had, in my opinion, brooded over the misty connection between his strange dream and his vile wife, until his mind was in a state of partial delusion on that subject. I was quite willing to help him with a trifle of money, and to recommend him to the kindness of my lawyer, if he was really in any danger and wanted advice. There my idea of my duty toward this afflicted person began and ended.

Confronted with this sensible view of the matter, Mrs. Fairbank's romantic temperament rushed, as usual, into extremes. "I should no more think of losing sight of Francis Raven when his next birthday comes round," says my wife, "than I should think of laying down a good story with the last chapters unread. I am positively determined, Percy, to take him back with us when we return to France, in the capacity of groom. What does one man more or less among the horses matter to people as rich as we are?" In this strain the partner of my joys and sorrows ran on, perfectly impenetrable to everything that I could say on the side of common sense. Need I tell my married brethren how it ended? Of course I allowed my wife to irritate me, and spoke to her sharply.

Of course my wife turned her face away indignantly on the conjugal pillow, and burst into tears. Of course upon that, "Mr." made his excuses, and "Mrs." had her own way.

Before the week was out we rode over to Underbridge, and duly offered to Francis Raven a place in our service as supernumerary groom.

At first the poor fellow seemed hardly able to realize his own extraordinary good fortune. Recovering himself, he expressed his gratitude modestly and becomingly. Mrs. Fairbank's ready sympathies overflowed, as usual, at her lips. She talked to him about our home in France, as if the worn, gray-headed hostler had been a child. "Such a dear old house, Francis; and such pretty gardens! Stables! Stables ten times as big as your stables here—quite a choice of rooms for you. You must learn the name of our house—

Maison Rouge. Our nearest town is Metz. We are within a walk of the beautiful River Moselle. And when we want a change we have only to take the railway to the frontier, and find ourselves in Germany."

Listening, so far, with a very bewildered face, Francis started and changed color when my wife reached the end of her last sentence. "Germany?" he repeated.

"Yes. Does Germany remind you of anything?"

The hostler's eyes looked down sadly on the ground. "Germany reminds me of my wife," he replied.

"Indeed! How?"

"She once told me she had lived in Germany—long before I knew her—in the time when she was a young girl."

"Was she living with relations or friends?"

"She was living as governess in a foreign family."

"In what part of Germany?"

"I don't remember, ma'am. I doubt if she told me."

"Did she tell you the name of the family?"

"Yes, ma'am. It was a foreign name, and it has slipped my memory long since. The head of the family was a wine grower in a large way of business—I remember that."

"Did you hear what sort of wine he grew? There are wine growers in our neighborhood. Was it Moselle wine?"

"I couldn't say, ma'am, I doubt if I ever heard."

There the conversation dropped. We engaged to communicate with Francis Raven before we left England, and took our leave. I had made arrangements to pay our round of visits to English friends, and to return to Maison Rouge in the summer. On the eve of departure, certain difficulties in connection with the management of some landed property of mine in Ireland obliged us to alter our plans. Instead of getting back to our house in France in the Summer, we only returned a week or two before Christmas. Francis Raven accompanied us, and was duly established, in the nominal capacity of stable keeper, among the servants at Maison Rouge.

Before long, some of the objections to taking him into our employment, which I had foreseen and had vainly mentioned to my wife, forced themselves on our attention in no very agreeable form. Francis Raven failed (as I had feared he would) to get on smoothly with his fellow-servants They were all French; and not one of them understood English. Francis, on his side, was equally ignorant of French. His reserved manners, his melancholy temperament, his solitary ways—all told against him. Our servants called him "the English Bear." He grew widely known in the neighborhood under his nickname. Quarrels took place, ending once or twice in blows. It became plain, even to Mrs. Fairbank herself, that some wise change must be made. While we were still considering what the change was to be, the unfortunate hostler was thrown on our hands for some time to come by an accident in the stables. Still pursued by his proverbial ill-luck, the poor wretch's leg was broken by a kick from a horse.

He was attended to by our own surgeon, in his comfortable bedroom at the stables. As the date of his birthday drew near, he was still confined to his bed.

Physically speaking, he was doing very well. Morally speaking, the surgeon was not satisfied. Francis Raven was suffering under some mysterious mental disturbance, which interfered seriously with his rest at night. Hearing this, I thought it my duty to tell the medical attendant what was preying on the patient's mind. As a practical man, he shared my opinion that the hostler was in a state of delusion on the subject of his Wife and his Dream. "Curable delusion, in my opinion," the surgeon added, "if the experiment could be fairly tried."

"How can it be tried?" I asked. Instead of replying, the surgeon put a question to me, on his side.

"Do you happen to know," he said, "that this year is Leap Year?"

"Mrs. Fairbank reminded me of it yesterday," I answered. "Otherwise I might *not* have known it."

"Do you think Francis Raven knows that this year is Leap Year?"

(I began to see dimly what my friend was driving at.)

"It depends," I answered, "on whether he has got an English almanac. Suppose he has *not* got the almanac—what then?"

"In that case," pursued the surgeon, "Francis Raven is innocent of all suspicion that there is a twenty-ninth day in February this year. As a necessary consequence—what will he do? He will anticipate the appearance of the Woman with the Knife, at two in the morning of the twenty-ninth of February, instead of the first of March. Let him suffer all his superstitious terrors on the wrong day. Leave him, on the day that is really his birthday, to pass a perfectly quiet night, and to be as sound asleep as other people at two in the morning. And then, when he wakes comfortably in time for his breakfast, shame him out of his delusion by telling him the truth."

I agreed to try the experiment. Leaving the surgeon to caution Mrs. Fairbank on the subject of Leap Year, I went to the stables to see Mr. Raven.

XV

The poor fellow was full of forebodings of the fate in store for him on the ominous first of March. He eagerly entreated me to order one of the men servants to sit up with him on the birthday morning. In granting his request, I asked him to tell me on which day of the week his birthday fell. He reckoned the days on his fingers; and proved his innocence of all suspicion that it was Leap Year, by fixing on the twenty-ninth of February, in the full persuasion that it was the first of March. Pledged to try the surgeon's experiment, I left his error uncorrected, of course. In so doing, I took my first step blindfold toward the last act in the drama of the Hostler's Dream.

The next day brought with it a little domestic difficulty, which indirectly and strangely associated itself with the coming end.

My wife received a letter, inviting us to assist in celebrating the "Silver Wedding" of two worthy German neighbors of ours—Mr. and Mrs. Beldheimer. Mr. Beldheimer was a large wine grower on the banks of the Moselle. His house was situated on the frontier line of France and Germany; and the distance from our house was sufficiently considerable to make it necessary for us to sleep under our host's roof. Under these circumstances, if we accepted the invitation, a comparison of dates showed that we should be away from home on the morning of the first of March. Mrs. Fairbank—holding to her absurd resolution to see with her own eyes what might, or might not, happen to Francis Raven on his birthday—flatly declined to leave Maison Rouge. "It's easy to send an excuse," she said, in her off-hand manner.

I failed, for my part, to see any easy way out of the difficulty. The celebration of a "Silver Wedding" in Germany is the celebration of twenty-five years of happy married life; and the host's claim upon the consideration of his friends on such an occasion is something in the nature of a royal "command." After considerable discussion, finding my wife's obstinacy invincible, and feeling that the absence of both of us from the festival would certainly offend our friends, I left Mrs. Fairbank to make her excuses for herself, and directed her to accept the invitation so far as I was concerned. In so doing, I took my second step, blindfold, toward the last act in the drama of the Hostler's Dream.

A week elapsed; the last days of February were at hand. Another domestic difficulty happened; and, again, this event also proved to be strangely associated with the coming end.

My head groom at the stables was one Joseph Rigobert. He was an ill-conditioned fellow, inordinately vain of his personal appearance, and by no means scrupulous in his conduct with women. His one virtue consisted of his fondness for horses, and in the care he took of the animals under his charge. In a word, he was too good a groom to be easily replaced, or he would have quitted my service long since. On the occasion of which I am now writing, he was reported to me by my steward as growing idle and disorderly in his habits. The principal offense alleged against him was, that he had been seen that day in the city of Metz, in the company of a woman (supposed to be an Englishwoman), whom he was entertaining at a tavern, when he ought to have been on his way back to Maison Rouge. The man's defense was that "the lady" (as he called her) was an English stranger, unacquainted with the ways of the place, and that he had only shown her where she could obtain some refreshments at her own request. I administered the necessary reprimand, without troubling myself to inquire further into the matter. In failing to do this, I took my third step, blindfold, toward the last act in the drama of the Hostler's Dream.

On the evening of the twenty-eighth, I informed the servants at the stables that one of them must watch through the night by the Englishman's bedside. Joseph Rigobert immediately volunteered for the duty—as a means, no doubt, of winning his way back to my favor. I accepted his proposal.

That day the surgeon dined with us. Toward midnight he and I left the smoking room, and repaired to Francis Raven's bedside. Rigobert was at his post, with no very agreeable expression on his face. The Frenchman and the Englishman had evidently not got on well together so far. Francis Raven lay helpless on his bed, waiting silently for two in the morning and the Dream Woman.

"I have come, Francis, to bid you good night," I said, cheerfully. "To-morrow morning I shall look in at breakfast time, before I leave home on a journey."

"Thank you for all your kindness, sir. You will not see me alive to-morrow morning. She will find me this time. Mark my words—she will find me this time."

"My good fellow! she couldn't find you in England. How in the world is she to find you in France?"

"It's borne in on my mind, sir, that she will find me here. At two in the morning on my birthday I shall see her again, and see her for the last time."

"Do you mean that she will kill you?"

"I mean that, sir, she will kill me—with the knife."

"And with Rigobert in the room to protect you?"

"I am a doomed man. Fifty Rigoberts couldn't protect me."

"And you wanted somebody to sit up with you?"

"Mere weakness, sir. I don't like to be left alone on my deathbed."

I looked at the surgeon. If he had encouraged me, I should certainly, out of sheer compassion, have confessed to Francis Raven the trick that we were playing him. The surgeon held to his experiment; the surgeon's face plainly said—"No."

The next day (the twenty-ninth of February) was the day of the "Silver Wedding." The first thing in the morning, I went to Francis Raven's room. Rigobert met me at the door.

"How has he passed the night?" I asked.

"Saying his prayers, and looking for ghosts," Rigobert answered. "A lunatic asylum is the only proper place for him."

I approached the bedside. "Well, Francis, here you are, safe and sound, in spite of what you said to me last night."

His eyes rested on mine with a vacant, wondering look.

"I don't understand it," he said.

"Did you see anything of your wife when the clock struck two?"

"No, sir."

"Did anything happen?"

"Nothing happened, sir."

"Doesn't *this* satisfy you that you were wrong?"

His eyes still kept their vacant, wondering look. He only repeated the words he had spoken already: "I don't understand it."

I made a last attempt to cheer him. "Come, come, Francis! keep a good heart. You will be out of bed in a fortnight."

He shook his head on the pillow. "There's something wrong," he said. "I don't expect you to believe me, sir. I only say there's something wrong—and time will show it."

I left the room. Half an hour later I started for Mr. Beldheimer's house; leaving the arrangements for the morning of the first of March in the hands of the doctor and my wife.

XVI

The one thing which principally struck me when I joined the guests at the "Silver Wedding" is also the one thing which it is necessary to mention here. On this joyful occasion a noticeable lady present was out of spirits. That lady was no other than the heroine of the festival, the mistress of the house!

In the course of the evening I spoke to Mr. Beldheimer's eldest son on the subject of his mother. As an old friend of the family, I had a claim on his confidence which the young man willingly recognized.

"We have had a very disagreeable matter to deal with," he said; "and my mother has not recovered the painful impression left on her mind. Many years since, when my sisters were children, we had an English governess in the house. She left us, as we then understood, to be married. We heard no more of her until a week or ten days since, when my mother received a letter, in which our ex-governess described herself as being in a condition of great poverty and distress. After much hesitation she had ventured—at the suggestion of a lady who had been kind to her—to write to her former employers, and to appeal to their remembrance of old times. You know my mother: she is not only the most kind-hearted, but the most innocent of women—it is impossible to persuade her of the wickedness that there is in the world. She replied by return of post, inviting the governess to come here and see her, and inclosing the money for her traveling expenses. When my father came home, and heard what had been done, he wrote at once to his agent in London to make inquiries, inclosing the address on the governess' letter. Before he could receive the agent's reply the governess, arrived. She produced the worst possible impression on his mind. The agent's letter, arriving a few days later, confirmed his suspicions. Since we had lost sight of her, the woman had led a most disreputable life. My father spoke to her privately: he offered—on condition of her leaving the house—a sum of money to take her back to England. If she refused, the alternative would be an appeal to the authorities and a public scandal. She accepted the money, and left the house. On her way back to England she appears to have stopped at Metz. You will understand what sort of woman she is when I tell you that she was seen the other day in a tavern, with your handsome groom, Joseph Rigobert."

While my informant was relating these circumstances, my memory was at work. I recalled what Francis Raven had vaguely told us of his wife's experience in former days as governess in a German family. A suspicion of the truth suddenly flashed across my mind. "What was the woman's name?" I asked.

Mr. Beldheimer's son answered: "Alicia Warlock."

I had but one idea when I heard that reply—to get back to my house without a moment's needless delay. It was then ten o'clock at night—the last train to Metz had left long since. I arranged with my young friend—after duly informing him of the circumstances— that I should go by the first train in the morning, instead of staying to breakfast with the other guests who slept in the house.

At intervals during the night I wondered uneasily how things were going on at Maison Rouge. Again and again the same question occurred to me, on my journey home in the early morning—the morning of the first of March. As the event proved, but one person in my house knew what really happened at the stables on Francis Raven's birthday. Let Joseph Rigobert take my place as narrator, and tell the story of the end to You—as he told it, in times past, to his lawyer and to Me.

FOURTH (AND LAST) NARRATIVE

STATEMENT OF JOSEPH RIGOBERT: ADDRESSED TO THE ADVOCATE WHO DEFENDED HIM AT HIS TRIAL

Respected Sir,—On the twenty-seventh of February I was sent, on business connected with the stables at Maison Rouge, to the city of Metz. On the public promenade I met a magnificent woman. Complexion, blond. Nationality, English. We mutually admired each other; we fell into conversation. (She spoke French perfectly—with the English accent.) I offered refreshment; my proposal was accepted. We had a long and interesting interview—we discovered that we were made for each other. So far, Who is to blame?

Is it my fault that I am a handsome man—universally agreeable as such to the fair sex? Is it a criminal offense to be accessible to the amiable weakness of love? I ask again, Who is to blame? Clearly, nature. Not the beautiful lady—not my humble self.

To resume. The most hard-hearted person living will understand that two beings made for each other could not possibly part without an appointment to meet again.

I made arrangements for the accommodation of the lady in the village near Maison Rouge. She consented to honor me with her company at supper, in my apartment at the stables, on the night of the twenty-ninth. The time fixed on was the time when the other servants were accustomed to retire—eleven o'clock.

Among the grooms attached to the stables was an Englishman, laid up with a broken leg. His name was Francis. His manners were repulsive; he was ignorant of the French language. In the kitchen he went by the nickname of the "English Bear." Strange to say, he was a great favorite with my master and my mistress. They even humored certain superstitious terrors to which this repulsive person was subject—terrors into the nature of which I, as an advanced freethinker, never thought it worth my while to inquire.

On the evening of the twenty-eighth the Englishman, being a prey to the terrors which I have mentioned, requested that one of his fellow servants might sit up with him for that night only. The wish that he expressed was backed by Mr. Fairbank's authority. Having already incurred my master's displeasure—in what way, a proper sense of my own dignity forbids me to relate—I volunteered to watch by the bedside of the English Bear. My object was to satisfy Mr. Fairbank that I bore no malice, on my side, after what had occurred between us. The wretched Englishman passed a night of delirium. Not understanding his barbarous language, I could only gather from his gesture that he was in deadly fear of some fancied apparition at his bedside. From time to time, when this madman disturbed my slumbers, I quieted him by swearing at him. This is the shortest and best way of dealing with persons in his condition.

On the morning of the twenty-ninth, Mr. Fairbank left us on a journey. Later in the day, to my unspeakable disgust, I found that I had not done with the Englishman yet. In Mr. Fairbank's absence, Mrs. Fairbank took an incomprehensible interest in the question of my delirious fellow servant's repose at night. Again, one or the other of us was to watch at his bedside, and report it, if anything happened. Expecting my fair friend to supper, it was necessary to make sure that the other servants at the stables would be safe in their beds that night. Accordingly, I volunteered once more to be the man who kept watch. Mrs. Fairbank complimented me on my humanity. I possess great command over my feelings. I accepted the compliment without a blush.

Twice, after nightfall, my mistress and the doctor (the last staying in the house in Mr. Fairbank's absence) came to make inquiries. Once *before* the arrival of my fair friend—and once *after*. On the second occasion (my apartment being next door to the Englishman's) I was obliged to hide my charming guest in the harness room. She consented, with angelic resignation, to immolate her dignity to the servile necessities of my position. A more amiable woman (so far) I never met with!

After the second visit I was left free. It was then close on midnight. Up to that time there was nothing in the behavior of the mad Englishman to reward Mrs. Fairbank and the doctor for presenting themselves at his bedside. He lay half awake, half asleep, with an odd wondering kind of look in his face. My mistress at parting warned me to be particularly watchful of him toward two in the morning. The doctor (in case anything happened) left me a large hand bell to ring, which could easily be heard at the house.

Restored to the society of my fair friend, I spread the

supper table. A pâté, a sausage, and a few bottles of generous Moselle wine, composed our simple meal. When persons adore each other, the intoxicating illusion of Love transforms the simplest meal into a banquet. With immeasurable capacities for enjoyment, we sat down to table. At the very moment when I placed my fascinating companion in a chair, the infamous Englishman in the next room took that occasion, of all others, to become restless and noisy once more. He struck with his stick on the floor; he cried out, in a delirious access of terror, "Rigobert! Rigobert!"

The sound of that lamentable voice, suddenly assailing our ears, terrified my fair friend. She lost all her charming color in an instant. "Good heavens!" she exclaimed. "Who is that in the next room?"

"A mad Englishman."

"An Englishman?"

"Compose yourself, my angel. I will quiet him."

The lamentable voice called out on me again, "Rigobert! Rigobert!"

My fair friend caught me by the arm. "Who is he?" she cried. "What is his name?"

Something in her face struck me as she put that question. A spasm of jealousy shook me to the soul. "You know him?" I said.

"His name!" she vehemently repeated; "his name!"

"Francis," I answered.

"Francis—*what*?"

I shrugged my shoulders. I could neither remember nor pronounce the barbarous English surname. I could only tell her it began with an "R."

She dropped back into the chair. Was she going to faint? No: she recovered, and more than recovered, her lost color.

Her eyes flashed superbly. What did it mean? Profoundly as I understand women in general, I was puzzled by *this* woman!

"You know him?" I repeated.

She laughed at me. "What nonsense! How should I know him? Go and quiet the wretch."

My looking-glass was near. One glance at it satisfied me that no woman in her senses could prefer the Englishman to Me. I recovered my self-respect. I hastened to the Englishman's bedside.

The moment I appeared he pointed eagerly toward my room. He overwhelmed me with a torrent of words in his own language. I made out, from his gestures and his looks, that he had, in some incomprehensible manner, discovered the presence of my guest; and, stranger still, that he was scared by the idea of a person in my room. I endeavored to compose him on the system which I have already mentioned— that is to say, I swore at him in *my* language. The result not proving satisfactory, I own I shook my fist in his face, and left the bedchamber.

Returning to my fair friend, I found her walking backward and forward in a state of excitement wonderful to behold. She had not waited for me to fill her glass—she had begun the generous Moselle in my absence. I prevailed on her with difficulty to place herself at the table. Nothing would induce her to eat. "My appetite is gone," she said. "Give me wine."

The generous Moselle deserves its name—delicate on the palate, with prodigious "body." The strength of this fine wine produced no stupefying effect on my remarkable guest. It appeared to strengthen and exhilarate her—nothing more. She always spoke in the same low tone, and always, turn the conversation as I might, brought it back with the same dexterity to the subject of the Englishman in the next room.

In any other woman this persistency would have offended me. My lovely guest was irresistible; I answered her questions with the docility of a child. She possessed all the amusing eccentricity of her nation. When I told her of the accident which confined the Englishman to his bed, she sprang to her feet. An extraordinary smile irradiated her countenance. She said, "Show me the horse who broke the Englishman's leg! I must see that horse!" I took her to the stables. She kissed the horse—on my word of honor, she kissed the horse! That struck me. I said. "You *do* know the man; and he has wronged you in some way." No! she would not admit it, even then. "I kiss all beautiful animals," she said. "Haven't I kissed *you*?" With that charming explanation of her conduct, she ran back up the stairs. I only remained behind to lock the stable door again. When I rejoined her, I made a startling discovery. I caught her coming out of the Englishman's room.

"I was just going downstairs again to call you," she said. "The man in there is getting noisy once more."

The mad Englishman's voice assailed our ears once again. "Rigobert! Rigobert!"

He was a frightful object to look at when I saw him this time. His eyes were staring wildly; the perspiration was pouring over his face. In a panic of terror he clasped his hands; he pointed up to heaven. By every sign and gesture that a man can make, he entreated me not to leave him again. I really could not help smiling. The idea of my staying with *him*, and leaving my fair friend by herself in the next room!

I turned to the door. When the mad wretch saw me leaving him he burst out into a screech of despair—so shrill that I feared it might awaken the sleeping servants.

My presence of mind in emergencies is proverbial among

those who know me. I tore open the cupboard in which he kept his linen—seized a handful of his handkerchiefs—gagged him with one of them, and secured his hands with the others. There was now no danger of his alarming the servants. After tying the last knot, I looked up.

The door between the Englishman's room and mine was open. My fair friend was standing on the threshold—watching *him* as he lay helpless on the bed; watching *me* as I tied the last knot.

"What are you doing there?" I asked. "Why did you open the door?"

She stepped up to me, and whispered her answer in my ear, with her eyes all the time upon the man on the bed:

"I heard him scream."

"Well?"

"I thought you had killed him."

I drew back from her in horror. The suspicion of me which her words implied was sufficiently detestable in itself. But her manner when she uttered the words was more revolting still. It so powerfully affected me that I started back from that beautiful creature as I might have recoiled from a reptile crawling over my flesh.

Before I had recovered myself sufficiently to reply, my nerves were assailed by another shock. I suddenly heard my mistress's voice calling to me from the stable yard.

There was no time to think—there was only time to act. The one thing needed was to keep Mrs. Fairbank from ascending the stairs, and discovering—not my lady guest only—but the Englishman also, gagged and bound on his bed. I instantly hurried to the yard. As I ran down the stairs I heard the stable clock strike the quarter to two in the morning.

My mistress was eager and agitated. The doctor (in

attendance on her) was smiling to himself, like a man amused at his own thoughts.

"Is Francis awake or asleep?" Mrs. Fairbank inquired.

"He has been a little restless, madam. But he is now quiet again. If he is not disturbed" (I added those words to prevent her from ascending the stairs), "he will soon fall off into a quiet sleep."

"Has nothing happened since I was here last?"

"Nothing, madam."

The doctor lifted his eyebrows with a comical look of distress. "Alas, alas, Mrs. Fairbank!" he said. "Nothing has happened! The days of romance are over!"

"It is not two o'clock yet," my mistress answered, a little irritably.

The smell of the stables was strong on the morning air. She put her handkerchief to her nose and led the way out of the yard by the north entrance—the entrance communicating with the gardens and the house. I was ordered to follow her, along with the doctor. Once out of the smell of the stables she began to question me again. She was unwilling to believe that nothing had occurred in her absence. I invented the best answers I could think of on the spur of the moment; and the doctor stood by laughing. So the minutes passed till the clock struck two. Upon that, Mrs. Fairbank announced her intention of personally visiting the Englishman in his room. To my great relief, the doctor interfered to stop her from doing this.

"You have heard that Francis is just falling asleep," he said. "If you enter his room you may disturb him. It is essential to the success of my experiment that he should have a good night's rest, and that he should own it himself, before I tell him the truth. I must request, madam, that you will not disturb the man. Rigobert will ring the alarm bell if anything happens."

My mistress was unwilling to yield. For the next five minutes, at least, there was a warm discussion between the two. In the end Mrs. Fairbank was obliged to give way—for the time. "In half an hour," she said, "Francis will either be sound asleep, or awake again. In half an hour I shall come back." She took the doctor's arm. They returned together to the house.

Left by myself, with half an hour before me, I resolved to take the Englishwoman back to the village—then, returning to the stables, to remove the gag and the bindings from Francis, and to let him screech to his heart's content. What would his alarming the whole establishment matter to *me* after I had got rid of the compromising presence of my guest?

Returning to the yard I heard a sound like the creaking of an open door on its hinges. The gate of the north entrance I had just closed with my own hand. I went round to the west entrance, at the back of the stables. It opened on a field crossed by two footpaths in Mr. Fairbank's grounds. The nearest footpath led to the village. The other led to the highroad and the river.

Arriving at the west entrance I found the door open—swinging to and fro slowly in the fresh morning breeze. I had myself locked and bolted that door after admitting my fair friend at eleven o'clock. A vague dread of something wrong stole its way into my mind. I hurried back to the stables.

I looked into my own room. It was empty. I went to the harness room. Not a sign of the woman was there. I returned to my room, and approached the door of the Englishman's bedchamber. Was it possible that she had remained there during my absence? An unaccountable reluctance to open the door made me hesitate, with my hand on the lock. I listened. There was not a sound inside. I called softly. There was no answer. I drew back a step, still hesitating. I noticed something dark moving slowly in the crevice between the

218

bottom of the door and the boarded floor. Snatching up the candle from the table, I held it low, and looked. The dark, slowly moving object was a stream of blood!

That horrid sight roused me. I opened the door. The Englishman lay on his bed—alone in the room. He was stabbed in two places—in the throat and in the heart. The weapon was left in the second wound. It was a knife of English manufacture, with a handle of buckhorn as good as new.

I instantly gave the alarm. Witnesses can speak to what followed. It is monstrous to suppose that I am guilty of the murder. I admit that I am capable of committing follies: but I shrink from the bare idea of a crime. Besides, I had no motive for killing the man. The woman murdered him in my absence. The woman escaped by the west entrance while I was talking to my mistress. I have no more to say. I swear to you what I have here written is a true statement of all that happened on the morning of the first of March.

Accept, sir, the assurance of my sentiments of profound gratitude and respect.

JOSEPH RIGOBERT.

LAST LINES.

—ADDED BY PERCY FAIRBANK

Tried for the murder of Francis Raven, Joseph Rigobert was found Not Guilty; the papers of the assassinated man presented ample evidence of the deadly animosity felt toward him by his wife.

The investigations pursued on the morning when the crime was committed showed that the murderess, after leaving the stable, had taken the footpath which led to the river. The river was dragged—without result. It remains doubtful to this day whether she died by drowning or not. The one thing certain is—that Alicia Warlock was never seen again.

So—beginning in mystery, ending in mystery—the Dream Woman passes from your view. Ghost; demon; or living human creature—say for yourselves which she is. Or, knowing what unfathomed wonders are around you, what unfathomed wonders are *in* you, let the wise words of the greatest of all poets be explanation enough:

"We are such stuff
As dreams are made of, and our little life
Is rounded with, a sleep."

PART V

THE DEVIL

GOBLIN MARKET

BY
CHRISTINA ROSSETTI

Morning and evening
Maids heard the goblins cry:
"Come buy our orchard fruits,
Come buy, come buy:
Apples and quinces,
Lemons and oranges,
Plump unpeck'd cherries,
Melons and raspberries,
Bloom-down-cheek'd peaches,
Swart-headed mulberries,
Wild free-born cranberries,
Crab-apples, dewberries,
Pine-apples, blackberries,
Apricots, strawberries;—
All ripe together
In summer weather,—
Morns that pass by,
Fair eves that fly;
Come buy, come buy:
Our grapes fresh from the vine,
Pomegranates full and fine,

Dates and sharp bullaces,
Rare pears and greengages,
Damsons and bilberries,
Taste them and try:
Currants and gooseberries,
Bright-fire-like barberries,
Figs to fill your mouth,
Citrons from the South,
Sweet to tongue and sound to eye;
Come buy, come buy."

Evening by evening
Among the brookside rushes,
Laura bow'd her head to hear,
Lizzie veil'd her blushes:
Crouching close together
In the cooling weather,
With clasping arms and cautioning lips,
With tingling cheeks and finger tips.
"Lie close," Laura said,
Pricking up her golden head:
"We must not look at goblin men,
We must not buy their fruits:
Who knows upon what soil they fed
Their hungry thirsty roots?"
"Come buy," call the goblins
Hobbling down the glen.

"Oh," cried Lizzie, "Laura, Laura,
You should not peep at goblin men."
Lizzie cover'd up her eyes,
Cover'd close lest they should look;

Laura rear'd her glossy head,
And whisper'd like the restless brook:
"Look, Lizzie, look, Lizzie,
Down the glen tramp little men.
One hauls a basket,
One bears a plate,
One lugs a golden dish
Of many pounds weight.
How fair the vine must grow
Whose grapes are so luscious;
How warm the wind must blow
Through those fruit bushes."
"No," said Lizzie, "No, no, no;
Their offers should not charm us,
Their evil gifts would harm us."
She thrust a dimpled finger
In each ear, shut eyes and ran:
Curious Laura chose to linger
Wondering at each merchant man.
One had a cat's face,
One whisk'd a tail,
One tramp'd at a rat's pace,
One crawl'd like a snail,
One like a wombat prowl'd obtuse and furry,
One like a ratel tumbled hurry skurry.
She heard a voice like voice of doves
Cooing all together:
They sounded kind and full of loves
In the pleasant weather.

Laura stretch'd her gleaming neck
Like a rush-imbedded swan,

Like a lily from the beck,
Like a moonlit poplar branch,
Like a vessel at the launch
When its last restraint is gone.

Backwards up the mossy glen
Turn'd and troop'd the goblin men,
With their shrill repeated cry,
"Come buy, come buy."
When they reach'd where Laura was
They stood stock still upon the moss,
Leering at each other,
Brother with queer brother;
Signalling each other,
Brother with sly brother.
One set his basket down,
One rear'd his plate;
One began to weave a crown
Of tendrils, leaves, and rough nuts brown
(Men sell not such in any town);
One heav'd the golden weight
Of dish and fruit to offer her:
"Come buy, come buy," was still their cry.
Laura stared but did not stir,
Long'd but had no money:
The whisk-tail'd merchant bade her taste
In tones as smooth as honey,
The cat-faced purr'd,
The rat-faced spoke a word
Of welcome, and the snail-paced even was
    heard;
One parrot-voiced and jolly

Cried "Pretty Goblin" still for "Pretty Polly;"—
One whistled like a bird.

But sweet-tooth Laura spoke in haste:
"Good folk, I have no coin;
To take were to purloin:
I have no copper in my purse,
I have no silver either,
And all my gold is on the furze
That shakes in windy weather
Above the rusty heather."
"You have much gold upon your head,"
They answer'd all together:
"Buy from us with a golden curl."
She clipp'd a precious golden lock,
She dropp'd a tear more rare than pearl,
Then suck'd their fruit globes fair or red:
Sweeter than honey from the rock,
Stronger than man-rejoicing wine,
Clearer than water flow'd that juice;
She never tasted such before,
How should it cloy with length of use?
She suck'd and suck'd and suck'd the more
Fruits which that unknown orchard bore;
She suck'd until her lips were sore;
Then flung the emptied rinds away
But gather'd up one kernel stone,
And knew not was it night or day
As she turn'd home alone.

Lizzie met her at the gate
Full of wise upbraidings:

"Dear, you should not stay so late,
Twilight is not good for maidens;
Should not loiter in the glen
In the haunts of goblin men.
Do you not remember Jeanie,
How she met them in the moonlight,
Took their gifts both choice and many,
Ate their fruits and wore their flowers
Pluck'd from bowers
Where summer ripens at all hours?
But ever in the noonlight
She pined and pined away;
Sought them by night and day,
Found them no more, but dwindled and grew grey;
Then fell with the first snow,
While to this day no grass will grow
Where she lies low:
I planted daisies there a year ago
That never blow.
You should not loiter so."
"Nay, hush," said Laura:
"Nay, hush, my sister:
I ate and ate my fill,
Yet my mouth waters still;
To-morrow night I will
Buy more;" and kiss'd her:
"Have done with sorrow;
I'll bring you plums to-morrow
Fresh on their mother twigs,
Cherries worth getting;
You cannot think what figs
My teeth have met in,

What melons icy-cold
Piled on a dish of gold
Too huge for me to hold,
What peaches with a velvet nap,
Pellucid grapes without one seed:
Odorous indeed must be the mead
Whereon they grow, and pure the wave they drink
With lilies at the brink,
And sugar-sweet their sap."

Golden head by golden head,
Like two pigeons in one nest
Folded in each other's wings,
They lay down in their curtain'd bed:
Like two blossoms on one stem,
Like two flakes of new-fall'n snow,
Like two wands of ivory
Tipp'd with gold for awful kings.
Moon and stars gaz'd in at them,
Wind sang to them lullaby,
Lumbering owls forbore to fly,
Not a bat flapp'd to and fro
Round their rest:
Cheek to cheek and breast to breast
Lock'd together in one nest.

Early in the morning
When the first cock crow'd his warning,
Neat like bees, as sweet and busy,
Laura rose with Lizzie:
Fetch'd in honey, milk'd the cows,
Air'd and set to rights the house,

Kneaded cakes of whitest wheat,
Cakes for dainty mouths to eat,
Next churn'd butter, whipp'd up cream,
Fed their poultry, sat and sew'd;
Talk'd as modest maidens should:
Lizzie with an open heart,
Laura in an absent dream,
One content, one sick in part;
One warbling for the mere bright day's delight,
One longing for the night.

At length slow evening came:
They went with pitchers to the reedy brook;
Lizzie most placid in her look,
Laura most like a leaping flame.
They drew the gurgling water from its deep;
Lizzie pluck'd purple and rich golden flags,
Then turning homeward said: "The sunset flushes
Those furthest loftiest crags;
Come, Laura, not another maiden lags.
No wilful squirrel wags,
The beasts and birds are fast asleep."
But Laura loiter'd still among the rushes
And said the bank was steep.

And said the hour was early still
The dew not fall'n, the wind not chill;
Listening ever, but not catching
The customary cry,
"Come buy, come buy,"
With its iterated jingle
Of sugar-baited words:

Not for all her watching
Once discerning even one goblin
Racing, whisking, tumbling, hobbling;
Let alone the herds
That used to tramp along the glen,
In groups or single,
Of brisk fruit-merchant men.

Till Lizzie urged, "O Laura, come;
I hear the fruit-call but I dare not look:
You should not loiter longer at this brook:
Come with me home.
The stars rise, the moon bends her arc,
Each glowworm winks her spark,
Let us get home before the night grows dark:
For clouds may gather
Though this is summer weather,
Put out the lights and drench us through;
Then if we lost our way what should we do?"

Laura turn'd cold as stone
To find her sister heard that cry alone,
That goblin cry,
"Come buy our fruits, come buy."
Must she then buy no more such dainty fruit?
Must she no more such succous pasture find,
Gone deaf and blind?
Her tree of life droop'd from the root:
She said not one word in her heart's sore ache;
But peering thro' the dimness, nought discerning,
Trudg'd home, her pitcher dripping all the way;
So crept to bed, and lay

Silent till Lizzie slept;
Then sat up in a passionate yearning,
And gnash'd her teeth for baulk'd desire, and
    wept
As if her heart would break.

Day after day, night after night,
Laura kept watch in vain
In sullen silence of exceeding pain.
She never caught again the goblin cry:
"Come buy, come buy;"—
She never spied the goblin men
Hawking their fruits along the glen:
But when the noon wax'd bright
Her hair grew thin and grey;
She dwindled, as the fair full moon doth
    turn
To swift decay and burn
Her fire away.

One day remembering her kernel-stone
She set it by a wall that faced the south;
Dew'd it with tears, hoped for a root,
Watch'd for a waxing shoot,
But there came none;
It never saw the sun,
It never felt the trickling moisture run:
While with sunk eyes and faded mouth
She dream'd of melons, as a traveller sees
False waves in desert drouth
With shade of leaf-crown'd trees,
And burns the thirstier in the sandful breeze.

She no more swept the house,
Tended the fowls or cows,
Fetch'd honey, kneaded cakes of wheat,
Brought water from the brook:
But sat down listless in the chimney-nook
And would not eat.

Tender Lizzie could not bear
To watch her sister's cankerous care
Yet not to share.
She night and morning
Caught the goblins' cry:
"Come buy our orchard fruits,
Come buy, come buy;"—
Beside the brook, along the glen,
She heard the tramp of goblin men,
The yoke and stir
Poor Laura could not hear;
Long'd to buy fruit to comfort her,
But fear'd to pay too dear.
She thought of Jeanie in her grave,
Who should have been a bride;
But who for joys brides hope to have
Fell sick and died
In her gay prime,
In earliest winter time
With the first glazing rime,
With the first snow-fall of crisp winter time.

Till Laura dwindling
Seem'd knocking at Death's door:
Then Lizzie weigh'd no more

Better and worse;
But put a silver penny in her purse,
Kiss'd Laura, cross'd the heath with clumps of furze
At twilight, halted by the brook:
And for the first time in her life
Began to listen and look.

Laugh'd every goblin
When they spied her peeping:
Came towards her hobbling,
Flying, running, leaping,
Puffing and blowing,
Chuckling, clapping, crowing,
Clucking and gobbling,
Mopping and mowing,
Full of airs and graces,
Pulling wry faces,
Demure grimaces,
Cat-like and rat-like,
Ratel- and wombat-like,
Snail-paced in a hurry,
Parrot-voiced and whistler,
Helter skelter, hurry skurry,
Chattering like magpies,
Fluttering like pigeons,
Gliding like fishes,—
Hugg'd her and kiss'd her:
Squeez'd and caress'd her:
Stretch'd up their dishes,
Panniers, and plates:
"Look at our apples
Russet and dun,

Bob at our cherries,
Bite at our peaches,
Citrons and dates,
Grapes for the asking,
Pears red with basking
Out in the sun,
Plums on their twigs;
Pluck them and suck them,
Pomegranates, figs."—

"Good folk," said Lizzie,
Mindful of Jeanie:
"Give me much and many: —
Held out her apron,
Toss'd them her penny.
"Nay, take a seat with us,
Honour and eat with us,"
They answer'd grinning:
"Our feast is but beginning.
Night yet is early,
Warm and dew-pearly,
Wakeful and starry:
Such fruits as these
No man can carry:
Half their bloom would fly,
Half their dew would dry,
Half their flavour would pass by.
Sit down and feast with us,
Be welcome guest with us,
Cheer you and rest with us."—
"Thank you," said Lizzie: "But one waits
At home alone for me:

So without further parleying,
If you will not sell me any
Of your fruits though much and many,
Give me back my silver penny
I toss'd you for a fee."—
They began to scratch their pates,
No longer wagging, purring,
But visibly demurring,
Grunting and snarling.
One call'd her proud,
Cross-grain'd, uncivil;
Their tones wax'd loud,
Their looks were evil.
Lashing their tails
They trod and hustled her,
Elbow'd and jostled her,
Claw'd with their nails,
Barking, mewing, hissing, mocking,
Tore her gown and soil'd her stocking,
Twitch'd her hair out by the roots,
Stamp'd upon her tender feet,
Held her hands and squeez'd their fruits
Against her mouth to make her eat.

White and golden Lizzie stood,
Like a lily in a flood,—
Like a rock of blue-vein'd stone
Lash'd by tides obstreperously,—
Like a beacon left alone
In a hoary roaring sea,
Sending up a golden fire,—
Like a fruit-crown'd orange-tree

White with blossoms honey-sweet
Sore beset by wasp and bee,—
Like a royal virgin town
Topp'd with gilded dome and spire
Close beleaguer'd by a fleet
Mad to tug her standard down.

One may lead a horse to water,
Twenty cannot make him drink.
Though the goblins cuff'd and caught her,
Coax'd and fought her,
Bullied and besought her,
Scratch'd her, pinch'd her black as ink,
Kick'd and knock'd her,
Maul'd and mock'd her,
Lizzie utter'd not a word;
Would not open lip from lip
Lest they should cram a mouthful in:
But laugh'd in heart to feel the drip
Of juice that syrupp'd all her face,
And lodg'd in dimples of her chin,
And streak'd her neck which quaked like curd.
At last the evil people,
Worn out by her resistance,
Flung back her penny, kick'd their fruit
Along whichever road they took,
Not leaving root or stone or shoot;
Some writh'd into the ground,
Some div'd into the brook
With ring and ripple,
Some scudded on the gale without a sound,
Some vanish'd in the distance.

In a smart, ache, tingle,
Lizzie went her way;
Knew not was it night or day;
Sprang up the bank, tore thro' the furze,
Threaded copse and dingle,
And heard her penny jingle
Bouncing in her purse,—
Its bounce was music to her ear.
She ran and ran
As if she fear'd some goblin man
Dogg'd her with gibe or curse
Or something worse:
But not one goblin scurried after,
Nor was she prick'd by fear;
The kind heart made her windy-paced
That urged her home quite out of breath with haste
And inward laughter.

She cried, "Laura," up the garden,
"Did you miss me?
Come and kiss me.
Never mind my bruises,
Hug me, kiss me, suck my juices
Squeez'd from goblin fruits for you,
Goblin pulp and goblin dew.
Eat me, drink me, love me;
Laura, make much of me;
For your sake I have braved the glen
And had to do with goblin merchant men."

Laura started from her chair,
Flung her arms up in the air,

Clutch'd her hair:
"Lizzie, Lizzie, have you tasted
For my sake the fruit forbidden?
Must your light like mine be hidden,
Your young life like mine be wasted,
Undone in mine undoing,
And ruin'd in my ruin,
Thirsty, canker'd, goblin-ridden?"—
She clung about her sister,
Kiss'd and kiss'd and kiss'd her:
Tears once again
Refresh'd her shrunken eyes,
Dropping like rain
After long sultry drouth;
Shaking with aguish fear, and pain,
She kiss'd and kiss'd her with a hungry
   mouth.

Her lips began to scorch,
That juice was wormwood to her tongue,
She loath'd the feast:
Writhing as one possess'd she leap'd and sung,
Rent all her robe, and wrung
Her hands in lamentable haste,
And beat her breast.
Her locks stream'd like the torch
Borne by a racer at full speed,
Or like the mane of horses in their flight,
Or like an eagle when she stems the light
Straight toward the sun,
Or like a caged thing freed,
Or like a flying flag when armies run.

Swift fire spread through her veins, knock'd at her heart,
Met the fire smouldering there
And overbore its lesser flame;
She gorged on bitterness without a name:
Ah! fool, to choose such part
Of soul-consuming care!
Sense fail'd in the mortal strife:
Like the watch-tower of a town
Which an earthquake shatters down,
Like a lightning-stricken mast,
Like a wind-uprooted tree
Spun about,
Like a foam-topp'd waterspout
Cast down headlong in the sea,
She fell at last;
Pleasure past and anguish past,
Is it death or is it life?

Life out of death.
That night long Lizzie watch'd by her,
Counted her pulse's flagging stir,
Felt for her breath,
Held water to her lips, and cool'd her face
With tears and fanning leaves:
But when the first birds chirp'd about their eaves,
And early reapers plodded to the place
Of golden sheaves,
And dew-wet grass
Bow'd in the morning winds so brisk to pass,
And new buds with new day
Open'd of cup-like lilies on the stream,
Laura awoke as from a dream,

Laugh'd in the innocent old way,
Hugg'd Lizzie but not twice or thrice;
Her gleaming locks show'd not one thread of
    grey,
Her breath was sweet as May
And light danced in her eyes.

Days, weeks, months, years
Afterwards, when both were wives
With children of their own;
Their mother-hearts beset with fears,
Their lives bound up in tender lives;
Laura would call the little ones
And tell them of her early prime,
Those pleasant days long gone
Of not-returning time:
Would talk about the haunted glen,
The wicked, quaint fruit-merchant men,
Their fruits like honey to the throat
But poison in the blood;
(Men sell not such in any town):
Would tell them how her sister stood
In deadly peril to do her good,
And win the fiery antidote:
Then joining hands to little hands
Would bid them cling together,
"For there is no friend like a sister
In calm or stormy weather;
To cheer one on the tedious way,
To fetch one if one goes astray,
To lift one if one totters down,
To strengthen whilst one stands."

THE TAPESTRIED CHAMBER

BY

SIR WALTER SCOTT

T he following narrative is given from the pen, so far as
memory permits, in the same character in which it was
presented to the author's ear; nor has he claim to further
praise, or to be more deeply censured, than in proportion to the
good or bad judgment which he has employed in selecting his
materials, as he has studiously avoided any attempt at ornament
which might interfere with the simplicity of the tale.

At the same time, it must be admitted that the particular class
of stories which turns on the marvellous possesses a stronger influence when told than when committed to print. The volume taken
up at noonday, though rehearsing the same incidents, conveys a
much more feeble impression than is achieved by the voice of the
speaker on a circle of fireside auditors, who hang upon the narrative
as the narrator details the minute incidents which serve to give it
authenticity, and lowers his voice with an affectation of mystery
while he approaches the fearful and wonderful part. It was with
such advantages that the present writer heard the following events
related, more than twenty years since, by the celebrated Miss Seward
of Litchfield, who, to her numerous accomplishments, added, in a
remarkable degree, the power of narrative in private conversation.
In its present form the tale must necessarily lose all the interest

which was attached to it by the flexible voice and intelligent features of the gifted narrator. Yet still, read aloud to an undoubting audience by the doubtful light of the closing evening, or in silence by a decaying taper, and amidst the solitude of a half-lighted apartment, it may redeem its character as a good ghost story. Miss Seward always affirmed that she had derived her information from an authentic source, although she suppressed the names of the two persons chiefly concerned. I will not avail myself of any particulars I may have since received concerning the localities of the detail, but suffer them to rest under the same general description in which they were first related to me; and for the same reason I will not add to or diminish the narrative by any circumstance, whether more or less material, but simply rehearse, as I heard it, a story of supernatural terror.

About the end of the American war, when the officers of Lord Cornwallis's army, which surrendered at Yorktown, and others, who had been made prisoners during the impolitic and ill-fated controversy, were returning to their own country, to relate their adventures, and repose themselves after their fatigues, there was amongst them a general officer, to whom Miss S. gave the name of Browne, but merely, as I understood, to save the inconvenience of introducing a nameless agent in the narrative. He was an officer of merit, as well as a gentleman of high consideration for family and attainments.

Some business had carried General Browne upon a tour through the western counties, when, in the conclusion of a morning stage, he found himself in the vicinity of a small country town, which presented a scene of uncommon beauty, and of a character peculiarly English.

The little town, with its stately old church, whose tower bore testimony to the devotion of ages long past, lay amidst pastures and cornfields of small extent, but bounded and divided with hedgerow timber of great age and size. There were few marks of modern improvement. The environs of the place intimated neither the solitude of decay nor the bustle of novelty; the houses were old, but in good repair; and the beautiful little river murmured freely on its way to the left of the town, neither restrained by a dam nor bordered by a towing-path.

Upon a gentle eminence, nearly a mile to the southward of the town, were seen, amongst many venerable oaks and tangled thickets, the turrets of a castle as old as the walls of York and Lancaster, but which seemed to have received important alterations during the age of Elizabeth and her successor, It had not been a place of great size; but whatever accommodation it formerly afforded was, it must be supposed, still to be obtained within its walls. At least, such was the inference which General Browne drew from observing the smoke arise merrily from several of the ancient wreathed and carved chimney-stalks. The wall of the park ran alongside of the highway for two or three hundred yards; and through the different points by which the eye found glimpses into the woodland scenery, it seemed to be well stocked. Other points of view opened in succession—now a full one of the front of the old castle, and now a side glimpse at its particular towers, the former rich in all the bizarrerie of the Elizabethan school, while the simple and solid strength of other parts of the building seemed to show that they had been raised more for defence than ostentation.

Delighted with the partial glimpses which he obtained of the castle through the woods and glades by which this ancient feudal fortress was surrounded, our military traveller was determined to inquire whether it might not deserve a nearer view, and whether it contained family pictures or other objects of curiosity worthy of a stranger's visit, when, leaving the vicinity of the park, he rolled through a clean and well-paved street, and stopped at the door of a well-frequented inn.

Before ordering horses, to proceed on his journey, General Browne made inquiries concerning the proprietor of the chateau which had so attracted his admiration, and was equally surprised and pleased at hearing in reply a nobleman named, whom we shall call Lord Woodville. How fortunate! Much of Browne's early recollections, both at school and at college, had been connected with young Woodville, whom, by a few questions, he now ascertained to be the same with the owner of this fair domain. He had been raised to the peerage by the decease of his father a few months before, and, as the General learned from the landlord, the term of mourning being ended, was now taking possession of his paternal estate in the jovial season of merry, autumn, accompanied by a select party of friends, to enjoy the sports of a country famous for game.

This was delightful news to our traveller. Frank Woodville had been Richard Browne's fag at Eton, and his chosen intimate at Christ Church; their pleasures and their tasks had been the same; and the honest soldier's heart warmed to find his early friend in possession of so delightful a residence, and of an estate, as the landlord assured him with a nod and a wink, fully adequate to maintain and add to his dignity. Nothing was more natural than that the traveller should suspend a journey, which there was nothing to render hurried, to pay a visit to an old friend under such agreeable circumstances.

The fresh horses, therefore, had only the brief task of conveying the General's travelling carriage to Woodville Castle. A porter admitted them at a modern Gothic lodge, built in that style to correspond with the castle itself, and at the same time rang a bell to give warning of the approach of visitors. Apparently the sound of the bell had suspended the separation of the company, bent on the various amusements of the morning; for, on entering the court of the chateau, several young men were lounging about in their sporting dresses, looking at and criticizing the dogs which the keepers held in readiness to attend their pastime. As General Browne alighted, the young lord came to the gate of the hall, and for an instant gazed, as at a stranger, upon the countenance of his friend, on which war, with its fatigues and its wounds, had made a great alteration. But the uncertainty lasted no longer than till the visitor had spoken, and the hearty greeting which followed was such as can only be exchanged betwixt those who have passed together the merry days of careless boyhood or early youth.

"If I could have formed a wish, my dear Browne," said Lord Woodville, "it would have been to have you here, of all men, upon this occasion, which my friends are good enough to hold as a sort of holiday. Do not think you have been unwatched during the years you have been absent from us. I have traced you through your dangers, your triumphs, your misfortunes, and was delighted to see that, whether in victory or defeat, the name of my old friend was always distinguished with applause."

The General made a suitable reply, and congratulated his friend on his new dignities, and the possession of a place and domain so beautiful.

"Nay, you have seen nothing of it as yet," said Lord Woodville, "and I trust you do not mean to leave us till you are better acquainted with it. It is true, I confess, that my present party is pretty large, and the old house, like other places of the kind, does not possess so much accommodation as the extent of the outward walls appears to promise. But we can give you a comfortable old-fashioned room, and I venture to suppose that your campaigns have taught you to be glad of worse quarters."

The General shrugged his shoulders, and laughed. "I presume," he said, "the worst apartment in your chateau is considerably superior to the old tobacco-cask in which I was fain to take up my night's lodging when I was in the Bush, as the Virginians call it, with the light corps. There I lay, like Diogenes himself, so delighted with my covering from the elements, that I made a vain attempt to have it rolled on to my next quarters; but my commander for the time would give way to no such luxurious provision, and I took farewell of my beloved cask with tears in my eyes."

"Well, then, since you do not fear your quarters," said Lord Woodville, "you will stay with me a week at least. Of guns, dogs, fishing-rods, flies, and means of sport by sea and land, we have enough and to spare—you cannot pitch on an amusement but we will find the means of pursuing it. But if you prefer the gun and pointers, I will go with you myself, and see whether you have mended your shooting since you have been amongst the Indians of the back settlements."

The General gladly accepted his friendly host's proposal in all its points. After a morning of manly exercise, the company met at dinner, where it was the delight of Lord Woodville to conduce to the display of the high properties of his recovered friend, so as to recommend him to his guests, most of whom were persons of distinction. He led General Browne to speak of the scenes he had witnessed; and as every word marked alike the brave officer and the sensible man, who retained possession of his cool judgment under the most imminent dangers, the company looked upon the soldier with general respect, as on one who had proved himself possessed of an uncommon portion of personal courage—that attribute of all others of which everybody desires to be thought possessed.

The day at Woodville Castle ended as usual in such mansions. The hospitality stopped within the limits of good order. Music, in which the young lord was a proficient, succeeded to the circulation of the bottle; cards and billiards, for those who preferred such amusements, were in readiness; but the exercise of the morning required early hours, and not long after eleven o'clock the guests began to retire to their several apartments.

The young lord himself conducted his friend, General Browne, to the chamber destined for him, which answered the description he had given of it, being comfortable, but old-fashioned, The bed was of the massive form used in the end of the seventeenth century, and the curtains of faded silk, heavily trimmed with tarnished gold. But then the sheets, pillows, and blankets looked delightful to the campaigner, when he thought of his "mansion, the cask." There was an air of gloom in the tapestry hangings, which, with their worn-out graces, curtained the walls of the little chamber, and gently undulated as the autumnal breeze found its way through the ancient lattice window, which pattered and whistled as the air gained entrance. The toilet, too, with its mirror, turbaned after the manner of the beginning of the century, with a coiffure of murrey-coloured silk, and its hundred strange-shaped boxes, providing for arrangements which had been obsolete for more than fifty years, had an antique, and in so far a melancholy, aspect. But nothing could blaze more brightly and cheerfully than the two large wax candles; or if aught could rival them, it was the flaming, bickering fagots in the chimney, that sent at once their gleam and their warmth through the snug apartment, which, notwithstanding the general antiquity of its appearance, was not wanting in the least convenience that modern habits rendered either necessary or desirable.

"This is an old-fashioned sleeping apartment, General," said the young lord; "but I hope you find nothing that makes you envy your old tobacco-cask."

"I am not particular respecting my lodgings," replied the General; "yet were I to make any choice, I would prefer this chamber by many degrees to the gayer and more modern rooms of your family mansion. Believe me that, when I unite its modern air of comfort with its venerable antiquity, and recollect that it is your lordship's property, I shall feel in better quarters here than if I were in the best hotel London could afford."

"I trust—I have no doubt—that you will find yourself as

comfortable as I wish you, my dear General," said the young nobleman; and once more bidding his guest good-night, he shook him by the hand, and withdrew.

The General once more looked round him, and internally congratulating himself on his return to peaceful life, the comforts of which were endeared by the recollection of the hardships and dangers he had lately sustained, undressed himself, and prepared for a luxurious night's rest.

Here, contrary to the custom of this species of tale, we leave the General in possession of his apartment until the next morning.

The company assembled for breakfast at an early hour, but without the appearance of General Browne, who seemed the guest that Lord Woodville was desirous of honouring above all whom his hospitality had assembled around him. He more than once expressed surprise at the General's absence, and at length sent a servant to make inquiry after him. The man brought back information that General Browne had been walking abroad since an early hour of the morning, in defiance of the weather, which was misty and ungenial.

"The custom of a soldier," said the young nobleman to his friends. "Many of them acquire habitual vigilance, and cannot sleep after the early hour at which their duty usually commands them to be alert."

Yet the explanation which Lord Woodville thus offered to the company seemed hardly satisfactory to his own mind, and it was in a fit of silence and abstraction that he waited the return of the General. It took place near an hour after the breakfast bell had rung. He looked fatigued and feverish. His hair, the powdering and arrangement of which was at this time one of the most important occupations of a man's whole day, and marked his fashion as much as in the present time the tying of a cravat, or the want of one, was dishevelled, uncurled, void of powder, and dank with dew. His clothes were huddled on with a careless negligence, remarkable in a military man, whose real or supposed duties are usually held to include some attention to the toilet; and his looks were haggard and ghastly in a peculiar degree.

"So you have stolen a march upon us this morning, my dear General," said Lord Woodville; "or you have not found your bed so much to your mind as I had hoped and you seemed to expect. How did you rest last night?"

"Oh, excellently well! remarkably well! never better in my life," said General Browne rapidly, and yet with an air of embarrassment which was obvious to his friend. He then hastily swallowed a cup of tea, and neglecting or refusing whatever else was offered, seemed to fall into a fit of abstraction.

"You will take the gun to-day, General?" said his friend and host, but had to repeat the question twice ere he received the abrupt answer, "No, my lord; I am sorry I cannot have the opportunity of spending another day with your lordship; my post horses are ordered, and will be here directly."

All who were present showed surprise, and Lord Woodville immediately replied "Post horses, my good friend! What can you possibly want with them when you promised to stay with me quietly for at least a week?"

"I believe," said the General, obviously much embarrassed, "that I might, in the pleasure of my first meeting with your lordship, have said something about stopping here a few days; but I have since found it altogether impossible."

"That is very extraordinary," answered the young nobleman. "You seemed quite disengaged yesterday, and you cannot have had a summons to-day, for our post has not come up from the town, and therefore you cannot have received any letters."

General Browne, without giving any further explanation, muttered something about indispensable business, and insisted on the absolute necessity of his departure in a manner which silenced all opposition on the part of his host, who saw that his resolution was taken, and forbore all further importunity.

"At least, however," he said, "permit me, my dear Browne, since go you will or must, to show you the view from the terrace, which the mist, that is now rising, will soon display."

He threw open a sash-window, and stepped down upon the terrace as he spoke. The General followed him mechanically, but seemed little to attend to what his host was saying, as, looking across an extended and rich prospect, he pointed out the different objects worthy of observation. Thus they moved on till Lord Woodville had attained his purpose of drawing his guest entirely apart from the rest of the company, when, turning round upon him with an air of great solemnity, he addressed him thus:—

"Richard Browne, my old and very dear friend, we are now alone. Let me conjure you to answer me upon the word of a friend, and the honour of a soldier. How did you in reality rest during last night?"

"Most wretchedly indeed, my lord," answered the General, in the same tone of solemnity—"so miserably, that I would not run the risk of such a second night, not only for all the lands belonging to this castle, but for all the country which I see from this elevated point of view."

"This is most extraordinary," said the young lord, as if speaking to himself; "then there must be something in the reports concerning that apartment." Again turning to the General, he said, "For God's sake, my dear friend, be candid with me, and let me know the disagreeable particulars which have befallen you under a roof, where, with consent of the owner, you should have met nothing save comfort."

The General seemed distressed by this appeal, and paused a moment before he replied. "My dear lord," he at length said, "what

253

happened to me last night is of a nature so peculiar and so unpleasant, that I could hardly bring myself to detail it even to your lordship, were it not that, independent of my wish to gratify any request of yours, I think that sincerity on my part may lead to some explanation about a circumstance equally painful and mysterious. To others, the communication I am about to make, might place me in the light of a weak-minded, superstitious fool, who suffered his own imagination to delude and bewilder him; but you have known me in childhood and youth, and will not suspect me of having adopted in manhood the feelings and frailties from which my early years were free." Here he paused, and his friend replied,—

"Do not doubt my perfect confidence in the truth of your communication, however strange it may be," replied Lord Woodville. "I know your firmness of disposition too well, to suspect you could be made the object of imposition, and am aware that your honour and your friendship will equally deter you from exaggerating whatever you may have witnessed."

"Well, then," said the General, "I will proceed with my story as well as I can, relying upon your candour, and yet distinctly feeling that I would rather face a battery than recall to my mind the odious recollections of last night."

He paused a second time, and then perceiving that Lord Woodville remained silent and in an attitude of attention, he commenced, though not without obvious reluctance, the history of his night's adventures in the Tapestried Chamber.

"I undressed and went to bed so soon as your lordship left me yesterday evening; but the wood in the chimney, which nearly fronted my bed, blazed brightly and cheerfully, and, aided by a hundred exciting recollections of my childhood and youth, which had been recalled by the unexpected pleasure of meeting your lordship, prevented me from falling immediately asleep. I ought, however, to say that these reflections were all of a pleasant and agreeable kind, grounded on a sense of having for a time exchanged the labour, fatigues, and dangers of my profession for the enjoyments of a peaceful life, and the reunion of those friendly and affectionate ties which I had torn asunder at the rude summons of war.

"While such pleasing reflections were stealing over my mind, and gradually lulling me to slumber, I was suddenly aroused by a sound like that of the rustling of a silken gown, and the tapping of a pair of high-heeled shoes, as if a woman were walking in the apartment. Ere I could draw the curtain to see what the matter was, the figure of a little woman passed between the bed and the fire. The back of this form was turned to me, and I could observe, from the shoulders and neck, it was that of an old woman, whose dress was an old-fashioned gown, which I think ladies call a sacque— that is, a sort of robe completely loose in the body, but gathered into broad plaits upon the neck and shoulders, which fall down to the ground, and terminate in a species of train.

"I thought the intrusion singular enough, but never harboured for a moment the idea that what I saw was anything more than the mortal form of some old woman about the establishment, who had a fancy to dress like her grandmother, and who, having perhaps (as your lordship mentioned that you were rather straitened for room) been dislodged from her chamber for my accommodation, had forgotten the circumstance, and returned by twelve to her old haunt. Under this persuasion I moved myself in bed and coughed a little, to make the intruder sensible of my being in possession of the premises. She turned slowly round, but, gracious Heaven! my lord, what a countenance did she display to me! There was no longer any question what she was, or any thought of her being a living being. Upon a face which wore the fixed features of a corpse were imprinted the traces of the vilest and most hideous passions which had animated her while she lived. The body of some atrocious criminal seemed to have been given up from the grave, and the soul restored from the penal fire, in order to form for a space a union with the ancient accomplice of its guilt. I started up in bed, and sat upright, supporting myself on my palms, as I gazed on this horrible spectre. The hag made, as it seemed, a single and swift stride to the bed where I lay, and squatted herself down upon it, in precisely the same attitude which I had assumed in the extremity of horror, advancing her diabolical countenance within half a yard of mine, with a grin which seemed to intimate the malice and the derision of an incarnate fiend."

Here General Browne stopped, and wiped from his brow the cold perspiration with which the recollection of his horrible vision had covered it.

"My lord," he said, "I am no coward, I have been in all the mortal dangers incidental to my profession, and I may truly boast that no man ever knew Richard Browne dishonour the sword he wears; but in these horrible circumstances, under the eyes, and, as it seemed, almost in the grasp of an incarnation of an evil spirit, all firmness forsook me, all manhood melted from me like wax in the furnace, and I felt my hair individually bristle. The current of my life-blood ceased to flow, and I sank back in a swoon, as very a victim to panic terror as ever was a village girl, or a child of ten years old. How long I lay in this condition I cannot pretend to guess.

"But I was roused by the castle clock striking one, so loud that it seemed as if it were in the very room. It was some time before I dared open my eyes, lest they should again encounter the horrible spectacle. When, however, I summoned courage to look up, she was no longer visible. My first idea was to pull my bell, wake the servants, and remove to a garret or a hay-loft, to be ensured against a second visitation. Nay, I will confess the truth that my resolution was altered, not by the shame of exposing myself, but by the fear that, as the bell-cord hung by the chimney, I might, in making my way to it, be again crossed by the fiendish hag, who, I figured to myself, might be still lurking about some corner of the apartment.

"I will not pretend to describe what hot and cold fever-fits tormented me for the rest of the night, through broken sleep, weary vigils, and that dubious state which forms the neutral ground between them. A hundred terrible objects appeared to haunt me; but there was the great difference betwixt the vision which I have described, and those which followed, that I knew the last to be deceptions of my own fancy and over-excited nerves.

"Day at last appeared, and I rose from my bed ill in health and humiliated in mind. I was ashamed of myself as a man and a soldier, and still more so at feeling my own extreme desire to escape from the haunted apartment, which, however, conquered all other considerations; so that, huddling on my clothes with the most careless haste, I made my escape from your lordship's mansion, to seek in the open air some relief to my nervous system, shaken as it was by this horrible rencounter with a visitant, for such I must believe her, from the other world. Your lordship has now heard the cause of my discomposure, and of my sudden desire to leave your hospitable castle. In other places I trust we may often meet, but God protect me from ever spending a second night under that roof!"

Strange as the General's tale was, he spoke with such a deep air of conviction that it cut short all the usual commentaries which are made on such stories. Lord Woodville never once asked him if he was sure he did not dream of the apparition, or suggested any of the possibilities by which it is fashionable to explain supernatural appearances as wild vagaries of the fancy, or deceptions of the optic nerves, On the contrary, he seemed deeply impressed with the truth and reality of what he had heard; and, after a considerable pause regretted, with much appearance of sincerity, that his early friend should in his house have suffered so severely.

"I am the more sorry for your pain, my dear Browne," he

continued, "that it is the unhappy, though most unexpected, result of an experiment of my own. You must know that, for my father and grandfather's time, at least, the apartment which was assigned to you last night had been shut on account of reports that it was disturbed by supernatural sights and noises. When I came, a few weeks since, into possession of the estate, I thought the accommodation which the castle afforded for my friends was not extensive enough to permit the inhabitants of the invisible world to retain possession of a comfortable sleeping apartment. I therefore caused the Tapestried Chamber, as we call it, to be opened, and, without destroying its air of antiquity, I had such new articles of furniture placed in it as became the modern times. Yet, as the opinion that the room was haunted very strongly prevailed among the domestics, and was also known in the neighbourhood and to many of my friends, I feared some prejudice might be entertained by the first occupant of the Tapestried Chamber, which might tend to revive the evil report which it had laboured under, and so disappoint my purpose of rendering it a useful part or the house. I must confess, my dear Browne, that your arrival yesterday, agreeable to me for a thousand reasons besides, seemed the most favourable opportunity of removing the unpleasant rumours which attached to the room, since your courage was indubitable, and your mind free of any preoccupation on the subject. I could not, therefore, have chosen a more fitting subject for my experiment."

"Upon my life," said General Browne, somewhat hastily, "I am infinitely obliged to your lordship—very particularly indebted indeed. I am likely to remember for some time the consequences of the experiment, as your lordship is pleased to call it."

"Nay, now you are unjust, my dear friend," said Lord Woodville. "You have only to reflect for a single moment, in order to be convinced that I could not augur the possibility of the pain to which you have been so unhappily exposed. I was yesterday morning a complete sceptic on the subject of supernatural appearances. Nay, I am sure that, had I told you what was said about that room, those very reports would have induced you, by your own choice, to select it for your accommodation. It was my misfortune, perhaps my error, but really cannot be termed my fault, that you have been afflicted so strangely."

"Strangely indeed!" said the General, resuming his good temper; "and I acknowledge that I have no right to be offended with your lordship for treating me like what I used to think myself—a man of some firmness and courage. But I see my post horses are arrived, and I must not detain your lordship from your amusement."

"Nay, my old friend," said Lord Woodville, "since you cannot stay with us another day—which, indeed, I can no longer urge—give me at least half an hour more. You used to love pictures, and I have a gallery of portraits, some of them by Vandyke, representing ancestry to whom this property and castle formerly belonged. I think that several of them will strike you as possessing merit."

General Browne accepted the invitation, though somewhat unwillingly. It was evident he was not to breathe freely or at ease till he left Woodville Castle far behind him. He could not refuse his friend's invitation, however; and the less so, that he was a little ashamed of the peevishness which he had displayed towards his well-meaning entertainer.

The General, therefore, followed Lord Woodville through several rooms into a long gallery hung with pictures, which the latter pointed out to his guest, telling the names, and giving some account of the personages whose portraits presented themselves in progression. General Browne was but little interested in the details which these accounts conveyed to him. They were, indeed, of the kind which are usually found in an old family gallery. Here was a Cavalier who had ruined the estate in the royal cause; there a fine lady who had reinstated it by contracting a match with a wealthy Roundhead.

There hung a gallant who had been in danger for corresponding with the exiled Court at Saint Germain's; here one who had taken arms for William at the Revolution; and there a third that had thrown his weight alternately into the scale of Whig and Tory.

While lord Woodville was cramming these words into his guest's ear, "against the stomach of his sense," they gained the middle of the gallery, when he beheld General Browne suddenly start, and assume an attitude of the utmost surprise, not unmixed with fear, as his eyes were suddenly caught and riveted by a portrait of an old lady in a sacque, the fashionable dress of the end of the seventeenth century.

"There she is!" he exclaimed—"there she is, in form and features, though Inferior in demoniac expression to the accursed hag who visited me last night!"

"If that be the case," said the young nobleman, "there can remain no longer any doubt of the horrible reality of your apparition. That is the picture of a wretched ancestress of mine, of whose crimes a black and fearful catalogue is recorded in a family history in my charter-chest. The recital of them would be too horrible; it is enough to say, that in yon fatal apartment incest and unnatural murder were committed. I will restore it to the solitude to which the better judgment of those who preceded me had consigned it; and never shall any one, so long as I can prevent it, be exposed to a repetition of the supernatural horrors which could shake such courage as yours."

Thus the friends, who had met with such glee, parted in a very different mood—Lord Woodville to command the Tapestried Chamber to be unmantled, and the door built up; and General Browne to seek in some less beautiful country, and with some less dignified friend, forgetfulness of the painful night which he had passed in Woodville Castle.

THE TELL-TALE HEART

BY

EDGAR ALLEN POE

TRUE!—nervous—very, very dreadfully nervous I had been and am; but why will you say that I am mad? The disease had sharpened my senses—not destroyed—not dulled them. Above all was the sense of hearing acute. I heard all things in the heaven and in the earth. I heard many things in hell. How, then, am I mad? Hearken! and observe how healthily—how calmly I can tell you the whole story.

It is impossible to say how first the idea entered my brain; but once conceived, it haunted me day and night. Object there was none. Passion there was none. I loved the old man. He had never wronged me. He had never given me insult. For his gold I had no desire. I think it was his eye! yes, it was this! He had the eye of a vulture—a pale blue eye, with a film over it. Whenever it fell upon me, my blood ran cold; and so by degrees—very gradually—I made up my mind to take the life of the old man, and thus rid myself of the eye forever.

Now this is the point. You fancy me mad. Madmen know nothing. But you should have seen me. You should have seen how wisely I proceeded—with what caution—with what foresight—with what dissimulation I went to work! I was never kinder to the old man than during the whole week before I killed him. And every night, about midnight, I turned the latch of his door and opened it—oh so gently! And then, when I had made an opening sufficient for my head, I put in a dark lantern, all closed, closed, that no light shone out, and then I thrust in my head. Oh, you would have laughed to see how cunningly I thrust it in! I moved it slowly—very, very slowly, so that I might not disturb the old man's sleep. It took me an hour to place my whole head within the opening so far that I could see him as he lay upon his bed. Ha! would a madman have been so wise as this? And then, when my head was well in the room, I undid the lantern cautiously—oh, so cautiously—cautiously (for the hinges creaked)—I undid it just so much that a single thin ray fell upon the vulture eye. And this I did for seven long nights—every night just at midnight—but I found the eye always closed; and so it was impossible to do the work; for it was not the old man who vexed me, but his Evil Eye. And every morning, when the day broke, I went boldly into the chamber, and spoke courageously to him, calling him by name in a hearty tone, and inquiring how he has passed the night. So you see he would have been a very profound old man, indeed, to suspect that every night, just at twelve, I looked in upon him while he slept.

Upon the eighth night I was more than usually cautious in opening the door. A watch's minute hand moves more quickly than did mine. Never before that night had I felt the extent of my own powers—of my sagacity. I could scarcely contain my feelings of triumph. To think that there I was, opening the door, little by little, and he not even to dream of my secret deeds or thoughts. I fairly chuckled at the idea; and perhaps he heard me; for he moved on the bed suddenly, as if startled. Now you may think that I drew back—but no. His room was as black as pitch with the thick darkness, (for the shutters were close fastened, through fear of robbers,) and so I knew that he could not see the opening of the door, and I kept pushing it on steadily, steadily.

I had my head in, and was about to open the lantern, when my thumb slipped upon the tin fastening, and the old man sprang up in bed, crying out—"Who's there?"

I kept quite still and said nothing. For a whole hour I did not move a muscle, and in the meantime I did not hear him lie down. He was still sitting up in the bed listening;—just as I have done, night after night, hearkening to the death watches in the wall.

Presently I heard a slight groan, and I knew it was the groan of mortal terror. It was not a groan of pain or of grief—oh, no!—it was the low stifled sound that arises from the bottom of the soul when overcharged with awe. I knew the sound well. Many a night, just at midnight, when all the world slept, it has welled up from my own bosom, deepening, with its dreadful echo, the terrors that distracted me. I say I knew it well. I knew what the old man felt, and pitied him, although I chuckled at heart. I knew that he had been lying awake ever since the first slight noise, when he had turned in the bed. His fears had been ever since growing upon him. He had been trying to fancy them causeless, but could not. He had been saying to himself—"It is nothing but the wind in the chimney—it is only a mouse crossing the floor," or "It is merely a cricket which has made a single chirp." Yes, he had been trying to comfort himself with these suppositions: but he had found all in vain. All in vain; because Death, in approaching him had stalked with his black shadow before him, and enveloped the victim. And it was the mournful influence of the unperceived shadow that caused him to feel—although he neither saw nor heard—to feel the presence of my head within the room.

When I had waited a long time, very patiently, without hearing him lie down, I resolved to open a little—a very, very little crevice in the lantern. So I opened it—you cannot imagine how stealthily, stealthily—until, at length a simple dim ray, like the thread of the spider, shot from out the crevice and fell full upon the vulture eye.

It was open—wide, wide open—and I grew furious as I gazed upon it. I saw it with perfect distinctness—all a dull blue, with a hideous veil over it that chilled the very marrow in my bones; but I could see nothing else of the old man's face or person: for I had directed the ray as if by instinct, precisely upon the damned spot.

And have I not told you that what you mistake for madness is but over-acuteness of the sense?—now, I say, there came to my ears a low, dull, quick sound, such as a watch makes when enveloped in cotton. I knew that sound well, too. It was the beating of the old man's heart. It increased my fury, as the beating of a drum stimulates the soldier into courage.

But even yet I refrained and kept still. I scarcely breathed. I held the lantern motionless. I tried how steadily I could maintain the ray upon the eye. Meantime the hellish tattoo of the heart increased. It grew quicker and quicker, and louder and louder every instant. The old man's terror must have been extreme! It grew louder, I say, louder every moment!—do you mark me well I have told you that I am nervous: so I am. And now at the dead hour of the night, amid the dreadful silence of that old house, so strange a noise as this excited me to uncontrollable terror. Yet, for some minutes longer I refrained and stood still. But the beating grew louder, louder! I thought the heart must burst. And now a new anxiety seized me—the sound would be heard by a neighbour! The old man's hour had come! With a loud yell, I threw open the lantern and leaped into the room. He shrieked once—once only. In an instant I dragged him to the floor, and pulled the heavy bed over him. I then smiled gaily, to find the deed so far done. But, for many minutes, the heart beat on with a muffled sound. This, however, did not vex me; it would not be heard through the wall. At length it ceased. The old man was dead. I removed the bed and examined the corpse. Yes, he was stone, stone dead. I placed my hand upon the heart and held it there many minutes. There was no pulsation. He was stone dead. His eye would trouble me no more.

If still you think me mad, you will think so no longer when I describe the wise precautions I took for the concealment of the body. The night waned, and I worked hastily, but in silence. First of all I dismembered the corpse. I cut off the head and the arms and the legs.

I then took up three planks from the flooring of the chamber, and deposited all between the scantlings. I then replaced the boards so cleverly, so cunningly, that no human eye—not even his—could have detected any thing wrong. There was nothing to wash out— no stain of any kind—no blood-spot whatever. I had been too wary for that. A tub had caught all—ha! ha!

When I had made an end of these labors, it was four o'clock—still dark as midnight. As the bell sounded the hour, there came a knocking at the street door. I went down to open it with a light heart,—for what had I now to fear? There entered three men, who introduced themselves, with perfect suavity, as officers of the police. A shriek had been heard by a neighbour during the night; suspicion of foul play had been aroused; information had been lodged at the police office, and they (the officers) had been deputed to search the premises.

I smiled,—for what had I to fear? I bade the gentlemen welcome. The shriek, I said, was my own in a dream. The old man, I mentioned, was absent in the country. I took my visitors all over the house. I bade them search—search well. I led them, at length, to his chamber. I showed them his treasures, secure, undisturbed. In the enthusiasm of my confidence, I brought chairs into the room, and desired them here to rest from their fatigues, while I myself, in the wild audacity of my perfect triumph, placed my own seat upon the very spot beneath which reposed the corpse of the victim.

The officers were satisfied. My manner had convinced them. I was singularly at ease. They sat, and while I answered cheerily, they chatted of familiar things. But, ere long, I felt myself getting pale and wished them gone. My head ached, and I fancied a ringing in my ears: but still they sat and still chatted. The ringing became more distinct:—It continued and became more distinct: I talked more freely to get rid of the feeling: but it continued and gained definiteness—until, at length, I found that the noise was not within my ears.

No doubt I now grew *very* pale;—but I talked more fluently, and with a heightened voice. Yet the sound increased—and what could I do? It was a low, dull, quick sound—much such a sound as a watch makes when enveloped in cotton. I gasped for breath—and yet the officers heard it not. I talked more quickly—more vehemently; but the noise steadily increased. I arose and argued about trifles, in a high key and with violent gesticulations; but the noise steadily increased. Why would they not be gone? I paced the floor to and fro with heavy strides, as if excited to fury by the observations of the men—but the noise steadily increased. Oh God! what could I do? I foamed—I raved—I swore! I swung the chair upon which I had been sitting, and grated it upon the boards, but the noise arose over all and continually increased. It grew louder—louder—louder! And still the men chatted pleasantly, and smiled. Was it possible they heard not? Almighty God!—no, no! They heard!—they suspected!—they knew!—they were making a mockery of my horror!—this I thought, and this I think. But anything was better than this agony! Anything was more tolerable than this derision! I could bear those hypocritical smiles no longer! I felt that I must scream or die! and now—again!—hark! louder! louder! louder! louder!

"Villains!" I shrieked, "dissemble no more! I admit the deed!—tear up the planks! here, here!—It is the beating of his hideous heart!"